Praise for M.D. Lake
and the PEGGY O'NEILL Mysteries

Grave Choices

M.D. LAKE

AVON BOOKS ◆ NEW YORK

GRAVE CHOICES is an original publication of Avon Books. This work has never before appeared in book form. This work is a novel. Any similarity to actual persons or events is purely coincidental.

AVON BOOKS
A division of
The Hearst Corporation
1350 Avenue of the Americas
New York, New York 10019

Copyright © 1995 by Allen Simpson
Published by arrangement with the author
Library of Congress Catalog Card Number: 95-94307
ISBN: 0-380-77521-2

First Avon Books Printing: November 1995

AVON TRADEMARK REG. U. S. PAT. OFF. AND IN OTHER COUNTRIES, MARCA REGISTRADA, HECHO EN U.S.A.

Printed in the U.S.A.

RA   10 9 8 7 6 5 4 3 2 1

Acknowledgments

Peggy's words about the fictional museum in this novel—"an ornament, a fantasy castle that had fallen from the Christmas tree and landed in the snow"— express my feelings about the Frederick R. Weisman Art Museum at the University of Minnesota in Minneapolis, inside and out the most beautiful museum in the country. I'm grateful to Dr. Lyndel King, director of the Weisman, and her staff, for tolerating me and my questions, and for sharing their love for the museum with me.

One

It was a few minutes after eleven and the other cops had already gone out on their patrols, but I was still in the squad room fiddling with the Christmas tree, blissfully unaware that on the New Campus across the river, a man was about to be murdered.

Jesse Porter had dragged the tree in on the morning watch, set it up next to the coffee urn, and trimmed it. Although it was a scraggly thing, I was glad he'd brought in a real tree instead of using the plastic one that's gathering dust in a storage closet in the basement. Christmas has never been my season, but I do enjoy the sight and smell of a real Christmas tree, properly trimmed.

I didn't like the way Jesse had hung the lights: in plain view on the ends of the limbs. Christmas lights shouldn't be seen directly, only their soft glow, as if coming from mysterious little communities scattered throughout an enchanted forest. As a kid, stringing the lights had been my job, since we couldn't count on my dad being sober enough to stand on a chair.

I looked around, saw that I was alone in the squad room, and decided to rearrange the lights. Lieutenant Bixler was officer in charge that night, but he'd disappeared into his office immediately after roll call, probably to thumb through his hunting or girlie magazines, so I thought I could stay a while in the squad room undisturbed.

The tree was a little sparse in places, which posed a challenge to my light-hanging talents. And, of course, to get the lights where I wanted them, I had to rearrange some of the ornaments too.

I lost track of the time after a few minutes, as I lost myself in the greenery and the memories of Christmases past—they weren't all horrible—that the smell of fresh pine always brings out: the laughter of my cousins, Bing Crosby crooning "White Christmas" in sunny southern California department stores, Mom quarrelling with her sisters-in-law, finding toys I'd actually asked for under the tree on Christmas morning, Dad and the other adult males drinking whiskey and churning ice cream in the garage. Females weren't allowed to touch the ice cream churn in my family. It wouldn't freeze, or something, if we did. The women could make the custard for it, though, since that was kitchen work.

"That in your job description, O'Neill?"

Lieutenant Bixler's raspy voice hacked into my reverie, and I jumped a foot. He'd managed to creep up behind me without my hearing him. He's a balding, red-faced man of about fifty-five, with piggy, close-set eyes. His attempt to hold in his belly gives him a chest like a rooster, which is what we call him behind his back.

"I was just leaving, Lieutenant," I said. Lying to Bixler becomes automatic after a while, like brushing your teeth.

"I don't know if you *were* leaving, O'Neill," he grated dully, "I just know you *are* leaving."

Under Bixler's baleful glare, I shrugged into my lambskin jacket, put on my hat and gloves, and stomped out into the night. I didn't need a scarf, since the woolly inside of my coat collar turns up to cover my mouth, letting me breathe warm air over the rest of my face.

It had snowed earlier that day, leaving a layer of powder on the sidewalks that concealed patches of ice from last week's thaw and made walking dangerous. A cold wind gusted around the buildings and swirled clouds of snow into the air, and ice crystals like tiny fireflies caught the lights of the city in the distance.

My assignment was the New Campus, not my favorite

beat. It's mostly graceless high-rises built in the '60s, with pavement instead of grass, no trees or shrubbery— perfectly suited to science, technology, and the law. I had to walk through the Old Campus to get there, my favorite part of the University. The street lights are far apart, and they cast their soft glow on the snow-covered shrubbery to create moody shadows. It's a little like living in a properly decorated Christmas tree. I even caught myself humming carols as I strolled along the winding paths. "You're getting soft, O'Neill," I muttered to myself, when I heard what I was doing.

The campus was more deserted than usual at that hour, not only because it was so cold but also because it was Christmas vacation. I love walking alone in the Midwestern winter night. I grew up in southern California, and I spent most of the four years I was in the navy in the Caribbean, but I've been here a long time now and my blood's grown thick. I also love to step out of a hot and stuffy building, especially one containing Bixler, into a night below freezing.

I'd toyed for a while with the idea of becoming a detective. I was feeling pressure from friends who thought my abilities were "underutilized" as a beat cop. But detectives do most of their work during the day, whereas I like having my afternoons and evenings free. So my better judgment prevailed and I'm still on the dog watch, from eleven P.M. to seven A.M. Not every woman enjoys being out alone in the middle of the night, but not every woman is armed and dangerous either.

A few minutes before midnight I crossed the bridge over the river to the New Campus and headed for the Student Union, dark except for a few lights in the halls and stairwells. I was only a few feet from the entrance when one of the doors opened and a man in a wide-brimmed hat and earmuffs stalked out, his coat collar turned up and a scarf covering the lower half of his face, his head down against the cold.

To avoid a collision, I flinched to one side, sliding on a patch of ice like a skater. At the sound, the man's head jerked up, his feet went out from under him, and arms flailing, he landed hard on his butt.

Winter rendezvous, Midwestern style.

I held out my hand to him, asked him if he was all right. If looks could kill, I would have died on the spot, but then he seemed to come to his senses. "Fine!" he said testily. Ignoring my hand, he got awkwardly to his feet.

I retrieved a cardboard tube he'd dropped that had rolled a few feet away and handed it to him. He tucked it under his arm like a baton and muttered "Thanks," the murderous look gone from his face, but an edge to his voice still.

I thought I knew what he was feeling. Slipping on ice is a shocking experience, bone-jarring and sometimes bone-breaking. It feels like a pie in the face thrown by a vicious god, and I always want to destroy anyone standing near me, no matter how blameless, on those rare occasions when I do it.

Breathing heavily, he said, in a rich, bluff voice I thought sounded Bostonian: "Wasn't looking where I was going, officer—must be getting absent-minded in my old age. An occupational hazard for the professor, I suppose." His chuckle was deep and fatuous.

Suddenly we were caught in the glare of headlights coming from the bridge behind me. It was Lawrence in the squad car. He pulled up next to us, leaned out his window and raised an inquiring eyebrow.

"Everything's okay, Lawrence," I told him. "Thanks."

With a brief glance at Lawrence, the man readjusted the scarf over his mouth and nose, said good night, and turned and marched off across the plaza, watching his feet. The back of his dark overcoat was stained with dirty snow.

"Who was that masked man, kemosabe?" Lawrence asked me.

"A law professor, I guess. Working late, neglecting the wife and kids. He slipped on the ice and landed on his ego. That could be Paula in a few years, you know—

except for the rich baritone voice, of course."

Lawrence is engaged to Paula Henderson, one of my best friends, who quit the campus police last year to go to law school. I don't approve, but she claims she's going to use her vast knowledge of the judicial system only in the service of the Good, the True and the Beautiful. We'll see.

"Paula's like that already," Lawrence replied. "I've hardly seen her the last three months. She only comes home to sleep."

"You'll see her tomorrow night, at least," I said.

Paula and Lawrence and my lover, Gary, and I were taking dancing lessons at a church in their neighborhood, and we'd agreed to meet to practice the next evening. We needed it, God knows. We'd been learning ballroom dance steps the last month.

We talked for a few more minutes and then he drove off and I used my passkey to enter the Union. You can't get in without a key after ten, although you don't need one to come out if you're already inside. The Law School is connected to the Union by a long underground tunnel, and a lot of people leave through those doors if they're going across the bridge to the Old Campus, or into the neighborhood behind the New Campus.

I spent about fifteen minutes in the Union, and then walked through the tunnel over to the Law School, which would normally be bustling with pettifoggers in embryo even after midnight on the weekend, but with finals just completed and Christmas coming up, I encountered only a few of the more eager or desperate among them.

I wandered the Law School halls for a few minutes, wondering, not for the first time, why the place resembles a penitentiary, then escaped through one of the downstairs doors and crossed a small snow-covered plaza to the Studio Arts Building, one of my favorites.

It's an old warehouse the University turned over to the artists fifty or sixty years ago and then promptly forgot. Although I had my passkey out, I tried the door first and it opened. That was no surprise. It's supposed to be kept locked at night, but the artists usually forget. They aren't the only ones, of course: the academic mind, trained in the science of exploring ways to maximize salary while minimizing contact hours with students, has no time for such mundane concerns as building security.

The entrance hall was dimly lit by a fluorescent fixture in the high ceiling. I glanced into the secretary's office and then went through the door that leads back into the studios. I get a certain voyeuristic pleasure from peeking into them when the artists aren't there, and trying to make sense of their work while it's still in progress.

As I stepped into the last studio in the row and flipped on the light, several things happened at once: I saw the body on the floor and the bright blood around its head, the overturned easel, the palette on the table with its gouts of color—the violent fragments of a savage interior—and then the door was torn from my hand and smashed back into me, knocking me out of the room.

I hit the floor hard, banging my shoulders and head on the opposite wall, then lay there a moment, stunned and breathless. A figure, a blur of motion, jumped over my legs and fled. I scrambled to one knee, groping for my pistol. The running man hesitated at the end of the hall, glanced quickly back at me, his face a mask of horror, then turned and disappeared, slamming the door closed behind him.

Still on my knee, pistol in my hand, I called for backup and an ambulance, then stood up shakily and went back into the studio and over to the figure on the floor. I'd thrown up once when I found a corpse. I wanted to throw up this time too but resisted the urge. There was enough color in the room already.

I forced myself to check for vital signs, even though I knew there wouldn't be any, for this man's head was almost completely severed from his body.

Two

Buck Hansen, a homicide lieutenant I know well, was finishing his interview with me in the secretary's office. I'd assured him I'd be able to recognize the man who'd rushed out of the studio and knocked me down if I saw him again. "He was Hispanic," I said, "with Indian features. Medium build, not tall—five-six or -seven, I think. I can't even guess how old. He was wearing a dark cap and a down jacket and he had dark eyes. I think he had a scar on the right side of his face, like this." I drew a line going from my cheekbone almost to my mouth. "But it may have been a shadow. Or blood," I added, because there had been a lot of blood in the studio.

The campus cops who'd answered my call for backup had searched unsuccessfully for the man. Now police dogs were being brought in to try to pick up his scent around the Studio Arts Building.

Buck listened and his assistant, Burke, made notes. Burke doesn't like me much. He thinks I'm responsible for the bodies I've found over the years I've been a campus cop and for the work they put him and his boss through. Whenever I catch him looking at me, he has a kill-the-messenger look on his face.

"And the front door was unlocked when you came in?" Buck asked again. "You're sure about that?"

I nodded.

"And that didn't alert you to the fact that you were confronting a situation, O'Neill?" That was Lieutenant Bixler's voice, the voice of the Rooster, as he stepped back into the office after viewing the crime scene.

"No," I said. And to Buck: "The doors are often left unlocked in buildings in which people work late. We send stern notes to their department heads, but it doesn't do any good."

"Yeah, fine," Bixler blustered on, "but this was Christmas break. Who'd expect an artist to be working late then?"

"I guess a murderer did," I answered.

That didn't stop him, the way it would in a movie. Nothing stops life's real Bixlers. "Right," he sneered, "a murderer that jumped you! You're lucky he ran, instead of taking your pistol and blowing you away. And you should've gone after him too. It wouldn't't've taken a genius to see that the stiff in the studio was a—a stiff."

"I felt I had to make sure the stiff in the studio was a—a stiff," I told Buck. "I don't have Lieutenant Bixler's physician's eye that tells me at a glance someone's dead."

Buck doesn't like getting between Bixler and me—professional clashing with personal loyalty—so he didn't say anything, just asked a few more questions and then said I could go.

Even though my head was aching from hitting the wall when I'd been knocked down and my elbow was still throbbing from its contact with the floor, I got up quickly and left the room. I wanted to get back outside, back into the night where it was clean and cold and where I see things more clearly than indoors. Bixler scowled at me as I passed him.

Then I remembered something and went back, pushing past Bixler again. Buck gave me a questioning look. I described my encounter with the man who'd slipped on the ice up on the plaza about three-quarters of an hour before I'd found the body.

"He was probably just a law professor who'd stayed late at his office," I added. "But—at least in retrospect—it seems odd that he was walking home instead of driving on a night this cold, and so late too. The Law School's garage is heated, and it's right under the building.''

"A lot of well-heeled faculty live in high-rises back behind the New Campus," Bixler said. "And you ain't the only person likes to walk around in the cold in the middle of the night, O'Neill.''

He had a point, of course, but I pretended I didn't hear it.

Buck asked me to describe the man. I said he'd been well bundled up, but his scarf had pulled away from his face when he'd fallen, and I was pretty sure I'd recognize him again if I saw him. He had a long face, a long, straight nose, and a wide mouth.

He was about six feet tall and I thought he was of average build, although it's hard to tell when someone's wearing a heavy winter overcoat. I could only guess at his age—anywhere between forty-five and sixty—and I couldn't tell the color of his hair, or how much of it he had, since it was dark and he was wearing a hat. "Oh," I added, "and he was carrying a long cardboard tube."

"The victim wasn't beaten to death with a long cardboard tube, O'Neill," Bixler stuck in, chuckling fatuously. "His throat was cut with a wire." He pantomimed looping a wire over someone's head, probably mine, and jerking it tight by its wooden handles.

I knew how the victim had been killed. I'd seen the wire and the handles when I'd knelt to check for vital signs.

"If he was the killer," I continued, in the voice of someone trying to pretend there isn't an elephant in the room, "then leaving campus through the Student Union via the Law School, the same way I came down here, would be the easiest way."

"The killer's the guy who took you by surprise and knocked you down back in the studio, O'Neill," Bixler blustered. "The guy you took by surprise and knocked down up on the plaza was just a law professor going home."

Before I could say anything I'd regret, Buck thanked

me again and I stalked out, muttering under my breath, wondering how it would feel to loop a wire around Bixler's fat neck and . . .

The Studio Arts parking lot at the side of the building was now cluttered with cop cars, their flashers coloring the snow red and yellow and blue like a holiday display in a bar, their radios muttering tinny obscurities. A television station's Crime Scene Cam was parked in the snow-covered area behind them, and the video camera itself came galloping donkeylike toward me, presumably being carried by someone behind it. Running alongside through the dirty snow, her hair blowing out behind her, came a woman I recognized, a well-known television reporter who always manages to look as though she's had to parachute in to bring us the story, even if it's only an ice cream social at the old folks home.

"Hey, Peggy! Over here, quick!" It was Lawrence, leaning out of his squad car.

I bolted for it. He had the passenger door open as I reached it, and pulled away as I rolled in.

"Break time!" he said. "The Donut Whole—my treat. You could probably use a cup of coffee and a little grease and sugar about now."

This wasn't the first time Lawrence had ridden to my rescue. He'd once carried me unconscious out of a burning building. I started to laugh and found I couldn't stop.

He darted me a concerned look. "What's so funny?"

"Oh, you know," I stammered, "being a campus cop, working the dog watch—it's such easy duty! First you trim the Christmas tree and get chased out into the cold night air by Bixler's wit, then you find a corpse in the Studio Arts Building with its head almost detached from its body—like a Picasso or something," I added, and laughed a little more at that. "Then you get knocked on your butt by the killer, who looks more terrified than you are, and then you go for coffee and doughnuts."

"Ssh!" Lawrence said. "Not so loud! You want people lining up for your job?"

Three

My phone rang at a little before noon the next day, a good two hours before I wanted to get up. Under normal circumstances, I roll over and go back to sleep when that happens, letting my answering machine take the call. But last night hadn't been normal circumstances, so I waited until I heard Buck's voice telling me to pick up my phone, and did.

Instead of saying hello, I mumbled, "When?"

"As soon as you've had some coffee. How'd you know we've got him?"

"I saw the look on his face and figured he wouldn't last long. He turn himself in?"

"No, we found him."

"The dogs?"

"No, it's a long story. Can you be here at two?"

"Sure."

I made a pot of coffee and drank it while staring out my big living-room window at the piece of Lake Eleanor I can see from there. It was Saturday morning, and the skating rink was alive with tiny people in colorful stocking caps, a Currier and Ives lithograph come to life. I would have liked to join them, but I had something ugly to do first.

I showered and dressed and drove downtown and used my shield to park in the official parking area below the Justice Building. It's not one of my favorite places. It's old and dark and obviously dispirited by the amount of misery it's seen and heard over ninety-odd years of dispensing what passes for justice in our world.

I called Buck from the front desk, and he came and led me down brightly lit halls and back to the lineup room, using a card to open doors on the way. A man was already in the witness room. Buck introduced him to me as a public defender appointed by the court to watch out for the suspect's rights. We sat and waited in uncomfortable silence for a few minutes, and then a cop pulled the curtain away from the one-way glass window and I looked out at the men in the lineup.

They were all Hispanic, of course, all about the same height and build, and they all had Band-Aids on their right cheeks where I thought the man who'd knocked me down had a scar. Only one of them had a defiant look on his face, though, and dark eyes that blinked nervously, but I would have recognized him anyway.

"You're sure?" the public defender asked.

"Yes," I said. I felt like I was being told to pull the switch at an execution. I don't believe in the death penalty because killing helpless people is murder no matter who does it.

I went back to Buck's office and signed the statement I'd given him the night before and another statement identifying the suspect, whose name was Daniel Sánchez.

"How'd you pick him up so soon?" I asked.

"A couple of months ago, he burst into a Studio Arts faculty meeting and threatened to kill Bell—with a clay cutter." The murdered man's name was Russell Bell.

"Good sleuthing!" I said, and managed a wry smile.

Buck offered to take me out for an espresso at a little place we go to sometimes not far from the Justice Building and tell me what he'd learned about the case so far. I usually take every opportunity I can to spend time with him, but for some reason I wanted to get away from cops and murder for a while, so I said no.

We agreed to meet for dinner the following Wednesday at a restaurant he's currently wild about, and then I drove back home, where I tried to catch up on my beauty sleep, since that night Gary and I were going to go over to Paula and Lawrence's to practice our dancing.

I slept poorly, haunted by the bloody scene in the studio and by the suspect's eyes—his eyes as he'd stood in the lineup and also last night, when he'd glanced back at me with an expression of horror on his face, as though he'd only just realized what he'd done a few minutes earlier.

I don't like being a part of putting people in jail, which is ridiculous for a cop—sort of like a bat who's afraid of the dark or a claustrophobic gopher.

There was a lot of talk in the squad room about the murder when I came in that night, although nobody acted as though I'd mishandled the situation, and I didn't think I had either. Rumor had it that Captain DiPrima, our chief, was annoyed that Bixler had let the city homicide cops take over the case. We had detectives now who were fully trained to investigate homicides—my friend Ginny Raines is one—and this one seemed made to order for us: it hadn't required any complicated forensics work, and even if it had, we could have brought in the county crime lab to do it.

So Bixler, probably having been royally chewed out by DiPrima, took his anger out on me at roll call, managing to imply that a good cop would have somehow sensed that something was wrong in the Studio Arts Building as soon as he got within a hundred feet of it. He admonished us never to take anything for granted. Just because a building is usually left unlocked by negligent faculty or students doesn't mean it always is—a negligent murderer could have forgotten to lock it after going in to do his dirty deed. And he tried to imply that I should have known the man on the floor was dead and not wasted time checking to be sure. I should have chased after the killer instead.

"He could have been a madman," he raved on, rocking back and forth on his Korfam shoes. "Professor Bell could have been just one in a long line of victims on his list. If anybody else had been murdered by the man, how would you sleep, O'Neill, knowing you'd shirked your chance to apprehend him?''

There'd been a time, early in my career as a campus cop, when Bixler could regress me to my days as a parochial school girl in the clutches of the Sisters Mary Attila and Mary Margaret the Hun, and I would have turned my toes in and lowered my head in shame, cheeks burning. But those days are past.

Bixler was waiting for my answer. "My life's so full of real questions, Lieutenant," I said, "that I don't have time for the hypothetical ones."

U PROF GARROTED, the headline read in the next morning's paper.

A photograph of Russell Bell, taken in the early '70s, showed a man with light curly hair and a conventionally handsome face, although the expression he'd put on it for the studio camera—staring intently at the camera with a slight frown on his full lips—suggested to me that creativity gave him gas. I wondered why there weren't any more recent photographs of him.

He was sixty-five when he'd been killed. Prior to coming here, he'd been considered a promising abstract expressionist painter in New York, where he palled around with the likes of Jackson Pollock, Robert Motherwell, David Smith, and Willem de Kooning, among others. He'd never been married and seemed to have left only one survivor, an older brother living in a retirement community in Arizona.

"Many in the art community will be shocked by the news of Russell Bell's tragic, violent death," the chairman of the Studio Arts Department was quoted as saying, which sounded like pretty tepid praise to me. "He will be mourned," a colleague in the department added, without going into detail. None of the famous artists Bell used to hang out with in New York were quoted, although I thought that some of them were alive and still fairly alert.

Bell had last been seen alive Friday night around five by the professor who shared the studio with him, a painter named Shannon Rider. He'd told her he was going to be working late. According to Professor Rider, he was struggling to complete a painting for the faculty show that was being held in conjunction with the opening of the University's new art museum in late December.

The article went on to say that Bell's body had been found by a campus policewoman, Peggy O'Neal, while on a routine check of the Studio Arts Building. Officer O'Neal had come upon Daniel Sánchez, at present being held as a material witness in the slaying, in Bell's studio with the dead man. Sánchez overcame the officer and made his escape. Officer O'Neal was unavailable for comment.

I sipped coffee through an annoyed grin, pleased that my name had been misspelled but not by much else in the story.

Sánchez allegedly held Bell responsible for his fiancée having been turned down for promotion in the Studio Arts Department two decades ago, when Bell had been the chairman. The woman, a sculptor named Kate Simons, was later killed in a burglary at her apartment, and the killer had never been apprehended. In October, Sánchez had burst into a meeting of the Studio Arts faculty and, according to the faculty members who'd been there, threatened to garrote Bell with a clay cutter. Sánchez was a potter, and the murder weapon was a wire clay cutter. The county crime lab was doing tests to determine if clay found on the murder weapon matched the formula of Sánchez's clay.

Sánchez was forty-nine, married with two children. In the late '60s, early '70s, he'd had several minor drug convictions, and he'd also been arrested twice for disorderly conduct.

The photograph of him, a mug shot, showed a man with a full head of dark hair streaked with gray, Hispanic-Indian features, and a mouth that looked sensitive in spite of the conditions under which the photograph had been taken, which would make even the Good Fairy look like a serial killer. The scar on his cheek didn't help either.

I sipped some cold but still tasty coffee and thought a moment, glancing across my living room at the big weed pot standing next to my fireplace, a pot Sandra Carr had given me—yes, *the* Sandra Carr. Then, with a sigh, I got up and went over to it, picked it up, and looked at the monogram stamped in the clay on the bottom: DS.

"Damn," I said, and put the pot back down.

I'd once saved Sandra's sister's life. Actually I'd been the one who'd put her life in jeopardy in the first place, but only I knew that. Sandra had been so grateful that she'd offered to completely redo my living room, which she thinks is boring. Since her books sell in the millions and are usually made into movies before the ink's dry on them, she could afford it, but I said no. My walls are white and the floor is wall-to-wall royal blue carpeting, all of which goes well with the art photography I buy occasionally—the only original art I can afford.

She'd had to content herself with giving me the weed pot.

A bold splash of crimson in its glaze served as a nice accent in the room and went well with some of the color in the tiles it sat on. As I stood there looking at it I couldn't help but think of other crimson splashes I'd seen recently, probably from the same potter's hands.

Four

It was the following Tuesday. When I woke up a little after two, I padded out into the kitchen, ground coffee, and started the coffeemaker, pretending I didn't see the angry little light on the answering machine winking like a pimple just before the senior prom. The phone ringing before I wanted to wake up had annoyed me, so I decided to take my time listening to the message.

I showered, etc., slipped into my white terry-cloth robe, and took a cup of coffee into the living room, where I skimmed through the newspaper. I noticed that Russell Bell's murder had been relegated to a small item in the back of the second section since—as far as the journalists were concerned—it was all over but the sentencing. After ten minutes of that, I refilled my coffee cup and, with a languid finger, pressed the button on the answering machine.

"Peggy!" the voice blared. "Sandra here. Call me as soon as you've had your coffee. It's urgent."

I glanced over at the weed pot, rolled my eyes, and dialed Sandra's number.

"Dan Sánchez," she said, when we'd exchanged hellos. "You know who he is, don't you?"

"You know I do, Sandra," I replied calmly. "Among other more recent and lurid accomplishments, he made the pot you gave me. After the trial, I'm going to sell it at the spring yard sale, where it should bring a very high price—properly advertised, of course."

"You wouldn't do that, Peggy! Would you?"

"No."

"Good. I don't think he did it."

"You don't think he made my weed pot?"

"Killed that awful painter, Russell Bell."

"Sánchez only kills good painters?"

"He's a friend of mine, and you can see for yourself what a wonderful potter he is."

"You've convinced *me*!"

"How about dinner tonight? Now that you're no longer cocooning with Gary and being fattened up by his rich sauces and domestic bliss, you can probably get out more and reconnect with your friends."

Before I came along, Gary and Sandra had been lovers, and I have a hunch that Sandra would like him back—at least temporarily. They still get together once in a while too, for dinner.

I told her I had to work that night.

"Still out there, are you—a lone bulwark in the night between the academics and the hoodlums? How do you tell 'em apart?" She brayed her loud, raucous laugh. Sandra was proud of the fact that she'd graduated from the University in two and a half years, mostly by taking multiple-choice tests. "Well," she went on, "in that case, we'll meet for dinner at six. At Fatima's Veil—you won't have to dress up, but we can still get something edible."

She deplores my lack of interest in clothes. She thinks that if she put me in a novel, people would accuse her of not knowing how to create a believable female character. No interest in clothes, plus what passes for intelligence in genre fiction, are apparently necessary for a male character but unconvincing in a female. Maybe that's why I don't read much popular fiction.

Sandra was already seated, a martini in front of her, when I arrived at Fatima's, a popular Middle Eastern restaurant that must violate every dietary law in the Koran. Enormous velvet paintings of vaguely Arabic subjects hang askew on the walls, and what look like old bedsheets cover the ceiling to give the impression you're in a tent. Canned Middle Eastern music wafts softly through the room, but not softly enough. I ordered a sparkling water with a twist of lime from a big-boned blond college student in a belly dancer's costume.

Sandra Carr is in her early forties and six-one or -four, depending on whether she's wearing flats or heels, with an angular face and a strong chin, and she rides an exercycle just enough to keep from getting fat. She's got red hair and freckles, as I do, but her red's redder and her freckles are bigger and there are more of them. She's loud, egotistical, and gifted, and, in small doses, I like her a lot. I can't read her novels, though. They're too scary.

When we'd ordered, I asked her how her sister was doing.

"Happy as a cricket." She laughed, shaking her head in amazement. "Melody lost a lover, an ex-lover, a husband, and a friend—and almost lost her own life too, as you know. But she's a poet, and misery is meat to the rhymester's muse, so what might have sent an ordinary person spiraling into suicidal despair gave Melody the stuff for an entire chapbook. I understand it's getting good reviews in all the little poetry rags."

"I wonder what she'll do for an encore," I said.

"Let's not even think about it!"

Sandra, although she loves her sister and is quite protective of her, doesn't think much of poetry. Real writers, she thinks, bring their lines all the way over to the right margin.

I looked at her expectantly, and after some hemming and hawing, she got down to business, between mouthfuls of couscous and hummus and other exotic delicacies.

"It must have been awful for you, Peggy," she said. "Finding that body and then having Dan run over you like that."

"Yes, it was awful, as you put it."

"He's sorry. He thought you were the murderer, coming back. He was terrified, and he just wanted to get out of there alive. He said that if he'd had a knife, he might've stabbed you with it. He's glad he didn't.''

I paused in my chewing to say I was too.

"Peggy, I've known Dan a long time." She reached across the table to place a hand on mine. "He's one of the best potters in the state."

"He wouldn't be your friend otherwise, would he?"

"I can't help it if I only attract gifted people," she retorted.

"So what if he's a great potter? Can't great potters commit murder? Besides, what's all this got to do with me? You want me to deny I saw him there that night— or claim it was a tall Swede?''

"Of course not! I didn't say he didn't do it," she reminded me. "I said I don't think he did it, and I hope he didn't. He's hot-tempered, but he works his anger off on his clay, not on people."

"He also seems to work off his anger by publicly threatening to garrote people."

She waved that away with a piece of pita bread dripping with baba ganusj in an elegant, freckled hand. "Blowing off steam's not the same thing as actually cutting somebody's throat. I want you to prove Dan didn't do it—or prove to my satisfaction that he did."

"Me!"

She flashed a grin full of fierceness and gums. "You! You saved Melody's life and figured out who murdered Cameron Harris. You're as good a snoop as I am a writer and as Dan is a potter. You said it yourself, Peggy: I don't have friends who aren't gifted. Why should I? Life's too short."

"According to the newspaper, he's an alcoholic, a drug abuser, and a barroom brawler."

"He *was*—a long time ago. The newspaper got it wrong. He quit doing drugs in the early '70s and quit drinking too. He's happily married now and has two beautiful children."

"If you believe so strongly in his innocence, Sandra, hire a private detective."

"I don't believe in private detectives," she said. "What are they good for? The best have the brains of newts, the worst earn their miserable livings trying to get photographs of people on disability lifting their kids! They carry guns to try to impress the aerobics instructors they meet in bars. What do they know about finding murderers?"

Absently shredding a piece of pita, she continued. "Besides, they don't know their way around the University the way you do or how to talk to those bozos on the faculty, either. All I want you to do is *try*, Peggy. Not spend a lot of time at it. Just snoop around the Studio Arts Department, see if you can pick up any gossip about who might've wanted Bell dead. It looks really bad for Dan. All I want is for you to come up with other possible suspects."

I shook my head. "I've had my fill of playing amateur sleuth, Sandra. I'm into dancing now."

"Dance—! You?"

"Gary and I," I amended smugly, "and some friends of ours."

"Gary too! He's never mentioned it to me—and with good reason." She shook her head sadly. "What kind of dancing?"

"All kinds. Right now, we're learning ballroom."

"Ballroom dancing isn't you, Peggy."

"It is for now," I said, bristling because I suspected she was right.

"Would you talk to Dan, please? I'll pay you for your time."

I asked her why she cared so much.

"Because I like him, that's why," she said, very soberly. "He's had a hell of a struggle in his life. He got off drugs and booze, and he's realized his dream of being self-supporting as a potter. Well, almost self-supporting, his wife works too. He deserves a better chance than he's going to get in court. I'd do the same for you, you know, Peggy," she said quietly.

I knew that was true.

"And no, Dan and I have never been lovers," she went on with a smile. "I don't go after happily married men. But I like his pottery a lot. I like him too—and Elena, of course, and the kids," she added as something of an afterthought.

"How'd you ever get to know him?"

She looked away uneasily. "I was doing a novel about a homicidal potter," she said finally. "I needed to talk to a potter and remembered Dan—I'd bought some of his things at an art fair. He was very helpful."

"I'll bet!"

She glared at me.

My voice rose as I ticked off the evidence against Sánchez. "He had a motive, the means, and the opportunity, Sandra. He threatened Bell in front of a lot of other people. I found him with the corpse, and he fled the scene of the crime!" I sometimes get a little hysterical arguing with her.

She shoved her plate away and stared morosely off into the distance. After a long silence, she looked at me as though she'd only just remembered I was there and said, "All right, Peggy. It was a stupid idea. I'll hire a private detective. Maybe two or three, if I can find that many who don't drag their knuckles on the sidewalk."

The waitress came up then and asked us if we wanted dessert.

"Nothing for me," Sandra said, "I'm not hungry. You go ahead, Peggy—I know how much you love baklava."

Give me a break! I thought. I told the waitress no, and she went away.

"I suppose he's still in jail," I said finally, when I couldn't stand the canned Middle Eastern music any longer.

"He's out on bail. The judge set it high, thinking Dan wouldn't be able to afford it."

"But you could."

She shrugged and seemed to find a camel in a velvet painting on the wall of great interest.

"I suppose I could talk to him," I said.

"Who?"

"Don't push it, Sandra."

Five

I agreed to spend a week on the case—more if I thought I was getting anywhere. If not, Sandra would have plenty of time to hire a real investigator, since Sánchez's case wouldn't go to court for at least two months.

She offered to come with me to talk to him, but I said no. I wanted to make up my own mind about him, without Sandra's ham-fisted efforts to sway me.

I rode over the next afternoon. If the wind's not blowing and the streets have been plowed, I like biking in the winter, and we hadn't had all that much snow yet anyway.

Sánchez lived on a street of old frame houses between the New Campus and downtown, in an area that was an uneasy mix of student housing and single-family homes whose owners were struggling to keep the neighborhood up. The Sánchez house looked recently painted, white with brown trim. Ceramic mobiles and bird feeders hung on ropes on the porch and three sets of old cross-country skis—one meant for a child—and a round red plastic sled leaned against the wall next to the front door.

I pulled my bike up onto the porch and rang the bell. I heard quick footsteps rattling down stairs and then the door opened on its chain and a woman peeked out. She was Hispanic, small and lithe, with delicate features, long, almost black hair, and large dark eyes.

She looked me up and down quickly and asked if I was a reporter. I assured her I wasn't, and when I added that I was a friend of Sandra Carr's, her expression softened. I told her I wanted to talk to her husband.

She unchained the door and let me in. "Are you a private detective?"

I shook my head, told her my name, and added, "I'm the campus cop who met your husband in the Studio Arts Building."

Her eyes grew large and then narrowed suspiciously again. "Are you here to question Dan?"

"Sandra wants me to talk to him, to see if I can help him."

"Help—how? Why?"

I laughed, hoping to put her more at ease. "Why? Because Sandra likes your husband. I don't know how, or even if, I can. Maybe I can't—and maybe, after I've talked to him, I won't want to."

She thought about that, then nodded, offering me her hand. "My name's Elena," she said. "Follow me, please."

As she led me through the house, she said over her shoulder, "You mustn't let Dan's attitude influence you. He's very upset, as you can imagine. He knows somebody is trying to make it seem like he killed that man. And he doesn't believe he will get a fair trial. And I don't think he will either."

The entire dining room of the house had been turned into a display room for Sánchez's pottery—pitchers, teapots, plates, goblets, vases and bowls of all sizes and shapes, and larger pots on the wood floor. An open door in the back wall led into a studio that had been added onto the house.

Dan Sánchez was sitting at a potter's wheel, scraping excess clay from the base of a pot, his long gray-flecked hair down around his face. He looked tired and defeated and not at all frightening.

"Dan," his wife said in the doorway, "this is a friend of Sandra's. She wants to talk to you."

"About what?" he asked roughly, gently lifting the pot from the wheel and putting it on the worktable next to him.

"Sandra asked her to help us."

He looked up. "What are you, a private eye?"

"No. I'm the campus cop you knocked down the other night in Russell Bell's studio."

He got off the wheel and stared at me. As his face darkened, the scar on his cheek became more prominent. "Sandy sent you? What the hell does she think she's doing?"

"Trying to help you, Dan," his wife said, an edge to her voice.

He glanced at her and back to me.

"Help me how?"

"I don't know yet," I said. "I'll have to hear your side of the story first. Sandra thinks I might be better than a private detective because I know my way around the University better than one of them would."

He laughed in spite of himself and shook his head. "A campus cop! What'll Sandra think of next! She's spent so much time writin' thrillers, she's confusin' 'em with real life."

He started to turn away, then remembered something. "Hey, I'm sorry I knocked you down and scared you. But I really thought you was the guy who killed Bell, comin' back."

"Then I guess I'm lucky you weren't armed," I said.

"I guess so," he agreed, and turned away again.

Two children came running in then, screeched to a stop next to Elena Sánchez, and looked at me warily. She introduced them and added, "Peggy's a friend of Sandra's." The girl smiled shyly, staying close to Mom; the boy nodded gravely.

"We have to go," Elena went on to me. "I work afternoons at a day care down the street. Now that school's out for the holidays, Carlos and Luisa are helping me."

She went over to Sánchez and put her arm around him. He stiffened, but she pulled him to her and held on until he put his arm around her too. The children pretended to find something on the worktable of great interest. Elena started to say something, caught herself when she began to tear up and, giving me a quick nod, hustled the children out of the studio.

Sánchez watched them go, then turned to me. "Pull up a stool. You can hang your hat and coat on one of those pegs over there if you want. How 'bout coffee, tea?"

I said coffee, and he handed it to me in a mug that looked nice and felt good in the hand.

It was warm in the studio. Sánchez was wearing clay-splattered jeans and a short-sleeved T-shirt that showed his arms—muscular as though he lifted weights. I didn't suppose he needed to, though: carrying around heavy bags of clay and throwing large pots like my weed pot could probably create muscles like those.

A big brick kiln formed one wall of the studio. A smaller electric kiln stood on the floor opposite, and there were shelves of bisque and unfired pottery, as well as sinks and worktables. Noticing a row of small electric wheels, I asked him if he taught pottery.

He nodded and laughed bitterly. "Did. None of my students showed up after they saw me bein' led into the police station in handcuffs on television. Can't say I blame 'em."

He picked up a wire clay cutter from a table. "Here's how you can know I didn't kill that bastard Bell. If I'd used one of these on him, his head wouldn't of still been attached to his body." With a sudden vicious jerk, he pulled it taut, his muscles bulging. His dark, angry eyes stayed on me the whole time, unblinking.

"That's very impressive," I said. "I'm sure a jury would enjoy seeing it too."

He looked embarrassed. "What difference does it make? I'll get a nice haircut and dig out the suit I was married in and those twelve nice blond Scandinavians on the jury'll take one look at me—they won't even have to go out and discuss it first. They're just going to stand up and say, 'This nice Mexican-American fella is not guilty, your honor!' " He laughed again and threw the clay cutter down. It clattered across the table like dice on a string.

He glared at me defiantly. I studied him a moment, but couldn't decide if his anger was real or bluster. I asked him why he'd been in the Studio Arts Building when Bell was killed.

He sighed as though he'd told this story many times recently, which I'm sure he had. "I got a call—eleven-thirty, eleven-forty, somewhere around then," he began. "That's no big deal, 'cause all my friends know I usually work late at night. Except it wasn't a friend. It was Bell—I mean, it was somebody *sayin'* he was Bell. He asked me to meet him at his studio."

"Did he tell you why?"

"He wanted to talk about what happened twenty-three years ago." Sánchez shot me a glance. "You know about that?"

"Just what was in the newspaper. It said you held a grudge against Bell for something that happened to your fiancée."

"Yeah. Bell was chairman of the Studio Arts Department back then. They turned Kate—that was my fiancée's name, Kate—down for promotion. They gave her job to a friend of Bell's instead. A little while after that, she got killed in a burglary."

"And after twenty-three years, he wanted to talk to you about it. Why now?"

"*Bell* didn't want to talk to me about it," Sánchez explained patiently. "The guy *pretendin'* to be Bell, the guy who killed him, said he wanted to talk to me about it."

"Did he say why?"

"Yeah—on account of what I did in October. I suppose you know about that?"

"The paper said you broke into a department meeting and threatened Bell."

"I didn't threaten him! Like I told the cops—"

"And in spite of *that*," I went on, ignoring his interruption, "you thought Bell called you and wanted you to come to his studio and talk about it—and you went, even though it was the middle of the night?" It was hard to keep the skepticism out of my voice.

"It's the truth!" he flared. I remembered his demonstration with the clay cutter and the effect a clay cutter had had on Russell Bell. "It's the truth," he went on more quietly, "except it wasn't Bell who called me. But I thought it was, and I started to tell him no—to fuck off. But I decided I'd go, instead."

"Why?"

"To see what he had to say."

"Why?"

He shook his head, his eyes brimming with exhaustion and pain. "I don't know if you'll understand this, Miss O'Neill. The cops didn't. You see, I'd hated that fucker for so long, and hate wasn't doin' nothin' for me. My life's been good since I stopped drinkin' and usin', and since Elena and I got together and the kids finally came."

He stopped, swallowed, looked at me. "But for some reason, every once in a while when I think of Kate and what happened to her, the anger grows in me like a—like I'm pregnant with somethin', some kind of monster. I can deal with it most of the time, talk it into goin' back where it came from. But that time I couldn't."

"What happened then that made you so angry?"

"I read in the *Daily*—the student newspaper—that this was gonna be Russell Bell's last year at the U. He was gonna retire 'after a long and distinguished career as an artist, teacher, and administrator.' I just snapped when I read that. I crashed their meetin', and stood in front of all the professors and told the fucker what I thought of him. I couldn't help it."

Long silence. He fiddled with a tool with a wooden handle, and a wire loop on the end. Good for scooping out an eye, probably.

"I could've helped it," he went on finally, "if I'd wanted to. I just didn't want to. Then somebody called the cops and one of 'em came to the Studio Arts Building an' handcuffed me an' drove me off campus. He could've taken me to jail, but he didn't 'cause none of the Studio Arts professors, not even Bell, wanted to press charges, so he just drove me off campus and gave me a warning. But bein' in those handcuffs, in the cage, scared me. I'd been there before—you know about that?"

I nodded. "The papers said you had some drug arrests and arrests for disorderly conduct."

"Yeah. A long time ago. Before Elena. So I was ashamed when I got back here, an' scared that I'd lost control of myself like that."

I thought he was finished, but he went on before I could ask another question: "An' there was somethin' else. When I broke into that meetin', that was the first time I'd seen Bell in twenty-three years—an' he looked so . . . so much smaller than I remembered, somehow. An' kinda like a plucked chicken. All the time I was standin' there screamin' at him and cursin' him, he just sat with his head down, not lookin' at me. Later, when the cop let me go and I got back here, I thought, Why do I let that poor old fucker live inside me without payin' rent?"

"And then," I said, "he called you Friday night—or somebody did who you thought was Bell?"

He nodded. "He asked me if I'd come over to his studio, said he wanted to talk to me. I asked him what about. He said he was upset about what happened to Kate—he never forgot it, or forgave himself. That's what he said, an' he sounded like he meant it. But it was all bullshit! Bell was already dead; it was the killer tellin' me that stuff. He was a good actor, though. Or maybe he wasn't a good actor, maybe I was just a good audience. A fool."

"And you're sure it wasn't Bell who called you?"

"I don't know what Bell sounds like—I ain't heard his voice in twenty-three years! But it wasn't Bell. It was whoever killed Bell, wantin' to pin it on me."

"Okay. So you dropped everything and went over there, even though it was almost midnight?"

He nodded wearily. He'd heard the question before, and the skepticism.

He'd always been a night owl, he said. And since he didn't spend his nights in bars anymore, he spent them in his studio, working. That gave him more time for his wife and kids during the day. Also, the Studio Arts Building was only a fifteen minute walk, and he liked walking around in the night. He walked a lot, when he'd been working hard and needed to get some fresh air to clear his head.

"The cops don't believe it," he said. "None of it. The jury's not gonna believe it, either."

Well, I believed the parts about liking to work nights and walk around in the dark.

"You say your friends all know you work late. How'd Bell know that—or the man you say wasn't Bell, the murderer?"

"I don't know. I even wondered about that as I walked over. I told myself I'd ask him about it when I saw him." Sánchez laughed tonelessly. "He told me he'd leave the front door unlocked so I could get in. He said his studio was the last one on the left. I'd been in the building before, of course, back when Kate and I were together, so I knew my way around. I went in and found him."

His dark eyes grew wide, the way I'd seen them the night of the murder. "I thought it was some kind of accident at first, or he'd had a stroke or somethin'. I went over and squatted down next to him and shook him—and then I saw what someone'd done to him." He seemed to stare into that scene again, then shook his head violently from side to side. "I couldn't do that to nobody, Miss O'Neill, no matter how much I hated 'em."

"What did you do then?"

"Nothin'! I wanted to throw up. Then I thought, Hey, I'm gonna be blamed for this! I even figured out, right then, that it probably wasn't Bell who'd called me. So I started to wipe my fingerprints off anything I might've touched—and then I heard you come into the building.

"Jesus, I was scared! I didn't know what to do, so I just turned off the lights, closed the studio door and waited. And then you opened the door to Bell's—''

I didn't need to hear the rest of that, since I'd lived it with him. ''Tell me what you said to him when you broke into the department meeting in October.''

He shook his head in disgust. ''I don't remember exactly. Somethin' about how he'd lived his whole life knowin' he was a no-talent, and now that his life was almost over, he didn't have nothin' to live for and nothin' to be proud of. He'd just stood in the way of artists like Kate who were better'n him.''

His voice rose and he started to get angry all over again. ''The guy'd had a nice tenured position at the U for forty years! He'd never had to worry about where his next meal was coming from, or his rent money or money for his medical bills—nothin'! An' he was gonna get a retirement income on top of all that! But even though he'd lived twenty-three years longer than Kate, he was just as unknown as her!''

''The people who were there said you threatened to kill him with a clay cutter.''

He hung his head. ''I didn't threaten him. I said somethin' about how when I slice clay sometimes, I pretend it's his neck.'' He looked up at me defiantly. ''And I did, damn it—but I'd never do anything like that, I was only pretending. Everybody does that, don't they?'' Without waiting for an answer, he went on: ''I probably told him he'd be better off dead than livin' the rest of his life knowin' what a failure he was, too. The homicide dick looked like he wanted to laugh in my face when I tried to explain that. He thinks I'm making all of this up—the phone call in the middle of the night, all of it.''

''Homicide cops are very literal,'' I said. ''They hear that you talked about cutting a man's head off with a clay cutter who ends up getting killed that way, they want to meet you. Call it a failure of imagination.''

''I didn't want him dead, damn it! You know the expression, 'put out of his misery'? I didn't want him put out of his misery—I wanted him to suffer!''

I controlled the impulse to roll my eyes. ''You hated

Bell because your fiancée didn't get promoted in the Studio Arts Department some two decades ago. Right?"

"Yeah."

"Tell me about it."

"Why? I didn't kill Bell, so it ain't important."

"Tell me anyway."

He looked at me thoughtfully, then got up and went over to the worktable in the middle of the room and began unwrapping something that stood on a kind of revolving pedestal and was covered with plastic and damp cloth. It was like unwrapping a mummy. A head of wet clay emerged. Dan Sánchez sat down in front of it and stared at it for a moment, then turned back to me.

"This is Kate. I'm tryin' to do a bust of her, but I'm not very good at sculpture. She was, though—she would've been a word-famous sculptor by now, if she'd lived. You would've heard of her, if you was into art."

He turned back to the bust, picked up the tool with the wire loop on the end and peeled a little clay off under the mouth.

"Kate," I said. "Kate what?"

"Simons. The Studio Arts Department fired her. That's not what they called it, of course—that don't sound classy enough for the University. She just didn't get promoted to associate professor, which meant she had to leave the U. They fired her, is what it amounts to."

"And she was killed soon afterward. You think there was a connection between her not getting promoted and her murder?"

"No! Like I told you, she was killed by a burglar."

"And they never caught him?"

He shook his head disgustedly. "For a while, they even thought I might've done it! The cops ain't gonna catch whoever killed Bell either, if they keep on thinkin' it was me."

"Why'd they think you might've killed Kate?"

Without looking up from the head, he said, " 'Cause

a couple of months before she got killed, she dumped me.''

"Oh? I thought you said she was your fiancée."

Sánchez ran his hands through his thick hair, then stared down wildly into them, as if they held some kind of answer to his misery. "I was into drugs, and she didn't like that. She gave me an ultimatum: quit usin' or get out. I tried to quit. I couldn't. It was the sixties."

I couldn't help it—I laughed. The '60s get blamed for a lot. I lost a father to booze, a stepbrother to drugs, a childhood to both in that decade.

Sánchez glanced at me, then quickly back at Kate Simons's clay head. "The cops were right, but not the way they thought," he said quietly. "I did kill Kate. I killed her on account of if I'd been able to quit usin' like she wanted me to, she wouldn't've kicked me out and I would've been there the night the burglar broke into her apartment."

"Where were you?"

He shrugged. "Home—a little dump I got after she threw me out."

"No alibi?"

"You on my side or theirs?"

"Nobody's side. I'm just running an errand for a friend."

"I'm really fucked now, aren't I? You don't believe my story, and I wouldn't believe it either if it happened to someone else."

He looked around his studio as if seeing it for the first time, which is probably how you see things for the last time too. "The cops came here, you know," he said, speaking so softly I could barely hear him. "They took samples of my clay. They're going to compare it with the clay on the murder weapon. I mix my own, in that clay mixer over there." He gestured to a thing that looked like a cement mixer. "It's my own formula."

"The clay cutter might have come from the ceramics studio in the Studio Arts Building," I said. I didn't think it would help him much if it had, since he could have used a clay cutter from there—by his own admission, he knew his way around the building—but at least it wouldn't add to the burden of evidence against him.

"Maybe," he said, his face lighting up momentarily. "Maybe the killer didn't know about clay." His face fell again. "But he probably did. I think somebody who knows somethin' about clay and who knows my routine stole one of my clay cutters and used it to kill Bell."

"Are you missing one?"

He laughed and pointed to the wall behind me. Four or five clay cutters dangled by their wires from the faucet over the sink. "How would I know? They break, they get lost, the students take 'em home. I got at least a dozen scattered around."

"How easy would it be to get in here and steal one?"

"Real easy. People come in here all the time—customers, people just passin' by who come in to look at the pottery and want to see the studio. I got—*had*—sixteen students who come here regularly, others who come now and then, just to use the wheels or the glazing room and to fire their pots. Lots of people know my schedule, and any of 'em could've taken a clay cutter out with 'em too.

"If I'd've killed Bell," he went on, "I wouldn't've used one of my own clay cutters. I wouldn't've used a clay cutter at all, of course. I'm not that stupid."

He'd been stupid enough to burst in on the department meeting when the rage got to be too much for him. For all I knew, he'd been drunk or high on something. I only had his word for it that he'd quit using. All addicts are stupid until they're forced to confront the consequences of their actions. Then they sometimes get very smart very fast. Sánchez's story of an elaborate frame could be the sober man's effort to cover up the drunk's stupidity.

I got up. "You leavin'?" he asked, getting up too. When I said yes, he said, "You don't believe me, do you?"

I didn't answer that. I'd heard more believable lies, less believable truths. "Can you think of anybody who'd want to kill Bell or who'd want to frame you for murder?"

"Nobody. I don't even know anybody anymore who knows Bell. And I don't have any enemies that I know of."

I went over to the table and looked down at the clay bust he'd said was Kate Simons.

Next to it was a five-by-seven black-and-white snapshot of a man and a woman standing on the shore of one of the city's lakes in swimsuits. The man was obviously Dan Sánchez when he was a lot younger. The woman looked a couple of inches taller, and she had one arm draped casually around his shoulder. They were both smiling and squinting into the sun. She had short, curly dark hair, broad shoulders, long arms, and sturdy legs that looked springy and athletic.

I studied the photograph for a long time, comparing it to the head Sánchez was sculpting.

"I started it a couple nights after I broke into the department meeting. I thought maybe it was time to try to work through what I was feelin' about her an' everything that happened."

"You haven't caught much of the vitality in the snapshot yet," I said.

"I know that. I'll never catch all of it."

I headed for the door. "Chin needs to be stronger too," I said.

He followed me. "Sorry I've wasted your time. Tell Sandy thanks."

I turned and looked at him. The grudge he'd held for twenty-three years had been against himself, not Russell Bell, because he hadn't been there for Kate Simons in her hour of need. But he didn't seem to understand that, which made him a potentially dangerous character. That was why he'd broken into the department meeting, and it was why he could have killed Bell too. Rage is always misdirected, I think.

"I don't know yet if I'm wasting my time," I said

finally. "I'll do some asking around at the University before I decide."

This wasn't my idea of how to get ready for Christmas, which was only five days away.

Out in the front room, I paused to look over his pottery. I picked up a jug. I like pots that look inviting and feel comfortable in the hand, and Sánchez's were like that, as the coffee mug had been. And they had the right heft to them. Bad potters throw pots that are either too light or too heavy for how they look, so you put either too much or not enough effort into lifting them. Sánchez's pots looked their weight.

"You can have that one," he said, "if you like it."

I told him I already owned one of his weed pots.

He tried a smile. "And one's enough, huh? Or maybe too many?"

I put the jug down.

"We'll see," I said.

Six

I rode my bike over to the Studio Arts Building, chained it to the rack beside the front door and went in. Two little plastic signs on the wall next to the main office said that its occupants were Lloyd Schaeffer, chairman, and Gloria Williams, secretary. The door to the secretary's office, where I'd spent a long, ghastly hour Saturday morning being interviewed by Buck, was open, and she was speaking on the phone.

She was a woman of about fifty, with short dark hair turning gray and an exasperated expression on her face that she aimed briefly at me as I came in. "I'll tell Professor Schaeffer you called," she was saying. She listened to the response as she used a finger with a square-cut, no-nonsense nail to page through a document on her computer screen. "Yes, Professor Bright, as soon as he comes in. Yes, I do understand the urgency and I'm sure Professor Schaeffer will too when I have an opportunity to explain it to him."

She listened some more, absently, then said, "No, I won't forget. Good-bye, Professor Bright," and hung up quickly and let out a long sigh, staring down at her desk for a moment, as if drawing strength from its steel to help her through crises without number. Fortified, she looked up at me and said, "Yes?" in a tone of voice that suggested she wasn't eager to be my friend.

I told her my name and that I wanted to talk to someone in the department who'd been a friend of Russell Bell's.

Her face darkened, and she took a second look at me.
"Are you a reporter?"

"I'm a friend of a friend of the man the police think
may have killed him. She doesn't think he did it, and
asked me if I'd look into it."

"A private detective?"

"No. I'm doing this on my own."

She looked me up and down, as though she'd missed
something the first time. "I really don't think Professor
Bell had any close friends in the department," she said
finally. "Most of the faculty are away from the building
for the holidays in any case."

"Are you expecting Professor Schaeffer back today?"

"I hope so. He has a great deal of work waiting for
him," she said pointedly. "Even without the tragedy of
Professor Bell's death, there's so much to do to get ready
for next semester."

"How about Professor Bell's studio mate, Shannon
Rider? Does she come in during the holidays?"

"Usually. But I'm not sure if she's in today. However,
I cannot allow outsiders without official business to go
back into the studio area without an appointment." She
shook her head with feigned regret, and pointed to a wall
with mailboxes on it. "Why don't you leave a note in
Professor Rider's box? Her schedule is quite flexible during the holidays."

I was debating whether to do that or leave the office
and try to sneak into the studio area without Gloria Williams seeing me, when a man entered the building behind
me, stomped snow off his boots noisily in the hall, and
came into the office.

"Hallo, Gloria!" he shouted as he paused at the secretary's desk. "Sorry I'm a tad late. The dean took me
to the campus club for lunch, and I forgot all about the
time."

She glanced up at the clock on the wall. It was a little
before three. "Professor Bright called, Professor Schaeffer," she said evenly. "He wants to be included in the
selection process for a temporary replacement for Pro-

fessor Bell. Apparently he knows someone—''

Schaeffer swore without much heat. ''Vultures, all of 'em! Russ has barely shuffled off this mortal coil and already they're gathering! If that old fart calls again, tell him I'm in a meeting.'' He glanced at me, nodded vaguely, and started back toward his office.

''Excuse me, Professor Schaeffer,'' I said, pretending not to see the look of outrage on the secretary's face. ''My name's Peggy O'Neill. I'm the campus cop who found Professor Bell's body.''

I figured I needed to say something dramatic to stop his forward progress. That did it. It also made Gloria Williams sit up and take notice. I explained why I was there.

''Well,'' he said, ''I suppose you've earned the right to a little of my time. C'mon in.''

''You have to find someone to cover Professor Bell's classes next semester!'' Gloria Williams said through clenched teeth. ''It's very short notice!''

''I'll get to it, Gloria, I'll get to it—the woods are full of starving artists who'll jump at the chance to teach for a semester. If necessary, I'll teach the damned classes myself! It's just life drawing, composition.'' He laughed and led me around the secretary into his office.

''Don't mind Gloria,'' he said, breathing sherry fumes in my face. ''Even though she's been here thirty years, she still worries about deadlines. Sit down, sit down!'' He gestured to the straight-backed chair beside his desk.

He was in his early fifties, I guessed, medium height, stocky, and small-featured, with long untidy white hair and a button nose made rosy by Christmas cheer and the cold outside.

He asked me to tell him how I'd come to find Bell's body, and to soften him up I did, exaggerating only slightly. He listened raptly, his round, blinking eyes never leaving my face.

''And now,'' he said when I'd finished, ''you're trying to get the man who killed Bell and attacked you off— for a friend!''

"I'm not trying to get him off," I said. "I'm keeping an open mind. If I decide he really did kill Professor Bell, I'll drop it."

He considered that and nodded. "I suppose I can give you a few minutes," he said judiciously, "but then I have to look at what taskmaster Gloria has dumped on my plate." He glanced at the stack of paper in his in-box and gave an exaggerated shudder.

I asked him to describe the scene when Sánchez had interrupted the department meeting in October.

He sat back in his chair, gazing at the ceiling. "I'd have to say that, at the time, it was just embarrassing. Now, of course, I see it as the first act in a great tragedy. The fellow simply burst in and stood there, staring around. None of us, not even Russ, had the slightest idea who he was, of course—Russ said afterwards he couldn't remember if he'd ever met Sánchez. Then he spotted Russ, who fortunately was sitting in the back of the room, and started ranting and raving about what a great artist Kate Simons, his fiancée, had been and how Russ was a failure who'd kept Kate from getting promoted years ago, back when Russ was chairman. She had more talent in her little finger than he had in his whole body, and on and on."

Schaeffer threw out his hands as if trying to reason with Sánchez. "Most of the people in the room didn't have the foggiest notion of what he was talking about—it was so long ago, and they weren't even here back then."

I asked him if he'd heard Sánchez threaten Bell with a clay cutter. He nodded solemnly. "I certainly did! Said he sometimes imagined cutting off Russ's head with one. Said Russ would be better off dead."

Not exactly a threat, I thought, but there wasn't much point in splitting hairs with Schaeffer. Leave that to Sánchez's lawyer.

"How did Professor Bell take it?"

"Russ never said a word! Looked very uncomfortable, and a little scared too—who wouldn't be? Then one of your colleagues came in—thanks to Gloria's quick thinking,'' he added, unnecessarily raising his voice so Gloria could hear him through the half-open door. ''She'd called nine-one-one as soon as Sánchez charged past her up the stairs. Your man handcuffed him and drove him off campus. Russ refused to let me press charges against him for trespassing, which I was quite prepared to do.''

''Did Sánchez look like he might try to attack Professor Bell?''

Schaeffer pursed his lips, shaking his head. ''There were too many people between him and Russ, for one thing. For another, I don't think he knew *what* he was going to do. Frankly, I think he wished he'd never come and was just rambling on to cover his embarrassment.''

That sounded much the way Sánchez had described the incident too. I asked Schaeffer if he could tell me something of Bell's background, since the obituary had been a little short on detail.

''Russ was hired in nineteen sixty-two,'' he said. ''I know the year because I had to look it up for the journalists. Before coming here, he taught at City College in New York. He was considered quite a promising young painter back then.''

I said I'd never heard of him.

''You're not alone,'' Schaeffer said with a sad smile. He picked up a pencil and began to sketch something on his blotter. ''Oh, he did some good work in the late fifties and sixties, and one occasionally sees his work from those years in retrospectives, if they're inclusive enough, but I'm afraid he burned out early.'' He squinted up at me and went back to his sketching. ''The adjective most often used to describe Russ's work, even in his prime, was 'facile.' When I was going through his file I found a yellowed review that had been clipped from *Art News* from about twenty years ago. The reviewer said Bell's paintings reminded him of a mimic so skillful that he could never convince anybody when he was being sincere.''

''Ouch! That's pretty devastating. Did his work sell?''

''I know that several fairly prominent New York gal-

leries handled his work when he still lived there. After
he came here, some of the local galleries sold his stuff.
Of course, once you've left New York, they forget you
pretty damned quickly," he added with a tinge of bitter-
ness. "I can tell you that no major museums or other art-
purchasing institutions have acquired any of Russ's work
since the early seventies."

"How do you know that?"

Schaeffer smiled thinly and sketched away. "He
would have listed it on his faculty activities form—the
form we fill out at the end of each academic year to try
to convince the powers that be that we're still creatively
alive. Merit pay increases are based on them."

"He must not have received many merit increases
then," I said.

"Not in many years, I'm afraid. There are other ways
to earn smaller salary increases, of course. Good teaching
counts for something, and he was a good intro to painting
and drawing teacher. Of course, none of the graduate
students, the M.F.A. candidates, would have him as a
teacher or adviser since it no longer meant anything to a
young artist just starting out to have Russ Bell's name
on his résumé."

It sounded to me as though Russell Bell had had quite
a dreary career—pretty much the way Dan Sánchez had
described it to me—and to Bell's face too, in October. I
wondered how Kate Simons, the woman who hadn't been
promoted, would have fared if she'd had Bell's oppor-
tunities.

I asked Schaeffer if he'd known her and he hesitated
in his scribbling, looked up uncomfortably and replied
that he hadn't. "She was"—he seemed to grope for the
right word—"she died before I came aboard. Another
tragedy in our little temple of art." He seemed to be
working on my hair, to judge from the motions of his
hand. Either that or he was doing a Santa Claus with my
face.

"Your secretary told me that Bell didn't have any
close friends in the department," I said.

"No, he did not. Russ kept very much to himself. I know we should speak only well of the dead, but I don't think he would mind greatly if I told you that he contributed very little except sarcasm to department meetings. He seemed to delight in voting against whatever he perceived the majority of the faculty wanted. He was also quite contemptuous of the work of his colleagues—especially the younger ones. He cut rather a pathetic figure, and we were all looking forward to his leaving us."

He added hastily, "Not, of course, in the way he did leave—I don't mean that!" He sketched faster, shading something now. "I mean we were all quite frankly looking forward to his retirement at the end of this year with perhaps unseemly eagerness."

"And he had no friends you know about?"

Schaeffer shook his head. "No." Then his face lit up as something occurred to him. "But you might talk to the people over in the art museum—especially Laura Price, the associate director. It's my impression Russ got along quite well with her and with the other museum people. He was a docent over there, you know."

I didn't know. I also didn't know what a docent was.

"A tour guide. Russ was very good at it, I understand." Schaeffer didn't sound as though that impressed him much. "In the past few years, he put a lot more energy into the art museum than he did here—probably because he wasn't competing with the artists over there, since most of them are dead," he added with a moist chuckle.

He looked at his watch, then at me, and stood up, sliding a piece of paper over what he'd been sketching. "Time's up!" he said. "I hope I've been of some help to you. Russ was unpleasant, certainly, but he was retiring in six months, and I can't think of anybody who felt so strongly about him that he couldn't wait that long to see him out of here."

"According to the obituary," I said, "he never married. How about lovers? Was he gay? Straight?"

Schaeffer shook his head. "I'm sorry," he said a little

too quickly, "I know nothing about his sex life." He turned to Gloria Williams, who was doing something with columns of figures on her computer as we came out into her office. "Do you, Gloria?"

Without looking up from her work, she snapped, "The faculty does not discuss its private affairs with me, Professor Schaeffer, and I don't discuss mine with them."

As he opened his mouth to say something to that, a woman came into the office from the hall. She was wearing a down jacket and earmuffs, and her face was red with cold.

"Ah, Shannon!" Schaeffer exclaimed. "You're just the woman we're looking for, aren't we—Peggy O'Neill, is it?" When I nodded, he continued. "Peggy here is the campus policewoman who found poor Russ's body. She doesn't think the man the police have arrested did it—is that right, Peggy?"

Shannon Rider looked me up and down curiously as I explained to her about Sandra.

"Sandra Carr thinks the police have the wrong man?" she said. "That's a scary thought—but then, Sandra Carr has lots of scary thoughts, doesn't she? I hope she's wrong about that, because if the Sánchez character didn't kill Russ, it could've been somebody who has it in for the entire Studio Arts Department—in which case, who's next?" She grinned at Lloyd Schaeffer, who looked appalled. "C'mon back to my studio," she said to me.

If only everybody was so eager to help, I thought, the amateur sleuth's job would be so much easier. I resisted the temptation to stick my tongue out at Gloria Williams as I passed her desk, if only to try to melt the frosty expression on her face, and followed Shannon Rider back down the hall to the studio she'd shared—and I had too for a brief, shocking time—with the late Russell Bell.

Seven

"This would be a perfect setting for one of Carr's novels," she said as we stepped inside. "But I suppose you know that better than I. I can still smell Russ's blood. Can you, or is it just my imagination? I suppose it was worse when you were here last."

I couldn't smell anything but paint and turpentine now. "Much worse," I said.

She stuffed her earmuffs into her coat and draped the coat over a chair. "And you patrol the campus in the middle of the night? I couldn't do that—I love light too much, and I'd hate to have to sleep during the brightest part of the day."

Different strokes. Shannon Rider was in her late twenties, about my height, with shoulder-length light brown hair, restless blue eyes and a wide, expressive mouth. She was wearing an old white shirt and khaki slacks, both paint-stained.

I went over and stood in front of the painting on her easel. It was a portrait of a woman, staring straight out of the canvas, just her head, tightly framed. She looked to be in her late fifties, early sixties. It wasn't trompe l'oeil—I hate that—but it was some kind of super-realism: You could see the brush strokes that had created the portrait clearly, but you could also see every line, every wrinkle, in the woman's face, the fuzz and a few dark hairs on her chin in the bright, unforgiving light. Her mouth, a severe line, still somehow looked as though it was about to smile, and her dark eyes staring into mine burned with intelligent humor. It was a hypnotic painting, awful in the original meaning of the word, and I wasn't sure I could stand having it in my house. I'd stumble in front of it every time I passed it.

"This wasn't here Saturday," I said. "Even with everything else that was going on, I think I would have remembered."

"No it wasn't," Shannon Rider said with a laugh. "I started it yesterday."

"Yesterday!"

She smiled at my amazement. "It went a little faster than I expected it to."

"It's your mother, isn't it?" I said because I could see the resemblance.

"Yes."

When she didn't add anything to that, I walked over to where I'd found Russell Bell's body. "This was his half of the studio?"

"Right. The custodians got rid of most of the mess the murderer and the police made, but I've gone over it with a mop a couple of times too."

I asked her how she'd happened to share a studio with Bell.

"Someone had to, and I'm low painter on the totem pole." She gestured to canvases leaning against the wall next to a storage cabinet. "Those are his. The cops took the painting he was working on when he was killed as evidence of something. Took his easel too."

The blood splatters on the easel and painting probably indicated where Bell was standing when he'd been killed.

"Now," she said, getting all businesslike, "what can I tell you?"

"I'm trying to find out who besides Dan Sánchez might have had a reason to want to kill Bell. You shared a studio with him. What did he talk about, the last days of his life?"

She shook her head. "If I was one of the people closest to him, he was certainly a very lonely man. We didn't socialize, and we rarely spoke while we were working.

We didn't have anything in common. He didn't like my art; I didn't like his. I was warned that he'd been quite the womanizer in his younger days, hitting on his students, his models, anything young and female, but I guess I wasn't his type, or else he'd got religion or grown out of it. He never pestered me.''

"And he didn't seem worried about anything?''

"He seemed quite cheerful, mostly,'' she said. "The only worry he had, as far as I could tell, was finishing the painting he was working on in time for the faculty show. That's why he was working so late Friday night. He'd been working like a fiend all week to try to finish it.''

I said, as tactfully as possible, that surely a faculty show couldn't be that important, especially for a man about to retire.

She gave me a sardonic smile and said, "No, Peggy, faculty shows are usually in-house affairs that only our friends and families would see—and the occasional student looking for a quiet place to study. But this one means a lot more than that to us because it's going to be a kind of pendant—sideshow might be a more accurate description—to the main event, the opening of the University's new art museum. You know about that?''

"Sure. I'm even going to be there,'' I said modestly.

She raised an eyebrow. "To guard the U's treasures from the sticky fingers of the art lovers?''

"Nope. My aunt Tess has been a patron of the museum a long time, and she gets to bring a guest to the opening. I'm hers. We're even sitting with Dr. Fowler, the new director, at the head table at the banquet. My aunt's his old high school teacher.''

"Lucky you,'' she said. "What are you going as?''

The guests were expected to come as characters from works of art. "Renoir's *Portrait of a Young Woman in a Blue Hat*,'' I told her. "How about you?''

"I figure the museum'll be hot and crowded, so I'm dressing light, the woman in Hopper's *Summertime*. Put in a word for me with Fowler, will you?'' she added.

"The museum needs more women in its permanent collection, and I could use the money. Anyway, the Studio Arts faculty's been given a gallery of its own—off to the side, naturally, where we won't contaminate the art of the dead masters. All the biggest gallery owners in the state, museum heads, art critics, wealthy buyers—everybody who's anybody is going to be there."

She took the painting off her easel and leaned it against a wall, replacing it with a blank canvas. She looked at it longingly and then turned back to me. I wondered what she'd seen when she'd stared at the new surface to paint on.

"You'll even see one of Russ Bell's paintings in the show," she said. "Since he couldn't get the painting *he* wanted in the show, I picked one out of that pile up against the wall. Not all of them were finished, but a couple were. I took what I considered the best and sent it over to the museum." She looked up at the ceiling. "I hope he would approve."

I went over and flipped through Bell's paintings, which were all abstractions. I like the work of some of the abstract expressionists—Motherwell, de Kooning, Pollock, for instance, and especially Helen Frankenthaler, one of the few women abstractionists to make it. But Bell's paintings didn't do anything for me; they seemed more decorative than expressive. I wondered if that was because I knew they were by someone who hadn't become famous, whereas other paintings, not so different from his—to my eye, at least—were by artists who had.

"He seems very competent," I said, uncertainly.

"He was," Shannon Rider agreed, her back to me, looking at her canvas with her head cocked. "He was an unrepentant abstract expressionist long after almost everybody else had moved on. But the painting he was working on when he was killed seemed to be a new direction for him."

"What new direction?" I asked.

"It was quite figurative. Not like what I'm doing, though. His was 'realistic realistic,' if you know what I mean. Realism's making a comeback, and I've heard Bell was pretty versatile when it came to styles in art—according to the gossip around here, that was his problem. But whatever he thought he was doing, he was having a lot of trouble getting the painting to come out the way he wanted it to. Mumbling and swearing under his breath, scratching and scraping and starting over.''

I asked her to describe the scene when Sánchez had confronted Bell at the faculty meeting, and she told me the same story Schaeffer had: Sánchez seemed to have exhausted his rage just by breaking in and interrupting the meeting. She'd thought he was mostly just words. ''But getting him off isn't going to be easy,'' she added.

''Tell me about it, Shannon!'' I said. I figured I could call her by her first name, since she'd called me by mine.

''I'm surprised, after what you must have seen in here and what he did to you, you'd even consider the possibility he's innocent.''

''Somebody has to,'' I replied.

''If you really want to get the scoop on Bell's private life,'' she said, ''you should talk to the Emeriti.''

''I know what 'emeritus' means,'' I said. ''A pretentious word for 'retired.' Who are the Emeriti?''

''Our distinguished retired faculty members. Burned-out volcanos—although I don't think they did much in the way of erupting when they were younger either. Three of them are still around: Charlie Bright, Herb Sweeney, and Blair McFarlane. I think they were all here before Bell arrived. What they don't know about his personal life, I'm sure they'll be glad to make up for you.''

''How do I get hold of them?''

''Weekday mornings, they come toddling in early—right after Gloria brings in the pastries and makes the coffee. The department still lets Bright and Sweeney have precious studio space, and McFarlane's still permitted to use the etching stones and press.''

I made a mental note to return to the Studio Arts Building myself, maybe try to share a Danish with the Emeriti and pump their memories for information about Bell's private life. After all, wasn't I practically an honorary member of the faculty since I'd found his body? I also intended to go over and talk to the associate director of the art museum, Laura Price, since Bell had spent so much of his time there.

I asked Shannon if Bell had ever mentioned Kate Simons to her.

"Kate—? Oh, right, the murder suspect's fiancée or whatever. No, he never spoke to me about her—or about anything else, as I've told you."

"Not even after Sánchez broke into the department meeting and talked about her?"

"Uh-uh. He never mentioned that incident, and I certainly wouldn't have asked him about her after what Sánchez had said." She looked out into space for a long moment. "I wonder what her work was like. I asked one of the Emeriti about her the other day—Charlie Bright, whose main claim to fame is that fifteen years ago he decided that art would be better off without the curve and abandoned it in his painting. He just clucked and said that in his opinion Kate Simons hadn't been a very promising sculptor. The other candidate for the position seemed far stronger at the time, he added, although he hadn't amounted to much either, in the end."

"Who was the other candidate?"

She gave me a look—suddenly old and at once stern and humorous—that reminded me of her portrait of her mother. "Lloyd Schaeffer, our esteemed chairman, a painter of spectacular mediocrity."

Eight

Wondering about the significance, if any, of the fact that Schaeffer had got Kate Simons's position and hadn't mentioned it to me, I went back out to the main office and the welcoming hoarfrost of Gloria Williams, waved good-bye to her, and left.

I met Buck that night at Crouton's, his latest favorite restaurant, which seems to specialize in small portions at exorbitant prices of foodstuffs never seen in combination before last week.

"Shouldn't the chef have signed and numbered this in beet juice or something?" I asked as I picked at a slice of exotic mushroom tart perched negligently on a strange-looking leaf that constituted the appetizer. Having spent part of a day in the Studio Art Department had made me more aware of the art in everyday things, but exotic fungi always make me nervous.

Buck chewed for a moment before answering, gazing over the candle at me in the absent-minded, rather bovine way of the gourmand. "Smaller portions force you to savor each bite's subtle blend of textures and tastes," he said when he'd swallowed. "You're less apt to just fork it in."

"That's what my aunt Tess said about life," I said, "when she turned sixty."

Buck and I had met a few years ago under somewhat inauspicious circumstances. I was a rookie cop and I'd just come upon a corpse and thrown up. Our friendship had grown from there. Although he often treats me like a little sister or a daughter, I doubt that he's more than ten years older than me, but you never know in these days of diet and exercise.

I have no idea if he's ever been married. I once saw him at a concert with a tall, elegant, and unpleasantly beautiful woman with lovely silver hair but couldn't get to him to find out who she was before the crowd swept them away. Could've been his sister, I suppose. The next time we had dinner together, I mentioned seeing them and he just smiled and asked me what I'd thought of the music.

He's about five-ten, but lean and long-legged so he looks taller. His hair is blond paling to silver, and he has laugh wrinkles at the corners of blue eyes that can turn cold very fast, like the lakes here. And his smile—I've never understood how a homicide cop could have such a beautiful smile.

I'm sure that if he ever made a pass at me, I'd forget all about Gary and propriety and fall straight into his arms. I might even cultivate a preference for endive over head lettuce. I've sent up trial balloons occasionally and watched them sail away in the sky above his head. We get together for dinner about once a month, sometimes at his place, sometimes at a restaurant, rarely at my place because he finds my cooking almost actionable.

I waited until after we'd finished dinner and he'd ordered an expensive brandy and I a cappuccino before mentioning that I was looking into Russell Bell's murder for Sandra Carr.

"Sandra—? Oh, right, the author of damsel-in-distress potboilers misnamed 'psychological thrillers.' Why?"

"She's a friend of Dan Sánchez's."

"I'm not surprised she has murder suspects among her friends," he said, his nose in his brandy bubble. "It's probably very trendy these days." His feelings for Sandra are almost as strong as hers for him. I sometimes wonder if I should try to fix them up with each other. It would serve them both right.

"I also talked to Sánchez."

He looked up. "That wasn't a very good idea. You might be called to testify at his trial."

"Too late to do anything about it now."

"You could find something else to occupy your time, Peggy. We found Bell's wallet in a dumpster in the alley behind Sánchez's home. The crime lab report's in on the clay on the murder weapon—it matches Sánchez's formula. And we found Bell's blood on Sánchez's boots."

"Were Sánchez's fingerprints on the wallet?"

"No, but that doesn't mean anything. By his own admission, he spent a few minutes trying to erase his fingerprints from Bell's studio before you came in. We think he took the wallet to try to make the murder look like robbery was the real motive."

"Gee," I said, "I thought Hispanics were supposed to be smart but hot-blooded—they kill in passion. If your guess is correct, Sánchez is just the opposite. Cold-blooded enough to think of trying to fake a robbery to cover the murder, but so dumb he left a long trail of clues: bursting into the department meeting, using a clay cutter—worse, using a clay cutter with his clay on it—and dumping the wallet close to home!"

"Who knows what he intended to do if you hadn't arrived when you did? For all we know, he might've been drunk, wandered over to the campus, found himself at the Studio Arts Building, gone in, encountered Bell, and killed him in a rage. I'm sure that's what his attorney's going to try to talk him into telling the jury, and in my opinion he'd be wise to do it. It's the only chance he's got."

"But it's not much of a chance, is it? Because the prosecutor's going to point out that he took a clay cutter with him and he managed to get behind Bell without Bell noticing—all of which spells premeditation."

Buck shrugged and didn't say anything.

I sat back and sighed. Sánchez's defense was going to have to come up with something quite remarkable to instill reasonable doubt in a jury that considers all the evidence.

There was another story, the one Sánchez had told me. And there were his children and his wife and his large eyes, full of pain and bewilderment, above the angry scar on his cheek.

"Sánchez lets anybody come back into his studio," I said. "Someone pretending to be a prospective customer could have taken one of his clay cutters. I could have when I was there."

"I'm sure his lawyer will impress that point on the jury," Buck said dryly.

"He says Bell—more likely, someone pretending to be Bell—called him and asked him to come over. Did you check to see if anybody made a call from the Studio Arts Building after hours that night?"

Buck nodded. "Nobody did."

I asked him if his investigation had turned up anyone else who might have wanted to kill Bell, before they settled on Sánchez.

"We didn't find anybody with a compelling reason to want to kill him—not now, at least. He was the oldest active member of the faculty. The younger faculty members hardly seemed to know he was still there—a lot of them were out of town, and could prove it, at the time he was killed too. He pretty much stayed away from the Studio Arts Department. He spent a lot of time at the University art museum as a guide."

I nodded. "He seems to have been a very big absence."

"A very *small* absence," Buck corrected me, "until Daniel Sánchez garroted him. Then he became a very big one—for a couple of days." He swirled brandy, sniffed fumes; I licked foam off my index finger. We were a pair.

" 'Not now, at least,' " I said.

He raised his eyebrows.

"You said you couldn't find anybody besides Sánchez with a compelling reason to want to kill Bell—'not now, at least.' When, then—and who?"

"After we arrested Sánchez, I went through the file on

the murder of his ex-fiancée, Kate Simons, just to see what that was all about. During the investigation back then, one of Bell's colleagues accused him of having an affair with Simons and, a few days before she was killed, of quarreling with her. Bell denied it hotly. He also had an alibi for the time of the murder that the detective was able to confirm.'' Buck gave me a cynical grin. ''In the course of the investigation, the detective learned that Bell was having an affair with the wife of his accuser.''

''Dear me!'' I exclaimed, throwing up my hands in horror. ''Just like the bohemian artists in Paris circa eighteen-ninety, wasn't it? Except the bohemians didn't have tenure. Who was Bell's accuser?''

''A printmaker named Blair McFarlane.''

''He's one of the Emeriti now,'' I said, and explained to Buck that that's what Shannon Rider had called the three retired faculty members who still had studio space in the Studio Arts Building.

''So the cops at the time decided McFarlane was trying to implicate Bell in Kate Simons's murder because his wife and Bell were having an affair?''

Buck smiled. ''Right. Except that McFarlane wasn't supposed to be aware of what was going on between his wife and Bell.''

''Sure! He must be pretty old now. Could he have killed Bell?''

''Physically, yes. He's tall enough—and whoever garroted Bell either had to be as tall as he, or else stand on a chair, which seems unlikely—and he wrestles lithography stones around, which means he's strong enough too.''

''Does he have an alibi?''

''His wife.''

''A new Mrs. McFarlane or the old Jezebel?''

''There's only been one.''

Not the strongest of alibis, but at least he had one. Dan Sánchez didn't. McFarlane also couldn't be placed at the crime scene, and there wasn't any other physical evidence to connect him to it either.

"And that's as far as you went before you settled on Sánchez as the perfect suspect," I said.

"Peggy," Buck replied, putting down his snifter with a dull thud, "we—you, that is—found Sánchez with the body, murdered with Sánchez's—"

"I know all that," I broke in. "I'm just saying it's too pat. If someone set Sánchez up for you to keep you from looking any further into Bell's life, then he succeeded, didn't he? Because your investigation came to a screeching halt the moment you found the Mexican—excuse me, I mean the Chicano—with the scar and the police record."

For a moment, I thought I'd gone too far as I watched Buck's fingers turn white on the snifter's thin stem. Luckily, it didn't break.

"You found him, Peggy," he said softly, "in the studio with the body. And we found the evidence. And he created his past history of drug and alcohol abuse and violence himself."

"A long time ago!"

"So he claims. You don't know he wasn't drinking or high on something last Friday night."

"You won't even consider the possibility that he's being framed for the murder?"

He leaned back in his chair, giving me a long look. "I could, Peggy," he said finally. He put a little extra emphasis on the pronoun, but I really had to strain to hear it. "In spite of a strong feeling that he's guilty as hell, I could. But the chief wouldn't let me spend any more time and manpower on it even if I wanted to. Bell's isn't the only murder I'm working on—it's the holiday season, and for a homicide cop, that's like the last act of *Hamlet*. It's not my job to try to clear suspects—you know that. It's my job to get enough evidence to bring them to trial. And in Sánchez's case, that's what I've done. Now he's in the hands of the justice system."

I'd really like to believe in that system since it's the only hope we have that justice will prevail in our world. But the trouble is, it depends on a population that knows how to think—how to weigh arguments rationally and separate facts from feelings. And where do we find that now? In my experience, any halfway competent lawyer can play a jury the way a used-car salesman plays a sucker, which is why so many used-car salesmen are changing careers.

Cops don't look gift horses in the mouth, and the case Sánchez had helped create against himself was a gift horse. For a cop, there's no such thing as a too-pat case— usually, a case isn't pat enough.

Buck and I talked about other things for a while before separating in the restaurant's parking lot with a quick, unsatisfying hug that mostly involved thick winter outerwear.

Nine

Taking the dog watch gives me a lot of free time to pursue my own interests during the day, when most people are locked into institutions of one sort or another, doing things they have no interest in to turn a profit for somebody else. For the time being, at least, my own interests included pursuing the murder of Russell Bell. Why? Not only because I'd promised Sandra Carr I'd do it but also because of Dan Sánchez's almost inarticulate rage at what had happened to his fiancée, Kate Simons.

There's something doubly moving about grief expressed poorly, emotion struggling to get through language, as unforgiving a medium as paint or stone to those with no gift for it. When he'd tried to tell me what he'd shouted at Bell, standing in that room full of mostly uncomprehending faculty members, I could feel his anger on behalf of someone he'd believed had been badly treated. Rape and abuse victims sound that way too sometimes because they have no talent for expressing the terrible violation they've experienced.

When they do try to express themselves, it comes out sounding embarrassing, as everybody I'd talked to who'd heard Sánchez—including Sánchez—had described the way he'd sounded.

Buck hadn't turned up any live suspects among Bell's colleagues or acquaintances. But then, once he'd got onto Dan Sánchez, he'd lost interest—or was ordered to lose interest—in other possibilities. I decided to take up where he'd left off, at least for a while.

Someone who knew a little about his habits could have framed Sánchez, as Sánchez wanted me to believe: his tirade against Bell in the faculty meeting gave the killer the idea, and everything else followed from that.

According to Buck, Bell had an affair with the wife of one of the retired faculty members, Blair McFarlane, twenty-three years ago. It was just as easy to believe McFarlane had borne a grudge against Bell all those years, and decided to kill him now, as to believe Dan Sánchez had. The catalyst for either of them could have been Bell's forthcoming retirement.

Shannon Rider had told me that some of the retired faculty members, the Emeriti, came in every weekday morning early enough to get the best selection of pastries before going off to the studio spaces they'd been allotted. So I didn't bother to go home after my shift was over the next morning; I just changed into slacks and a sweater in the women's lounge at headquarters, freshened up, and hung around the squad room, where I read the *Daily*, fussed with the Christmas tree, and gossiped with my friend Ginny Raines, who works days.

At 8:30, I bundled up and biked across the Old Campus to the Studio Arts Building. The sun had risen since I'd come in from my patrol, and it was a bright, crisp morning a few degrees below freezing. I was looking forward to the Studio Arts doughnuts and coffee—assuming I was able to get past Gloria Williams, of course.

She wasn't at her desk, which was fine with me. From my nocturnal wanderings through the building, I knew the faculty lounge was at the head of the stairs on the second floor. I walked up.

Three men were in there, two of them sitting on a couch, the third standing at the coffee urn, spooning whitener into a styrofoam cup. Who says artists don't suffer?

They looked me up and down. I smiled all around, told them my name, and explained that I was a campus cop looking into the murder of Russell Bell, hoping they'd assume I was on official business. "Both your chairman, Professor Schaeffer, and Professor Rider suggested to me that you were the people in the department who knew Bell the longest and might have the most to tell me about him," I added, dropping names the way scholars do to shore up thin arguments.

At the mention of Bell's name, the two men on the couch sat up straight—or, in the case of the short, fat one, tried to.

The tall man at the coffee urn said, "Really? What's wrong with the suspect you have now, that Mexican fellow—García or López or whatever it is?"

"Daniel Sánchez," the gawky one on the couch supplied. He was wearing a cheap hairpiece in a gaudy straw yellow that he must have bought before his own hair had begun to fade to gray.

"Did you know him, Herb?" the squat one asked.

"Certainly not," Hairpiece replied. "I told you so when he invaded the department meeting! The city's awash with murderous and disgruntled potters. How can I be expected to know them all?"

"Sánchez is still the prime suspect, of course," I assured them soothingly. "However, the police wouldn't be doing their jobs if they didn't explore other possibilities." Take that, Buck!

"Other possibilities?" the fat man on the couch said. "What other possibilities?"

"I'm sorry," I said, "but I don't know your names." I made a show of bringing out the little spiral notebook I keep in my shoulder bag and poised a pen over it earnestly.

"I'm Herb Sweeney," Hairpiece the potter said. "This tub of nastiness sitting next to me is Charlie Bright. And that's Blair McFarlane over by the goodies."

Of the three of them, McFarlane was the only one I'd ever heard of as an artist. I'd seen a show of his children's book illustrations at the downtown library a year or so ago.

Bright got up and came over and circled around me, squinting in the morning light from the dirty window behind the coffee urn. He was bald, with a ripple of fat on the back of his neck, and so round he looked as though he would roll across the room if you pushed him off his little legs. It occurred to me that he couldn't have garroted Bell unless he'd stood on a chair.

"You wouldn't pose for me, would you?" he asked.

"No." I'd heard from Shannon Rider that he'd abolished the curve in his paintings.

"Good for you!" Herb Sweeney exclaimed.

"Perhaps it's just as well," Bright said, unperturbed. "I don't think I have the color of your hair on my palette." He went over and poured himself a cup of coffee, plucked up a doughnut, and returned to the couch. Only the toes of his shoes touched the floor. "Help yourself," he said to me.

I got a cup of coffee and selected a doughnut heavy with grease and sugar glaze that makes even the worst coffee drinkable if you dunk the doughnut in it a few times first.

"You don't suspect anyone on the Studio Arts faculty of doing away with Bell, do you?" McFarlane asked, as he strode over to a window and parked himself on the sill. He was tall and lean, with a hooked nose, lantern jaw, and gray hair under a jaunty plaid tam-o'-shanter.

"Of course she does, Mac," Herb Sweeney said. "She suspects everyone. If she didn't, she wouldn't be a cop."

"Well she's wasting her time," Charlie Bright muttered. "I'm happy with the Mexican."

"But Charlie," Sweeney said, after biting into a cherry Danish, "if 'the Mexican,' as you so charmingly put it, isn't the killer, then it's not entirely out of the question that whoever is hasn't finished his task yet." He raised his shaggy eyebrows, wiped jam from his lips with the back of his hand, and looked around at the other two. "One of us might be next! I, for one, won't feel safe down in the studios late at night until the jury's spoken. Even then . . ." he added, and let the rest of the sentence trail off.

"You don't work late at night anymore anyway," Bright retorted. "As far as I'm concerned, the police have their man."

"Professor Bell lived here for almost thirty-five years," I said. "He didn't have any close family, according to the obituary, but he must have had friends. We'd like to talk to them, find out about his life—get some sense of the man."

"I haven't had anything to do with Russ, outside of this building, I mean, for many years," Bright said. "We didn't agree on art; we didn't agree on anything else either. Russ Bell had a second-rate talent and a second-rate mind. As far as I know, he disappeared into the woodwork about the time he stopped being chairman of the department."

He darted his mean little eyes around at the others. "Isn't that right? He used to have parties at his house sometimes, back when he had a house, but as soon as he stepped down as chairman, he seemed to dry up—in more senses than one."

I asked him what he meant by that.

"He stopped trying to push his work on an already indifferent public, stopped socializing—seemed to give up and crawl into a shell. Wouldn't you say that's true, Sweeney?"

Sweeney nodded, frowning hideously. "I rarely visited the painters' studios, and Russ never came down to mine either. He didn't think much of potters as artists. Ironic, isn't it, that a potter may have done him in!" He glanced around at the rest of us to see if we appreciated the irony as much as he did.

"But you must have known something about his life outside this building," I insisted. I looked at McFarlane, who hadn't spoken since I'd first come in. He returned my gaze calmly, said nothing, brought out a long-stemmed pipe, and began stuffing it with tobacco with slow, deliberate gestures.

"You mean, was he gay or straight or involved in a sex or drug ring—things like that?" Sweeney asked. "He wasn't gay. I couldn't honestly swear he wasn't part of a sex or dope ring, although that doesn't sound like Russ, somehow. He was an unhappy man, very bitter over the fact that his career never went anywhere.''

"When Russ first came into the department," Bright said, "he was full of energy and seemed glad to be out of the New York rat race. He continued to get the occasional respectful review from the New York critics for a while after that.''

"And what more can a painter want?" Sweeney asked rhetorically.

"But it didn't last," Bright went on. "New York's a fickle lover. Out of sight, out of mind. Russ's problem was that he had great facility but nothing to say." He looked at me as though he was disappointed I didn't write that down.

"That's true," Sweeney said mournfully. "He could paint in any style—just couldn't come up with one of his own.''

Bright chuckled maliciously. "I remember seeing him with a big canvas spread out on the floor, dribbling paint on it à la Jackson Pollock. 'Russ, stop that!' I told him. 'You're making a mess!' He just glared at me and went on squeezing and splattering and dribbling. He had no sense of humor at all.''

"And then there were those horrid paintings of women with spear-point breasts right out of de Kooning," Sweeney said.

"When you could find them," Bright sneered.

"The art world is lucky Russ didn't decide to become a forger," Sweeney said. "He would have made a great one."

I was glad Bright and Sweeney were sitting together on the sofa. I didn't have to swivel my head back and forth.

Bright laughed suddenly. "Remember the Georgia O'Keeffe he had hanging on his wall? He'd painted it himself. It was—''

"Bell couldn't *stand* O'Keeffe!" Sweeney broke in,

giving Bright a quick glance. " 'There are "holes" in her canvases,' he hollered." He turned to me. "You see, Officer O'Malley, real painters—like Charlie Bright here, and Russ Bell—don't like holes in paintings. By holes I mean the illusion of three-dimensional space. Poor Georgia O'Keeffe didn't seem to know what real painters know—or maybe she didn't care, since her paintings are full of great gaping holes, like mysterious hiding places and wounds."

I nodded. "O'Keeffe once said she thought holes were very expressive," I said a little smugly.

They all looked at me, startled that I had something to contribute. "And she was right!" Sweeney roared, his eyes sparkling. "As a potter, I've always been very fond of holes. And I've always liked Georgia O'Keeffe."

Something about the way he had interrupted Bright bothered me—that and the look they'd exchanged—as if Charlie Bright was about to put his foot in his mouth before Sweeney stopped him. "I don't get it. Why did Professor Bell paint an O'Keeffe?"

There was a long pause before Sweeney said, "It wasn't really an O'Keeffe. It was a painting Bell had done with an O'Keeffe in it, hanging on the wall—it was a parody, just his idea of a joke. As Charlie said, Russ had no sense of humor."

"The University had just purchased an O'Keeffe," Bright added sourly. "They decided they had to try to protect their investment, so they invited her here and gave her an honorary degree. 'Female flower painters do not receive honorary degrees,' Russ grumbled, when he heard about it. He painted a flower in the style of O'Keeffe to show that anybody could paint like her."

I looked at Bright and Sweeney in turn. They looked like two choirboys up to no good. McFarlane said nothing, his face an expressionless mask.

I was up to no good too. "You say he wasn't gay," I said to Sweeney. "Does that mean he had women lovers?"

McFarlane, red-faced, broke his silence. "I don't feel

comfortable speculating on a man's personal life so soon after he's been brutally murdered.''

"We no longer bury Caesar,'' Sweeney said lightly, "we peck him to death.''

I recalled that McFarlane, according to Buck, had felt comfortable speculating on Kate Simons's personal life back at the time of her murder. He'd told a detective that he thought she and Bell had been having an affair. His wife had had an affair with Bell too, according to the police report Buck had read.

"If Russ Bell's death had anything to do with some kind of sordid affair he was having,'' Bright said, his voice ringing with righteousness, "the police will have to unearth the evidence without any help from me.''

I pushed it a little. "Someone told me that Bell was quite a womanizer in his younger days.''

"It's no secret that Russ Bell loved women—how does it go?—'not wisely, but too often,' '' Bright said, licking his fingers.

"Who?'' I asked.

"You want names?'' he asked, laughing uneasily. "Ask Gloria for the class lists from twenty, twenty-five years ago! Or the names of his models.''

McFarlane took the pipe out of his mouth and blurted, "If you're looking for a woman behind Bell's murder, there was one! Kate Simons!''

We all three looked at him in surprise.

"She's the woman behind Bell's murder—the *only* woman. It's just as the police think: Sánchez killed Russell Bell on account of Kate Simons.''

"Yes,'' Bright said, "but if Sánchez flew into a murderous rage because Kate Simons didn't get promoted, Mac, why did he focus his anger just on Bell? Why isn't he out to kill the rest of us who were here back then too?'' He put his elbows on his fat knees and stared at McFarlane across the room, a little smile on his round, malicious face.

"Because *we* didn't take her to bed, Charlie!'' McFarlane answered. "Sánchez didn't kill Russ because

Kate didn't get promoted. That was just an excuse. He didn't want to tell us the real reason when he broke into our meeting in October.''

He lit his pipe with furious puffs and glared at us through the cloud of smoke. "I'm going to tell you something I've never told anybody in the department before. Shortly after she and the Mexican broke up, Russ and Kate had an affair. And a few days before she was murdered, I heard 'em quarreling! Frankly, I think Sánchez murdered Kate—if Russ didn't. And I think he bided his time and murdered Russ as well.''

"Why didn't you say something about it to the police back then?" Bright asked.

"I did," he replied. "I don't mind admitting it now. I don't know if the police followed up on it or not. If they did, they obviously couldn't find the proof. Sánchez may have been a little more careful back then—a little more in control." He gave me a pointed look. "And now I'm telling the police investigating Bell's murder the same thing.''

I took the hint, made a note.

"I remember Kate," Herb Sweeney said, screwing up his face in thought, "and I don't think she would have had an affair with Russ.''

"She may have thought it would enhance her chances of getting promoted," McFarlane said.

"No," Sweeney said, shaking his head stubbornly and looking like a clown about to cry. "She wouldn't have done that. I'm sorry, Mac, but I think she had too much pride!''

McFarlane's lips turned pale, and he started to say something. Before he could, Charlie Bright laughed, looked at McFarlane, and said, "If you did tell the police of your suspicions, Mac, you must have made things a little hot for Russ too, not just Sánchez, back then.''

McFarlane turned to him angrily. "That was his problem, Charlie. He made his bed.''

"Too bad his alibi seems to have held up," Bright said to nobody in particular. McFarlane glared at him.

I asked McFarlane why he'd thought Bell and Kate Simons were having an affair. He waved his pipe. "It was over twenty years ago. You can't expect me to remember the details after all this time."

"You heard them quarreling shortly before she died too. What about?"

"Couldn't hear," he replied indifferently. "Kate's office was next to mine, but the walls are thick."

I looked at him for a few moments. He stared back defiantly.

"What about gallery owners or painters not connected with the University? What about Bell's former students?"

"Former students!" Bright repeated, and laughed. "Russ Bell hasn't had a graduate student in fifteen years—and none of the ones he did have ever amounted to anything!"

"That's not quite true, Charlie," Herb Sweeney said. "There's always Tom Fowler."

"I mean as artists," Bright snapped. "Fowler amounted to something because he got *away* from Russ."

"Are you talking about the new director of the art museum?" I asked.

"You know who he is?" McFarlane asked, apparently impressed that a campus cop might know something about campus high culture.

"Yes."

"When I heard that Fowler had been appointed the new director," Sweeney said, "I asked Russ if he'd had anything to do with it. He was on the search committee, and Fowler had been his student. He implied that he'd had a little something to do with it and added that he was looking forward to working with Fowler at the museum after he retired."

"They had a lot in common," Bright said with a nasty laugh. "Neither of them could paint. And do remember, Herb," he added, "it's *Thomas* Fowler, not Tom. He insisted on that, even though he was just a student. 'Thomas, please'!"

Suddenly Gloria Williams materialized in the lounge. She stopped when she spotted me and looked surprised, or pretended to. She was carrying two mugs.

"Gloria!" Bright exclaimed. "You've been our faithful secretary since we were teaching drawing to cavemen. We're being grilled by a cop about Russ Bell's murder. She suspects us all." He pointed a pudgy finger at me and added, "This is the cop I'm referring to. Who could she talk to about Russ who might know all his dark secrets?"

She regarded me coolly for a moment. "I know who she is," she said. "She's the policewoman who found Professor Bell's body, and she's not investigating his murder officially; she's doing it on her own. You don't have to talk to her if you don't want to—in case she neglected to tell you that."

McFarlane took the pipe out of his mouth and said, "You found Russ's body?"

Bright gaped at me. "You're not here officially?"

Sweeney's monkey face split in a big grin. "How devious, Officer McDuff! But you never actually said you were, did you? I should have realized you weren't what you pretended to be. Your eyes are much too green and sly."

Gloria Williams filled the two mugs she was carrying with coffee, added sugar to one and, giving me a smile full of sweetness and light, marched out the door.

Bright called after her, "Don't think she doesn't suspect you too, Gloria!"

She turned. "Why?" she asked him. She waited until he'd shriveled up like a worm on a hot sidewalk, and then left the room.

McFarlane crumpled his coffee cup, stuffed his pipe into the pocket of his tweed jacket, and said to me in an offended tone of voice, "Well, I don't know what you're up to, wasting your time and ours on a wild goose chase, but I don't plan to indulge you any longer. I'm off to paint."

"Them that can't," Sweeney said, jumping up, "sit

around and speak ill of the dead; them that can, do.'' He marched to the door, turned back, and gave me his clownlike grin. ''Like Mac, I feel the prompting of the muse—and I am off to *do*!''

They marched out together, all apparently on much the same errand.

Ten

My body and brain were telling me that it was long past my bedtime as I followed them downstairs.

Something strange had passed between the three old men when they'd got on the subject of Georgia O'Keeffe. Apparently Bell had disliked her work and done a parody of it that Sweeney didn't want them to discuss with me. From the way they kept glancing at him, I suspected that it had something to do with Blair McFarlane.

If McFarlane was right about Bell and Kate Simons having had an affair, that could be another motive for Dan Sánchez to kill Bell. But McFarlane could have made the story up, and the story of the quarrel too, first to try to get Bell into trouble and, after he'd killed Bell himself, to add to Sánchez's motives.

I didn't know Kate Simons—hadn't heard her name until a few days ago. All I knew about her was that she hadn't got a promotion and got murdered soon afterward, apparently in a burglary that had turned violent. Mc-Farlane had implied that she'd used sex to try to influence the chairman, Bell. I didn't want it to be true—and not just because it wouldn't do Daniel Sánchez any good if it were.

I'd also learned from the Emeriti that Thomas Fowler, the new director of the art museum, had once been Bell's student. It might be worthwhile talking to him about Bell too, especially since I planned to visit the museum anyway to talk to Laura Price, the associate director.

Aunt Tess had one thing in common with Russell Bell: Fowler had been her student too, except that in her case it had been in high school and her influence on him had apparently been a lot more lasting than Bell's. According to her, she'd taken him to his first art museum.

I glanced into Gloria Williams's office. The door behind her was open, and the chairman, Lloyd Schaeffer, was sitting at his desk, frowning at something he was reading. Funny—he'd got the position Kate Simons thought she deserved twenty-three years ago. And that, if Buck's scenario was the right one, had culminated in the murder of Russell Bell.

Schaeffer looked a little like one of the minor characters in a tragedy, a Rosencrantz or Guildenstern. He had a vaguely nerdy look about him, like someone who'd wear a T-shirt that says I KISS MY DOG ON THE MOUTH. I wondered what type of artist he was and how successful he'd been in his career. I'd never heard of him. I wondered if, had she lived, I would have heard of Kate Simons.

Comfortably unaware of what was going on in my head, he glanced up and smiled when he saw me watching him. "Gloria tells me you've been upstairs," he called out, "grilling the Emeriti, giving them the impression you're on police business. Naughty, naughty! I'll bet they gave you an earful."

I oozed past Gloria and into his office before she could say anything. "According to the Emeriti," I said, "Bell seemed to dry up creatively and vanish into a shell around the time he stepped down as chairman. Do you know anything about that, Professor Schaeffer?"

He frowned and placed his plump hands on his blotter, covering the sketch he'd made the day before. "I suppose he did. I've heard rumors that he was quite the party animal back then, but I never saw any of that myself. It probably had more to do with the fact that his work wasn't getting noticed much any more, than that he had to step down as chairman. I got the feeling he'd come here as a kind of exile and had always hoped he'd be asked to return to New York, where he could live and work among his old friends again. But that never happened. I think he finally just gave up.''

I asked him when Bell had stepped down as chair. He said it was at the end of the academic year in 1972. ''I know because I arrived in September of that year, and Charlie Bright was already installed as the new chairman.''

''So practically the last official act of Russell Bell as chairman was hiring you,'' I said.

Schaeffer's smile was a little stiff. ''He could have done worse.''

I wondered if he could have done better. ''I understand,'' I said, ''that you got the job Kate Simons hoped to get. If Daniel Sánchez is Bell's killer,'' I rushed on, before he could say anything, ''he might have his sights set on you too.''

His face froze. ''It's kind of you to be concerned for my well-being, Officer. But you must remember that Sánchez directed his threats at Russ, not at me. He must have realized I had nothing to do with my hiring, other than demonstrate a strong talent for painting pictures that get noticed.''

He paused to gulp air. ''And if you're suggesting I got my position in this department on account of my friendship with Russ Bell, I assure you that wasn't so. Russ and I knew each other in New York, yes, but mostly through our work. I admired his; he admired mine. It took a majority of the faculty to vote against Kate Simons's promotion, and it also took a majority of the faculty to vote to hire me for the position.''

I leaned over his desk. In his agitation, he'd taken his hands off the sketch. He covered it quickly but not before I could see that, unlike Charlie Bright, he hadn't abandoned the curve.

''Nice,'' I said, and grinned at him and watched him turn red. ''Did you ever meet Kate Simons?''

He raised his eyes to mine briefly, then looked down. "No, she died before I arrived here. I wonder if you'd mind closing my door as you leave."

Touchy, touchy. But I did as he asked since I didn't want to annoy him so much that he might report me to Lieutenant Bixler, who disapproves of the personal errands I run, especially if there's any suggestion I'm passing my errands off as official.

I gave Gloria Williams my nicest smile and told her I thought her boss wanted a new blotter for his desk, and then I went home and to bed.

Eleven

We met that evening at Lillian Przynski's house—Gary and I, Paula and Lawrence—to practice the new ballroom steps we'd learned in the dance class we were taking together. It wasn't going well.

"One-two-three, one-two-three, *rock* back; one-two-three, one-two-three, *rock* back," Gary was muttering under his breath.

"Damn it, Gary!" I said, panting. "You're supposed to twirl me out on 'one,' not on 'two' or 'three'! And 'twirl' is the operative word here, not 'fling' or 'hurl.' "

Lawrence and Paula were on the other side of the room, Lawrence leading with grace and elegance and the slightly sheeplike look on his face that most ballroom dancers have except in the movies. When Lawrence launched Paula out, she would somehow manage a graceful twirl and end up back in his arms. When Gary did that to me, I was lucky to end up back in the same room.

"You're supposed to duck under my arm as you twirl," Gary replied. "Whoever created the swing probably didn't have a partner as tall as you."

"I wouldn't have to duck," I snarled elegantly, "if you'd lift your arm a little higher."

"Watch how Paula does it," Gary said.

"Watch how Lawrence does it!" I retorted.

"You all dance *very* nicely, for beginners," Lillian said, rocking vigorously to the big band sounds coming from her ancient hi-fi, her poodle, Rufus, asleep in her lap.

Lillian is someone I got to know when I set out to find who'd torched her brother's house, across the street from mine, with him in it.

She sighed dreamily. "Watching you dance certainly does take me back! Vince and I could really cut a rug in our day."

Vince was her late husband. I'd seen glossy black-and-white photographs of them doing the jitterbug: Lillian with the same short, curly hair she has now, but brown then, her skirt flared up around her tiny waist as Vince, in his World War II sailor suit, twirled her deftly—and she was wearing heels too! Today, bone disease has played havoc with her posture and agility but not her spirit.

Why were we doing this? Because Paula had decided she wanted a dance band at her wedding in June, and Lawrence didn't know how to dance. They'd signed up for a class at a neighborhood church and talked Gary and me into signing up too. I didn't go along with the idea because I had a burning desire to learn to dance but because Paula, since she quit the campus cops and started law school, didn't have much time for me, and I missed her.

And why were we practicing in Lillian Przynski's living room instead of at either my place or Paula and Lawrence's? First, because Lillian has a lot of LP records of swing music and the record player needed to play them on, and second, Gary's living in Lillian's house now.

We'd tried living together for a couple of months, Gary and I, but it didn't work out. My apartment's too small for two people who both need space, and I'm not ready to move yet. Just at the moment when having Gary underfoot was starting to drive me nuts, Lillian announced she was giving up her home and moving into an old people's high rise, since she couldn't afford the upkeep on the old house, or the rising property taxes.

"You're not going anywhere," Gary told her when he heard that. "You're taking in a boarder who's good at home repair."

"Where do I find one?" she'd asked.

"Right here," he answered, pointing to his manly chest.

Since Gary's a born handyman, it's working out well. He's also a sensible cook who deplores my eating habits, which involve a lot of take-out or, when I'm feeling creative and adventurous, microwaving.

All four of us got pretty good at some of the dances where each partner does her or his own thing, but ballroom dancing was harder, at least for Paula and me. Gary and Lawrence took to it like crocodiles to a swamp when they discovered how patriarchal it is. The guy stomps the rhythm and gets to make all the decisions, such as when and how often to fling the woman out and which way to turn. A strong implication is that, without him, the woman would fly off the planet in frivolous arabesques.

"What'd you think you're doing now?" I demanded. Instead of throwing me out where I could twirl around, Gary was sliding a hand sensuously down my shoulder and arm on the "*rock* back."

"Don't you remember?" he asked. "It's an alternative to flinging you out."

"Oh, yeah, right. But how am I supposed to know that's what you're going to do?"

"You're supposed to read and interpret his microscopically raised eyebrows," Paula hollered over, "the slight curl of his lips, the gentle pressure of his arm, and respond accordingly. Isn't that right, Lil?"

"Well, I don't know about that," she replied. "I always knew what Vince was going to do next because his face was so revealing. He could never keep anything from me, poor man."

"Whereas your face gives nothing away," I said to Gary. Although Gary has a lovely face—a little somber, slightly swarthy, with deep-set eyes and a sudden wicked smile—I didn't want to have to spend a lot of my life learning to read it. "I'm getting winded," I added. "Can't you put me into overdrive or something?"

"Do the tango again," Lillian said, scurrying over to

her stereo, Rufus under one arm, and putting on another record.

I do love the tango, although Gary and I have a long way to go to really do it well, because it's so hokey. The music began, and Gary and Lawrence promptly got smoldering looks on their faces as they swept Paula and me masterfully into their arms. A minute later, Gary guided me into the Christmas tree, which fortunately wasn't trimmed yet. I managed to catch it before it hit the floor.

When we'd exhausted ourselves and received Lillian's praise, she put Christmas music on the hi-fi and we trimmed the tree. Gary insisted on doing the lights, of course, and naturally he did them all wrong. That was okay, since they're easier to rearrange after someone else has strung them, wrapping them around and around the tree and getting all scratched up. I was prepared to wait.

Lillian brought out cider and the cookies she'd baked for the occasion, and we hung her ornaments, some of which had been in her family for over a century. Paula and Lawrence fought over how to hang tinsel. Lawrence's method is to stand back exactly three paces and fling clumps of it at the tree; Paula hangs each strand separately. Their engagement almost broke up during the ensuing discussion. The holiday season, as everyone knows, is hell on relationships.

At about nine-thirty, I left Lillian's and drove home, since I was on duty that night. It had snowed earlier—not much, just enough to whitewash the thin layer of snow we already had.

I parked in front of my house, the lower floor of a duplex. My landlady, Mrs. Hammer, lives on the second floor when she's in town, which she wasn't. She spends the winter in Florida and sends me weekly postcards describing her lazy days and reminding me not to forget to water her plants.

I paused on the sidewalk to admire the colored lights I'd hung in the snow-covered bushes beneath the porch windows. They glowed softly in the night—red, green, white and blue. Blue isn't a Christmas color, but I love the glow it throws on the snow around it anyway.

As I started up the walk, I noticed the porch was dark. I never leave my apartment without turning on the porch light if I know I won't be returning home until after dark. I can't remember the last time I forgot.

Then I realized I couldn't have forgotten to turn the light on since the outdoor Christmas lights were on, and they work off the same switch. Of course, I thought, it could have burned out. I'd never changed it, and I had no idea when Mrs. Hammer had either.

Going slowly up to the house, I looked down at the walk. I'd shoveled it before leaving for Lillian's, but a little more had fallen after that. I could see the faint imprint of my shoes coming away from the house. There hadn't been enough snow to bother with boots.

In the same patch of snow, next to mine, was the tread of boots going toward the house.

Moving more slowly now—dragging my feet, in fact—I wondered who'd come to my door, or Mrs. Hammer's, earlier that evening. As I reached the steps going up to the porch's screen door, I saw the boot tread going up, nothing coming down.

I backpedaled quickly, looking around. The street was deserted. The house on the left was dark, but in the front window of the yellow Victorian on the right the lights of a Christmas tree glowed.

I stared back at my house and tried to penetrate the gloom on the porch through the screens above the Christmas lights.

Like most sensible city dwellers these days, especially those who live alone, I have a burglar alarm system—an electric eye that notifies the cops if somebody breaks the light beam by walking across a room before turning off the system. So it was unlikely anyone was inside my apartment waiting for me, even if they'd managed somehow to get in. But the system doesn't extend to the front porch.

I felt foolish, standing out on the walk in the night, afraid to go into my own apartment, letting my imagination get the better of me. I work in the dark, I'm not afraid of it, but I respect it the way a sailor respects the sea. When I'm at work, I wear a uniform and carry a pistol, and I have a portable radio on my belt that provides comforting, tinny chatter. But now I was as helpless as any other unarmed woman—and most unarmed men too, except that I've never heard of a man who'd been raped by an intruder waiting for him on his front porch.

I thought I saw movement, something glitter, in the dark in the corner by Mrs. Hammer's door. I'm no hero. I turned and ran across my front yard to the house on the right. Keeping an eye on my porch, I rang the bell until the light went on above me and the elderly man who lives there with his wife came to the door and opened it as far as the chain would permit.

"Peggy!" he exclaimed. "What—?"

Just then my screen door opened and a figure slipped out and down the stoop, paused and glanced my way. Whoever it was was wearing a ski mask, and I saw stray light glitter in its slits. Then he—or she—turned and ran around the side of my apartment.

"Call nine-one-one," I told my neighbor. "Tell them there's an intruder next door."

I jumped off the stoop and ran across his lawn and my own, my feet slipping in the powdery snow, cursing myself for not having worn boots. Bare branches whipped my face and clumps of snow fell on my shoulders and slid down my back as I shoved my way through the lilac bushes between my house and the house next door. I didn't know what I'd do if whoever I was chasing stopped and waited for me.

I reached the alley behind my place. Halfway down, on the other side, a figure briefly silhouetted against the glow of the street light melted into the darkness. I ran after it, hesitated at the narrow opening between two garages, then plunged into it when I heard a dog start to bark wildly in the fenced yard in front of me. As I ran alongside a fence, the dog's body thudded against it.

I reached the street next to mine, stopped and looked

around, waiting for something to move. It was silent and empty, glittery with the lights of Christmas trees in windows and displays in yards. Something moved in the shadows of a creche across the street. I started toward it, but it was just a cat.

When I'd caught my breath, I retraced my steps, plodding back home past the barking dog still jumping against the fence in mindless, innocent savagery.

Twelve

I identified myself to the cops and described what had happened. They didn't bother searching the area; there wasn't much point in it. We looked at the porch light. The bulb had been loosened. Snow from the intruder's boots showed that he'd been waiting for me at the end of the porch, in the recess of the door that leads up to Mrs. Hammer's apartment, probably squatting below the porch screens.

"Good thing you didn't come up here," the female cop said a little unnecessarily. If I had, and the intruder had had a weapon, he could have done what he wanted with me—there or in my apartment—and nobody would have seen or heard it.

I wasn't able to give a description of the intruder, not even if it was a man or a woman. I said I thought it was a man and that he'd been above average in height but not tall—maybe five-ten—average build, but how can you tell when they're wearing heavy winter jackets? He'd been wearing a ski mask, but I was sure he'd worn glasses under it.

They came into my apartment with me, just to be on the safe side, and waited until I'd turned off the alarm system and checked to make sure nothing was missing or disturbed, and then we went back out and up the stairs to check Mrs. Hammer's place too. A waste of time, I knew, but it felt good to be doing something and to have company for a few more minutes.

There wasn't much else they could do. No assault, just

an intruder who'd fled. Even I, a cop who knew better, felt they should have brought in the crime scene unit, awakened everybody in the neighborhood and checked their boots—just for starters. Maybe helicopters too, and searchlights and dogs.

"You're a young woman who lives alone," the male cop said, telling me something I hadn't known. "Looks like someone knew that, had a good idea you were gonna be coming home soon—somebody who definitely wanted you tonight. You know of any suspicious characters who live in the neighborhood?"

"No," I said. I shuddered. *Somebody who definitely wanted you tonight.* It sounded like a line Sandra Carr might have put in one of her thrillers. Somebody who wanted me enough to unscrew the porch light and wait—who knows how long?—in the shadows for me to return home.

I shook myself. "This isn't normal behavior for a rapist," I said. "Whoever it was couldn't have been sure I'd come back home tonight. I might've gone straight to work."

The female cop shrugged. "What's normal? You say you have the dog watch at the University. If somebody's been watching you for a while, and saw you drive off at the same time every night, they could find out what you do for a living and when. And when he saw you drive off earlier tonight, he might've figured you'd come back here before going to work. Maybe thought you'd come back sooner than you did, but waited anyway."

"Some creeps are very methodical and patient," the male cop added, and with those cheery words, they gave me concerned, helpless looks, went out to their car, and drove away.

The thought that someone in the neighborhood—methodical and patient—someone I might even have nodded to or stopped to chat with, had kept watch on me, figured out my schedule, then waited on my porch for me to return home, was scary. It doesn't pay to fall into a comfortable routine, and yet civilization was created so we could.

Inside my house, alone, the door locked and bolted, I noticed there was a message on my answering machine. I pressed PLAY, and a voice jumped into the room that at first I didn't recognize.

"Hello, Miss O'Neill." Awkward pause. "How's it goin'?" Another awkward pause. "That was dumb! Like I'm actually talkin' to you!"

It took me a second to make the transition from one unreality to another. It was Dan Sánchez.

"Sorry to bother you at home, except Sandra said it'd be okay—you probably won't listen to this until you feel like it anyhow." Nervous laugh.

If only that were always so, I muttered to myself.

"I was thinkin' of somethin' after you left yesterday," he went on. "Tryin' to figure out who might know somethin' about Russell Bell's private life. Then I remembered a guy named Joel Osmond. He used to own an art gallery, and he was a friend of Bell's back when Kate and I were together. If you wanna know more about him, give me a call. Thanks."

I didn't have time to call him then; I had to get to work. I called campus police headquarters to tell them I'd be late.

"You're in luck," the dispatcher said. "Sergeant Hiller's the duty officer tonight, not Bixler. You must live right."

I told him I did and started to hang up and then, on a hunch, asked him if there'd been any phone calls for me.

"Yeah, must be a new boyfriend, huh? I told him you'd be coming in about ten-thirty. He said he'd call back then."

"What time did he call?"

He checked the log. "Five forty-two."

"What'd he sound like?"

"Like he had a bad cold or smoked a lot."

"You sure it was a man?"

"Could've been a woman, I guess—but if it was, she

must've had a really bad cold or a two-pack-a-day habit." It suddenly dawned on him that my questions were going beyond normal curiosity. "Why?" he asked. "Somethin' wrong?"

I told him no and asked him if the call had come from on or off campus.

"Off campus," he said.

Too bad. We can trace on-campus calls.

Sergeant Hiller, one of the good guys, rolled his eyes when I came in about twenty minutes after the other cops had left on their patrols. He filled me in on the new stuff to watch out for on mine. I had something of my own to add to the list.

Walking around campus in the middle of the night gives you plenty of time to think, even when you're looking over your shoulder a lot and approaching shadows warily—and there are a lot of shadows on a university campus, especially on the Old Campus, my assignment that night.

Assuming the anonymous phone caller was the man— if it was a man—who'd been waiting for me on my porch, then he'd called the campus police about ten minutes after I'd left to drive over to Lillian's. That meant he'd known I was a campus cop. When the dispatcher told him when I was expected in, he must have known enough about my habits to guess I'd return home first from wherever I'd gone.

Would a rapist go to so much trouble? Surely there were other women out there to assault, easier prey than I was, if that's what he'd wanted. "It was somebody who definitely wanted you tonight," the cops had told me. "Somebody patient and methodical."

It was possible, too, that he'd followed me to Lillian's, then come back to my place and waited for me to return home.

There are a lot of big old apartment buildings in my neighborhood and a lot of single men living in them. I've met them on my walks, nodded to them, smiled—even discouraged the attempts of a few to get closer. If one of them had been more than normally interested in me, he hadn't shown it.

I became aware that I was approaching the University's new art museum. It's a fantasy castle of stainless steel that rises unexpectedly—shockingly, even—among the Old Campus's ivy-covered buildings. I'd watched it being built over the past year, and I like it a lot. I usually don't like the appearance of new buildings on the Old Campus—the Psychology Building, for example, is an architectural disaster designed by a committee of cost accountants or, more appropriately, rat-maze builders.

The new museum makes no effort to imitate the styles of the old buildings around it. Instead, it somehow manages to be both serious and playful, fantasy and reality—one artist's vision of how the world could be if we were all more creative—or at least receptive to creativity. It's a perfect museum for our time, I think.

As I crossed the plaza in front of it, a figure came suddenly around a corner. The most unsettling part of patrolling the campus late at night, when there aren't a lot of people around, is coming upon someone entering or leaving a building, or meeting them on one of the dark paths. You just have to smile and say "Good evening" and continue on your way because what distinguishes universities from most businesses is that there are no regular hours.

It was a campus cop, Jesse Porter, who also had the dog watch that month.

"Duel in the dark," he said, and we both laughed.

Jesse's in his late twenties but looks sixteen—he's one of those guys you assume wears a baseball cap on backwards when he's not in uniform. Jesse does.

We stopped to talk. I told him about the museum opening the following Friday night and how I was going with my aunt Tess.

"A costume party, huh? What're you going as?"

"A woman in a painting by Renoir."

"Who's Renoir?"

"A French painter."

"The woman have red hair?"

"Not exactly, but close enough. I'll be wearing a big blue hat with roses, so nobody who knows the painting will notice. I couldn't find anybody with red hair I could dress up as—unless I wanted to go as one of Edvard Munch's vampire women who suck the blood out of their men. It somehow ends up in their hair."

"You wouldn't want to do that!" Jesse exclaimed, horrified.

I bared my fangs at him.

We both stood in the snow and stared into the museum's main gallery through one of the big plate-glass windows. There was still a week until the opening, and it looked as though they'd just started hanging the exhibition, selected from the University's permanent collection.

"Too bad we can't go inside and look around while we're warming up," Jesse said wistfully. "There's some nice stuff in there."

The campus cops have keys to almost all the buildings and classrooms but not to the museum, which has its own security system.

One of the paintings already up on the wall was a Georgia O'Keeffe. Although the light was dim in the gallery, I knew it was a painting called *Hibiscus with Rose* because I'd seen it hanging in the old museum sometimes, back when I was a student and I went there to study. It occurred to me that it must be the painting the Emeriti had talked about that morning, the one the University bought at the time O'Keeffe came here to get an honorary degree.

I asked Jesse if he liked O'Keeffe.

"Who's that?"

I pointed the painting out to him, and he put his face up to the glass and peered in. "Oh, yeah, my wife's got a poster of one of her flowers in the bedroom." He looked at it a little more, then stood back. "Nah," he said, finally, "I think it's kind of boring. How about you?"

I smiled to myself. In a lot of ways, Jesse's not a conventional man, but in that he was. Russell Bell wasn't the first man I'd heard of who'd disparaged O'Keeffe's work either. I don't like everything O'Keeffe's done myself—I can do without those cow skulls floating over New Mexican landscapes, for instance—but the lush flower paintings, like *Hibiscus with Rose*, and her landscapes, and the early New York cityscapes are beautiful, and they grow on you the more you look at them.

But what I admire most about her is that she seemed to be completely indifferent to what you and I think about what and how she painted and the way she lived her life.

Jesse pressed his nose against the window again. "She didn't sign it," he said.

"O'Keeffe never signed her paintings. Somebody once asked her why and she snapped, 'Why don't you sign your face?' "

Jesse thought about that. "Huh," he pronounced finally. "Wouldn't it be easy to fake, if you don't sign your name?"

"It would probably be easier to fake a signature than a painting." I took him by the elbow and pulled him away. "Come on, let's go over to Adamson Hall. I'll buy you a cup of coffee and tell you what's so great about Georgia O'Keeffe."

We walked over to Adamson and got cups of coffee out of the machine and took them into the banquet room where I'd once seen somebody murdered. Although there are lots of dark nooks and crannies in Adamson Hall, I've never sighted her ghost or that of her killer, and I'm very happy about that.

I tried to explain O'Keeffe in terms that might make Jesse give her a second look. When I got to calla lilies and clefts and folds—those "holes" in the canvases Russell Bell and his colleague Charlie Bright had hated—I had him blushing and hanging on my every word.

One nice thing about Jesse is that, among the other oddities rattling around in his big, round head, he keeps an open mind.

Thirteen

When I got up the next afternoon, I pulled a book of O'Keeffe's Hawaii paintings off my shelf, took it into my living room and looked through it as I drank my coffee. A pineapple company paid her to go there in the late '30s, in return for which she painted a pineapple for them to use in their advertising. I think the paintings she did during that short stay in Hawaii are among her best.

She seemed to paint from within whatever she painted, making of it a subject instead of an object. I think that's why the critics and scholars pay so little attention to her work: she makes them uneasy. They're accustomed to art in which the artist views things from a distance—makes objects of them.

But what do I know? I thought as I put the book away. I'm only a campus cop.

Then I biked over to Dan Sánchez's house. He was at his wheel, centering a spinning clump of clay, his face a mask of concentration. I watched fascinated as the clay rose in his hands into a tall cylinder, then ballooned into a graceful ellipsis as if he'd blown air into it. Finally his hands coaxed the top into a shoulder and neck and then he thickened the lip and sat back, his arms at his sides. I'd taken pottery lessons a couple of years ago, very briefly—the less said about that, the better—and knew how hard it was to do what I'd just witnessed.

As he turned to look at me, I wondered if he'd be allowed to work with clay in prison.

We talked awkwardly for a few minutes as he dried

his hands, and then I asked him to tell me about Joel Osmond.

"Back when me and Kate was together," he said, "Osmond owned an art gallery downtown. One of the biggest. He specialized in American art—twentieth century, especially. Modern stuff. He liked Kate's sculpture and had a few pieces of hers in his gallery sometimes."

He smiled at the memory. "It really looked great, sitting there in that big, ritzy place and surrounded by stuff he was sellin' by some of the big names from New York and Europe. He even sold one of her large pieces to some rich lady in town—the biggest sale Kate ever had, I think." His face darkened. "It was just before she was killed. She told me about it on the phone, one of the last times I talked to her."

He paused, looking down at his hands. "Anyway, Osmond always had some of Russell Bell's work in his gallery—he even gave him a couple of shows. Kate said she didn't understand why, and nobody else in the art department could either. They figured it was on account of Bell and Osmond was friends. Sometimes I'd see 'em together at the Factory."

"The Factory?"

"Yeah, a little bar where a lot of local artists hung out back then. Not Kate, though. She didn't like the place, but I'd go there sometimes by myself. Some of my friends went there too. It's gone now."

"But Osmond's gallery is still there?"

He shook his head. "Not that one. He got in trouble with the IRS—big-time trouble—an' went to prison. He lost everything, I heard, including the gallery."

"When was this?"

Shrug. "I dunno, exactly. About fifteen years ago, I guess. I heard he started up again when he got outta prison, sellin' posters and frames. When I remembered him yesterday, I looked him up in the phone book and seen he's got a gallery in Riverview Mall, so he must of come back up in the world."

We've got almost as many malls as lakes here now.

Riverview Mall is the most splendid of them all.

I got up to leave and decided I had to ask him if he thought Kate Simons had ever dated Russell Bell.

His eyes flicked up at me. "Funny you should ask," he said after a moment. "The cops asked me that back when Kate was killed. Like they wondered if I'd thought they were dating or somethin', and maybe I'd killed her on account of I was jealous. I told 'em I didn't know. An' that's the truth. But I don't think she would've dated that scumbag."

I biked across the river to the Old Campus and over to the art museum. In the dull light of a cloudy winter day reflected off its stainless steel sides, it all but vanished into its surroundings. I tied my bike up to a lamppost next to the entrance and tried the front door. It was locked, but I could see a few people in work clothes unpacking crates and hanging paintings or preparing the walls for installations of some kind. I rapped loudly on the glass, and a man carrying a clipboard looked up. I dangled my shield in front of my face, and he came over and let me in. He looked at my picture and compared it to the real thing, then asked me what I wanted.

I told him I wanted to talk to Laura Price, the associate director.

"Second floor," he said, and pointed to the stairs. Then he went back to where he was supervising the hanging of an immense Pop Art piece—Lichtenstein's giant cartoon portrait of Louisa Ferncliff—that I'd seen at the old museum and never liked very much. I think it takes up too much space for what little it has to say, and who's Louisa Ferncliff anyway?

I took the stairs, pausing on the balcony that runs around the second floor to look down at the galleries below. This was the first time I'd been inside the museum. I could see O'Keeffe's *Hibiscus with Rose*, the pinks and yellows glowing softly in the diffused light against the creamy whiteness of the walls.

I told the receptionist who I was and asked if I could

speak to Doctor Price. She gave me a doubtful look and reluctantly asked, "Is this official business?"

I hate that question just as much as I hate "why" questions. I started to reply—I have a variety of lies that float somewhere between barefaced and little white— when a woman emerged from a door down the hall and came toward us.

The receptionist's face brightened. "Doctor Price, this is a campus policewoman who wants to talk to you."

Laura Price was in her early fifties, tall, with salt-and-pepper hair cut short and wearing jeans and a beige wool sweater with holes in it. I'd seen her before when she'd been interviewed about the new museum on the public television channel I watch. She gave me a pleasant, somewhat preoccupied smile and said, "What about?"

"Russell Bell."

Some of the pleasant faded from her smile.

I told her my name and gave her my story about Sandra Carr not being convinced Dan Sánchez had killed Bell. She listened and when I was through, said she'd read a few of Sandra's novels. "She's not planning to set a thriller in here, is she? You're not just doing her legwork for her?"

I assured her I wasn't. "I can't find anyone in the Studio Arts Department who knows anything about Bell's personal life—or at least who's willing to talk about it. Several of the faculty over there suggested I talk to you. They said he spent more time here the past few years than in his own department."

"I'm afraid I'm not going to be of much help either," she said. "I liked Russ, but I never saw him outside the museum. He never spoke to me about anything personal."

"I'd still appreciate it if you'd tell me a little about this part of his life."

She made a face, shrugged, looked at her watch. "Okay, but would you mind talking downstairs? I was just going down to see how the installation's coming. We're way behind schedule."

As we walked down, she said, "I understand Russ could be quite nasty and destructive in his own department. And he made it clear to anyone who would listen that he had nothing but contempt for his colleagues' work. But he was incredibly useful to us. He started working at the old museum as a docent—a guide—years ago, and he was wonderful. He had a remarkable ability to communicate his knowledge of art to an audience of nonspecialists. His tours were always among the best-attended. We're going to miss him."

"It sounds like he got more attention as a docent than as an artist," I said, and she nodded, saying she thought that was true.

She stopped and watched as two men lifted a large painting by Edward Hopper into place on the wall, then dug a little notebook out of her jacket and scribbled something in it. "Too much outside light," she told me, "and coming from the wrong direction. Were you ever at our old museum?"

"Sure. It was cramped and dingy and tucked off in a corner of the campus so nobody knew where it was. I used to study there when I was a student because it was so quiet and there were so few people around. Better than the library."

She nodded and sighed. "Russ was as thrilled as I when we finally got funding for this building. He was looking forward to seeing the art he loved so much hanging in here, where there's so much more light and space. He even managed to get himself put on the committee that selected the new director—as a voice for the artist, he said."

Two workers who looked like students lifted a squarish abstract sculpture out of a crate and set it on a pedestal. They stood back and looked at it. "What d'ya think, Doctor Price. We got it upside down, or what?"

She squinted at it. "You must've got it right," she replied with a laugh, "since it's not falling over." Back to me, she said, "Doctor Fowler was Russ's student many years ago. Did you know that?"

I told her I'd heard it from some of the old faculty members in Studio Arts. "I'd like to talk to him about Bell. Is he in?"

"He hasn't arrived yet," she said, a slight edge to her voice. "One of the conditions he made when we offered him the position was that he would assume his duties effective the first of the year because of previous commitments he had in New York and abroad. But he'll be here for the opening next Friday, of course."

"How about you?" I asked. "Were you one of the candidates for the position?" I knew she'd been the museum's curator and associate director for years, and acting director since the old director's death last year.

Her face became a mask, and she gave me the bland smile that so many ambitious women learn to wear to cover their feelings. "It was felt," she replied, picking her words carefully, "that someone from the outside should be brought in. New blood for a new museum. I was never a serious candidate."

"Just a humorous one? Lots of belly laughs?"

"Doctor Fowler has a much better national reputation than I do," she recited, trying not to smile. "And far more contacts in the international art community. He'll make a fine director."

"Will you stay on as associate director and curator?"

"If Doctor Fowler wants me," she said. "But if not, I can always return to teaching art history. That was my first love anyway."

We'd come to O'Keeffe's *Hibiscus with Rose*. Another flower painting had just been removed from a wooden crate and was leaning against the wall beside it.

"I've seen that one at the old museum," I said, pointing, "but I don't think I've seen this one before."

"It only arrived yesterday. It's on indefinite loan from a local art collector, Dulcie Tyler Farr. Do you like O'Keeffe's paintings?"

"Very much," I said. The new painting was of a hibiscus all by itself.

It's easier for me to see O'Keeffe's flower paintings

as art first, flowers second, than it is for a lot of people I know, maybe because I didn't grow up liking flowers. My parents moved so often when I was a kid that we never had a garden, so I came to associate flowers only with funerals. It wasn't until after I'd started looking at O'Keeffe's paintings—really looking at them, I mean—that I began noticing real flowers, and began appreciating their beauty too. O'Keeffe once said that she wanted to paint flowers as she saw them, but large, to surprise the viewer into really seeing them too. She'd succeeded with me, at least.

"It was Russ who got Mrs. Farr to loan us her O'Keeffe for the museum opening," Doctor Price said. "He thought they'd make a nice pair. I was reluctant, at first, since we have so many deserving artists in the permanent collection. But in the end I agreed since, as Russ pointed out, we have so few women artists. The old director didn't think women had anything important to say in art."

She stepped back and looked at the two O'Keeffes. "Russ was right," she said. "They make a lovely pairing. There's a remarkable affinity between them. Too bad he didn't live to see it."

"I talked to a few of Bell's old colleagues yesterday," I said. "They told me he didn't like O'Keeffe's work at all—he even painted parodies of it."

"Really? How odd. Well, most people are capable of growth and change," she said. "Perhaps Russ was too."

Maybe he was. And maybe today Russell Bell would have worked for Kate Simons's promotion, instead of against it. Except that he obviously hadn't worked for Laura Price's candidacy for the directorship of the museum. As in the case of Kate Simons, he'd thrown his weight behind a man he'd known from his past.

I asked Doctor Price if she'd known Kate Simons.

It seemed to take a moment for the name to register. "Oh, you mean the woman Russ was supposedly murdered on account of." She shook her head. "No, she was here in the early seventies, wasn't she? I wasn't here then. I don't recall Russ ever mentioning her either."

"And I don't suppose you've ever seen her art."

She shook her head again. "She was a sculptor, wasn't she?"

"Yes."

She led the way into one of the smaller side galleries.

"This is where we're tucking the faculty show," she said. "Russ didn't want one at first—he said it was an insult to the new museum. But once it was a fait accompli, he must have decided to try to create something that would set the local art world on its ear. I understand it was quite a departure for him. Too bad he didn't get to finish it."

"His eagerness to finish it," I said, "seems to have been what got him killed, since he wouldn't have been working late last weekend otherwise."

We'd walked out into the main gallery again. A woman was standing just inside the entrance, holding two small children by the hand. When she saw Doctor Price, she started over toward us, dragging the children behind her.

"Oh, Lord!" Doctor Price changed direction and went over to meet them. "Hello, Mrs. Fowler," she said brightly.

"I'm sorry to burst in on you like this again, Laura," the woman said, not sounding the least sorry. "I know you're busy, but the children and I are at loose ends until Thomas gets here. I thought I'd show them their father's new museum. Do you mind? They miss their daddy so."

Laura Price introduced us. "This is Peggy O'Neill, a campus policewoman," she said. "Officer O'Neill, Kendra Fowler, the wife of our new director. And these are your children?"

Kendra Fowler was in her early thirties, tall, slender, and pale, with long mahogany hair and dark eyes. She was dressed in a coat that went to her ankles and must have cost some forest somewhere a number of its furrier denizens, with a hat made from one or more of the same poor creatures. A way of keeping a family together, I supposed. I wondered if Aunt Tess would approve of her prize student's wife. Quite a glamorous one for a small-town boy.

"How do you do," she said. "Yes, these are the twins, Caroline and Thomas Junior."

"Mrs. Fowler and the children arrived in town last week," Doctor Price explained to me. "They've just moved into their new home."

"It's a house, actually," Mrs. Fowler corrected her, "that Thomas rented for us when he was here in November. We don't plan to buy a home until we have the time to do some research into the private school situation here, since we don't want to live far from where the children attend school. The children and I have been rearranging furniture all week, getting ready for Thomas and Christmas."

I asked her where her husband was now.

She gave an exasperated sigh. "Where *isn't* he? He called from Paris yesterday to see how we were settling in. It was Berlin the day before—or was it Rome? No, Rome was last Saturday. He has so much business to clear up before he assumes his duties here, you see. But he promised he'd be here for Christmas Eve to help us trim the tree and open presents Christmas morning. Didn't he, children?"

The kids sucked their thumbs, mumbled something, and sulked.

"Would you excuse me," Doctor Price broke in, edging away.

"Of course, Laura," Mrs. Fowler said graciously. "Would you mind if I brought the children up to see their father's new office in a few minutes?"

"Not at all," Doctor Price gritted through smiling teeth, and vanished around a corner.

"I'm looking forward to meeting your husband at the opening," I said.

She gave me a puzzled look, from head to toe. "Are you a museum guard?"

"No, my Aunt Tess is bringing me. She was one of your husband's teachers in high school."

Her face lit up. "Of course—Tess O'Neill! He told me all about her after they met at the open house last month. She was the faculty advisor for the school plays Thomas starred in, and she drove the 'culture bus,' as he called it, that brought the country kids down to the big city to hear concerts and see plays and things of that sort."

"She told me she took him to his first art museum," I said, "in an old school bus."

"I'm sure she had no idea what *that* would lead to!" Kendra Fowler said with a laugh and a sweeping glance around the museum that was now her husband's. "I suppose you're here to guard the artwork while it's being installed. Don't the campus police wear uniforms?"

"I came over to ask Doctor Price about Russell Bell, the professor in Studio Arts who was murdered last week. I think your husband knew him too."

Her eyes widened. "Why, yes, he did! So terrible—it happened just a few days after the children and I arrived. And Thomas, you know, assured me there was hardly any crime here! Isn't it ironic?" She laughed. "When he called, right after I heard about Professor Bell's murder on television, I pointed out that nobody we knew in New York has ever been murdered!"

"Really?" I said, segueing into sleuth mode. "Did you know Professor Bell well?"

"*I* didn't know him at all, of course. I never even met him. But during the selection process for the directorship, he called Thomas at home once or twice." She smiled and put a well-manicured hand to her thin lips. "I hope I'm not giving away secrets."

Something seemed to occur to her. Her high, pale forehead wrinkled slightly. "You're here investigating Professor Bell's murder? I thought the police had already arrested someone, a Mexican who bore Professor Bell a grudge over some woman."

"We wouldn't be doing our jobs," I said piously, "if we didn't consider all the possibilities, however remote."

"I suppose not. Well, Thomas and Professor Bell were

never really friends. Frankly, I'd never heard his name until the museum directorship opened up. He'd been Thomas's teacher, back when Thomas thought he wanted to be an artist. He gave it up, he told me, when he realized he'd never be one of the great ones.''

As we spoke, she was dragging her children around the gallery, letting them touch things the way you're not supposed to. I spotted Laura Price occasionally, discussing some aspect of the installation with the workers or one of her assistants, darting quickly around corners when she saw us coming.

"Thomas has very definite ideas about what should and should not be in a museum," Mrs. Fowler went on, "and how things ought to be done. Frankly, I don't always agree with him—but what do I know? That Oldenburg *Fire Plug*, for example.''

She nodded up at it, a great soft thing dangling from the ceiling by wires. "Is it really art?" Without waiting for me to reply, she went on. "Thomas has wonderful ideas about ways to involve the community in the art experience too—and he's a very clever fund-raiser." She laughed. "That's probably a director's single most important talent, isn't it?''

She stood in the middle of the main gallery and did a slow 360-degree turn. "It is a beautiful museum. Much nicer than the one Thomas is leaving, and larger, so it really is a big step up for him. And that's important.''

I asked her what she was going to go as at the museum's opening.

"Thomas organized a similar costume party in New York last year," she said. "In fact, the one here was his idea. He likes to make museum attendance a carnival experience, he says. Since I haven't had time to come up with an idea for a new costume, much less make it, I'll just have to come in the costume I wore last year, Sargent's *Madame X*. Do you know it?''

I remembered it from the art history course I'd taken, one of those courses where you memorize the titles, artists' names, dates, and one thing to say about a million works of art and then have to identify them from slides for the final, which is always held on the hottest day of the year in an overcrowded room. I recalled *Madame X* as being a pointy-nosed, aristocratic woman in a low-cut black gown, with a white complexion and a prissy mouth—a snooty version of Snow White's wicked stepmother. I didn't think it would be a stretch for Mrs. Fowler.

She asked me what I was going as, and when I told her, she said vaguely, "That's nice." Then one of the children said he or she had to go to the bathroom, so they all went looking for Laura Price, to ask her where one was.

Fourteen

It was a little after three, plenty of time to follow the lead Dan Sánchez had given me. I used the museum's phone book to make sure the Osmond Gallery was where he'd said it was, and then biked over, following the River Road. Riverview Mall is an old warehouse complex that's been remodeled into an upscale shopping center on the riverbank a couple of miles west of the University. I'd been there once before, to exchange a gift I'd received.

I chained my bike to a lamppost near the entrance and went inside, where elegantly clad women, many in the Kendra Fowler mold, shopped to the rhythms of consumer-friendly Christmas music. Some of them looked at me as though wondering where I'd left my toolbox and ladder. Locating Osmond's gallery on a directory, I took an escalator to the second floor and found it at the end of a short, brightly lit hall.

As I entered, a willowy saleswoman with short, glossy black hair tucked behind her ears was showing a customer a painting on a panel she'd slid out of a wall. The customer was holding a small square of carpet up to it doubtfully. "Notice how the tiles on the villa roofs subtly bring out the reds," the saleswoman murmured.

"Too subtly, perhaps?" the customer wondered aloud, nibbling at a pretty lower lip.

I drifted around, looking at the art on the walls, sliding out a panel here and there as I worked my way to the back of the gallery. It was remarkable—it was all original art and expensive, and it all bore a strong resemblance to the work of artists who'd died anywhere from a hundred to five hundred years ago. They weren't copies, exactly, but if, say, Degas and Cezanne and Renoir popped into your mind as you gazed at them, I felt sure the artists wouldn't be dismayed.

"Do you like it?" a man asked, materializing beside me. He had a voice like the warm oil my mother used to pour into my ear when I had an earache as a child.

I was trying not to doze off while contemplating a painting of empty striped-canvas chairs on an empty deck that looked out onto an empty sea beneath an empty sky. A painting without a lot of content, in other words.

"Um," I said, thoughtfully.

"It's a Talbot French," he went on in a reverent voice. "His work is in great demand right now. These prices won't last."

A response to that sprang to my lips, but I suppressed it.

"Actually," I said, "I'm not here to buy art. Are you Joel Osmond?"

He cocked his head, and a watchful look appeared in his eyes. "Yes?" Maybe that's what the eyes of people who've been in prison do when someone asks them their name, but you couldn't really tell from looking at him that Joel Osmond had ever been in prison.

He was five-ten or so, in his late fifties, early sixties, with expensively cut gray hair brushed back from a high forehead and glasses in designer frames. His gray wool suit was beautifully tailored and almost concealed the thickening around his waist.

"My name's Peggy O'Neill," I began, and stopped because his eyes widened and his mouth opened. "What's the matter?"

"Nothing," he said, and tried a laugh and then had to clear his throat. "Why?" He still looked as though he'd seen a ghost.

"You know me," I said.

"No." He cleared his throat again. "I don't think so. Should I?"

He did know me. Or else I looked just like a long-dead loved one, and I doubted that. I told him I was investigating the murder of Russell Bell. I didn't show him my shield, and he didn't ask to see it either.

"Russell Bell?" He put surprise in his voice, the way a lounge singer adds heartbreak. "What's left to investigate? I thought a man had already been charged with his murder."

I smiled reassuringly and gave my spiel about wanting to cover all the bases, although from the look in his eyes, I knew he knew I was lying. He'd also recovered from the initial shock of hearing my name. "The accused has a good defense lawyer too," I added. "He'll try to sow doubts in the jury's mind. We're doing what we can to anticipate that."

"What kind of doubts?" he asked.

The elegant saleswoman and her prey had drifted down our way and were comparing another late-twentieth-century Impressionist to a swatch of sofa material. I asked Osmond if we could talk in his office. He thought about it a moment, then nodded and led the way to the back of the gallery and into a glass-enclosed office. He sat down behind a desk, and I took the chair beside it.

"What kind of doubts?" he repeated, and made a steeple of his fingers, set his long chin on it and, as if watching a performance, waited to hear what I'd have to say.

"We're concerned that the case is a little too tidy," I replied. "The murder weapon's from the suspect's studio, and other evidence linking him to the murder was found in a trash can near his home. These days, most people are too smart to make mistakes like that."

Osmond laughed quietly. "Looking a gift horse in the mouth, are you? Most likely he wasn't thinking at all. He was also a drug addict, wasn't he, this Mexican fellow? And, of course, there were the threats he made against Bell."

"You sound like you don't know 'this Mexican fellow,' " I said. "But didn't you know him twenty-three years ago, when he was engaged to Kate Simons?"

He blinked, then shrugged. "I remember *her*, of course, but not him. As you say, it's been twenty-three years."

"According to some of the people we've talked to, you were a good friend of Bell's—"

He broke in quickly. "No, our relationship was purely business."

"You handled his paintings," I said. "Even gave him a couple of one-man shows."

"Of course I did." He took off his glasses and polished them on a cloth he brought out of a desk drawer. "Russell Bell had a name twenty, twenty-five years ago—the biggest name in this town, at least. What's your point?"

"We just want to find out more about his private life—to see who else might have had a grudge against him besides Sánchez. After he stepped down as chairman of the department, he apparently became something of a recluse, and he dried up as a painter too. I was hoping you'd stayed friends with him—"

"As I said, Russ Bell and I were never friends. We did business together, that's all. He painted pictures, I sold them. What else have the gossips said about Bell and me?"

"That you were seen together a lot at a bar called the Factory."

"The Factory!" He smiled, seeming to relax a little. "I haven't thought of that place in years. I was seen with a lot of local artists in the Factory, not just Russ. It was a good place to discuss business when they weren't too drunk or fighting or hitting on women." He glanced at me and said, "I don't suppose you see the irony in it, do you?"

I shook my head. "No. What irony?"

"The Factory was the name of Andy Warhol's studio in New York. And here were all these local abstract expressionists hanging out in a bar named for one of the most important sources of Pop Art—and Pop Art, of course, was the beginning of the end for abstract expressionism."

Pretty funny, all right. Osmond's voice had grown stronger and more confident as he spoke, as though he felt on solid ground for the first time since I'd entered his gallery. Suddenly his gray eyes lit up.

"You say you're looking for other suspects besides Sánchez. Well, you've got your work cut out for you! Back when I knew him, Russ—Bell—was a womanizer. All the local artists were, of course. They were trying to ape the behavior of the New York artists to see who was the most macho. And the easiest way to demonstrate that, if you don't want to risk your life in a bull ring or a war, is to see how drunk you can get, how many of your friends you can beat up, and how many women you can take to bed. Isn't that right?"

I said I thought that was probably true enough and wondered why he was so at ease with me now.

"Russ didn't fight, and he didn't drink all that much, but he scored with the most women. After all, he had the biggest name. A lot of art students and models hung out at the Factory too, of course—groupies. So if you're looking for someone other than Sánchez who might've wanted to murder him, why not look among the girls he knew back then or the guys they're married to now?"

Well, why not? Daniel Sánchez didn't have to be the only man in the world who'd held a grudge against Bell. I thought of Charlie Bright's taunting advice, that I should go through Bell's class and model lists over the years. That seemed a hopeless task.

I told him I'd heard that Blair McFarlane's wife had had an affair with Bell.

Osmond laughed again. "I haven't thought of Mac in twenty years," he said. "He still at the U?"

"He's retired now."

He thought for a minute, as though flipping through possible things to say. "It's been a long time, but yes—

I seem to remember something.'' He shot me a cunning glance. ''McFarlane—Mac, they used to call him— didn't go to the Factory much, but his wife did. Sally, or Suzy—no, Sally. Mac stayed home with the kids; Sally hung out with the boys.'' The grin he gave me spoke volumes of X-rated material.

''And she was having affairs with the artists?''

''I don't know about 'artists,' but she sure as hell had an affair with Russ Bell! When Mac found out about it, there was a big scandal. I heard it was even the reason Russ had to step down as chairman of the department— even had to spend a night in jail. Mac too, I think. They destroyed a restaurant or something. Things were pretty tense in Studio Arts for a while, but they must've arrived at some kind of peace settlement since they continued on for the next twenty-some years under the same University roof. Until someone murdered Russ, of course,'' he added.

Again I'd got Osmond off on a subject he enjoyed talking about, digging up dirt on people who might have wanted to murder Bell. Now it was McFarlane.

''We've also heard Bell might have had an affair with Kate Simons,'' I said.

Osmond's eyes clouded, came to mine and moved away quickly. He stared out through the glass walls at his gallery and, still farther out, at the mall shoppers. ''She was a good-looking gal,'' he said reluctantly. ''I'd be surprised if Bell didn't at least try.''

I seemed to have awakened something in Joel Osmond that I hadn't seen in him before, some kind of genuine feeling.

''You liked her,'' I said.

He stiffened, then turned and looked at me, and whatever he'd let me catch a glimpse of was gone now, if it had ever been there. ''Maybe Russ did made a pass at her,'' he said. ''And maybe she fell for him—or pretended to, since he was chairman of the department and she wanted to get promoted.''

"You knew her," I said. "You handled her work. Do you think she was like that?"

He didn't like the question. He licked his lips and looked away again. "I'm just speculating, that's all. I didn't know her personally." He got up quickly. "I have to go back outside. There are customers in the store."

I got up too.

"It's a fact," he said, staring into my eyes. "A powerful man can look pretty attractive to an ambitious woman, isn't that right?" Without waiting for an answer, he plunged on. "And that's another reason why Sánchez might've wanted to kill Russ."

I asked him what Kate Simons's work was like.

"You ever hear of Louise Nevelson?" he asked.

I nodded. She was one of the few famous women sculptors.

"Simons was clearly under Nevelson's influence," he said, "but she was working her way free. She had a vision all her own, struggling to get out." He stood up straight. "I pushed her work," he added quietly. "I really did."

He looked at me as though begging me to believe him, and his eyes looked haunted. "I couldn't give her a one-man show though—my gallery was too small for most of her big pieces. But I displayed some of her smaller things and photographs of the larger installation pieces."

The saleswoman stuck her head in the door and said in a hushed voice that Doctor Pelletier's wife was in the gallery and asking for him personally. He gave her an angry look and said, "Tell her—tell her I'll just be a moment!"

He transferred his anger to me. "I've given you more of my time than I needed to," he said. "You're just fumbling in the dark, you know. You're just hoping to find something that'll get Sánchez off the hook!"

He turned and stalked out into his gallery.

"How do you know I'm trying to get Sánchez off?" I hollered after him. He spun around. "That's not what

I told you. I told you I was working with the police.''

"It was pretty obvious from your questions," he blustered, pale.

"No, it wasn't. You knew who I was as soon as I told you my name. Who told you?"

He ran a hand through his hair. "I don't have time for this; you're imagining things."

"I'm imagining the dampness on your forehead? I'm imagining the secrets you're keeping?"

He pulled a handkerchief out of his pocket and began mopping his head, as if removing evidence. "Get out," he said. Other people in the gallery were watching us curiously.

I walked up to him. "We lost a lot when we lost Kate Simons, didn't we?" I said, striking blindly into his fear, and into his wretchedness too.

"Get out," he said again, hoarsely, and reached up and straightened his tie, pasted a sick smile on his face, and went off to sell a couple of yards of color-coordinated art to Doctor Pelletier's wife.

Fifteen

He'd recognized my name as soon as I'd said it, and he'd known what I was up to. Who'd told him? Not Sánchez, surely, who'd suggested I talk to him. One of the Emeriti? And why hadn't they told me about Osmond— or about the Factory, for that matter? I didn't think Blair McFarlane would have told Osmond about me—not from the way Osmond talked about him. But you never know. Osmond looked like the kind of man who would throw his children off the sled, one at a time, if he saw the wolves gaining on him.

But there was more to him than that. I'd touched something genuine, something that was hurting, when I'd asked about Kate Simons. He'd obviously liked her work. But like Blair McFarlane before him, he'd acted as though she could have had an affair with Bell in an effort to get promoted in the department.

Or had he? Maybe he was just throwing her to the wolves too.

That was Friday afternoon. I had that night off and the next since I was working Christmas Eve and Christmas night—a choice I'd made before I knew Aunt Tess was coming down to spend the holidays with me. Because Christmas had never been my favorite holiday, I usually volunteered to work those nights so that cops with families could have them off. Besides, I was going to need the next Friday night off to attend the opening of the art museum with Tess—and you also get overtime pay for working holidays.

I had some last-minute Christmas shopping to do. I enjoy last-minute Christmas shopping: it gives Christmas a chaotic edge it wouldn't otherwise have, now that I no longer celebrate it with my family in southern California. Aunt Tess—she's my dad's sister, the only relative I'm on speaking terms with—was arriving in two days, Christmas Eve, and staying with me through the New Year. So I had to clean the house too.

I spent Friday evening and part of Saturday shopping and cleaning. Saturday evening, I drove over to Sandra Carr's place for dinner. She lives on the top floor of a very posh condo.

She has large pots scattered around her living room, some with weeds in them. I recognized Sánchez's—a couple of pots in the same style as the one she'd given me.

"I have a set of dinnerware he did for me a couple of years ago," she told me. "We'll eat off it tonight."

"To keep me motivated?"

"You're motivated enough," she retorted. "I can tell."

Maybe. I went over and looked at her Christmas tree. It was huge—her rooms are large and high-ceilinged— flocked and fake. The lights on it were those horrible kind that send up bubbles from little plastic tubes. There were no ornaments on it. It looked like a chemical experiment.

I glanced at the lurid posters on her walls of the movies that have been made of some of her books. Her books usually involve beautiful and highly successful women who somehow manage to get themselves into scary situations where they find themselves flinching away from shadows holding knives, guns, ropes, etc. I've never read one or seen any of the movies, but I've overheard people describing the plots in tiresome detail.

I filled her in on what I'd done since we'd last talked, ending with my visit to Joel Osmond's gallery. I told her he'd known who I was and why I was there.

She looked up from the cheese she was grating into a bowl. "You think he killed Bell? Does he have a motive?"

"I don't know. Sánchez thinks they were friends, but he denied it—vigorously. I'm pretty sure he knows something that's related to Bell's murder—maybe to Kate Simons's too. He doesn't like having to think about her."

"Dan's ex-fiancée?" Sandra stared at me. "What's she got to do with this?"

"I don't know. But talking about her brought Osmond close to tears once."

"That's interesting. What's his gallery like?"

"Art for the surgeon's second wife. But according to Sánchez, he had a really good gallery before he went to jail for tax evasion. He handled all the big names of the time, even took risks with younger artists like Simons."

Sandra's cats, Jim Bob and Pierre, strolled down the circular stairs from the second floor and into the room, yawning. I'm mildly allergic to cats. Pierre seems to respect that. He's the sort of cat who, if he were human, would wear glasses and carry a well-used library card. If Jim Bob were human, however, he'd drive a pickup with a gun rack in the back window, show a couple of inches of butt-cleavage when he bent over to pick something up he couldn't get his woman to pick up for him, and he'd think allergies are all in the mind. Sandra shooed him out of the room. He went slowly, with a swagger.

"Osmond knew who you were," she said thoughtfully. "The art community's a small one here, but it's a little spooky, isn't it—someone gossiping about you like that. You think you may be in danger?"

"I don't know." I told her about the person who'd gone to so much trouble to try to attack me on my porch the other night. "It doesn't have to be related to this," I said. "It probably isn't. There are guys out there stalking women even as we speak."

It occurred to me that Joel Osmond was the right size

and shape to be the man who'd waited for me on my porch, and he wore glasses too.

"Maybe you ought to carry your gun with you," Sandra said. "You're allowed to do that, aren't you?"

"Yeah, but I can't walk onto my porch every time I come home at night with my pistol out, can I? Besides, if I fired it and missed, I might hit a neighbor." I thought of the elderly man who'd called the police for me, his face illuminated by the lights on his Christmas tree.

"You wouldn't miss, Peggy," Sandra said.

While she was putting the final touches on dinner in her Eurotech kitchen, I went over to the big picture window in her front room and stared out. You can see a lot of the city from up there, including the University. I followed the lights of the bridge over the river that cuts it in half like a ragged scar and spotted the ugly concrete pile that constitutes the Law School and then the darker, smaller rectangle of the Studio Arts Building.

I thought about the night I'd found Bell's body and Sánchez, and recalled the man I'd encountered coming out of the Student Union who'd slipped on the ice. He'd said he was a professor. I remembered him because that encounter was the only unusual thing that happened that night—until I opened the door to Bell's studio.

Sandra called me to dinner. It seemed strange to be eating and drinking from dishes that might have sprung from the hands of a killer. But they were beautiful; they looked good to the eye and felt good to the hand, and after a while I forgot what their creator might have done to Russell Bell. Or to Kate Simons, for that matter.

"What else have you come up with?" Sandra asked me as she dug into a salad of marinated red and green vegetables, in honor of Christmas, I supposed. I don't know where people get these ideas.

"Fragments of a man's biography," I said. "Russell Bell came here from New York about the time the golden age of abstract expressionism was ending. New York forgot about him, and the times passed him by. He used his influence as chairman of the department to keep Kate

Simons from getting promoted, apparently because he wanted to bring in a man he knew from New York.''

I crunched a mouthful of beans and peppers, then chased it with Perrier. ''According to Joel Osmond, he had an affair with another faculty member's wife, and when it came out, it caused a big scandal and he had to step down as chairman. If you can believe the gossip, he never did anything worthwhile as an artist after that and became something of a recluse.''

''Because of no longer being chairman, or because the affair ended, or because of the scandal?'' Sandra asked, looking skeptical. ''You're implying the man had a soul.''

I laughed. ''Maybe he grew one. There are a couple of things about him that don't fit the picture. He became so interested in the University art museum that he ended up a tour guide. He even served on the committee that selected the new director.''

''That's not so strange,'' Sandra said with a shrug. ''If he couldn't *do* art anymore, he just wanted to be around it. There are lots of professors who only profess because they can't do. And a museum guide's kind of the same thing as a professor, isn't it?''

''I suppose.''

''Critics are like that too,'' she muttered under her breath as she went back to the kitchen. She returned after a few minutes with a large serving bowl and plopped spinach pasta on our plates, then slopped red sauce on top of it. It's people like Sandra who give Christmas a bad name.

''What else?'' she asked.

''He'd apparently become a kind of advocate for women artists. At least he argued for getting more of them into the new museum—and even went out and got a Georgia O'Keeffe for the opening show. But according to some of his old colleagues, he didn't like O'Keeffe.''

Sandra made a face. ''There's something about the floating skulls I like,'' she said, ''and the other bones she painted, but the flowers are just too pretty for my taste.''

"That doesn't surprise me," I said. "But Bell's behavior does."

"You think there's a clue there?"

"When you don't know what you're looking for, Sandra, everything's a clue."

"Oh, that's good! Can I have it?"

I sobered her up by telling her that one of the retired faculty members was convinced enough that Russell Bell had been having an affair with Kate Simons that he'd told the police.

"Oh." She played with her food in silence for a minute, then looked up at me. "That means Dan could have murdered Kate Simons back then—and got away with it—and murdered Bell now." She looked at me as though I'd hurt her feelings, although I hadn't spelled it out for her. She'd done that for herself.

"Dan's incapable of committing one murder," she said through clenched teeth, "much less two." She stared at the goblet he'd made for her, as if trying to reassure herself.

I told her that Buck Hansen's detectives had found Bell's wallet in a dumpster near Sánchez's home.

"Buck Hansen!" She spit out his name. "I saw enough of *him* last year to last me a lifetime. I can't understand why you'd have a civil servant like that for a friend, Peggy. If he hadn't had your help, Cameron Harris's ghost would still be wandering restlessly around crying 'Vengeance! Vengeance!' And my sister's ghost too."

"You're not writing tales from the crypt now, are you?" I asked her suspiciously.

"Of course not. There's no money in it."

"Has Sánchez ever talked to you about Kate Simons?"

"He's told me just enough so that I know he didn't kill her," she snapped.

I laughed. Being a writer of crime fiction, Sandra is incredibly naive. "You mean," I asked, "his eyelids didn't flicker as he told you about her? He didn't have trouble meeting your stern gaze?''

"I don't mean anything of the sort! Dan adored her. As far as he's concerned, she could do no wrong. He takes all the blame for the breakup of their relationship and for her death too. If he'd been there—"

"I know, I know," I interrupted her. "I've heard him sing that song too. I'll bet his wife enjoys hearing how he's still carrying a torch for poor Kate after all these years!"

"He doesn't 'sing that song' all the time! Dan loves Elena and she loves him—Kate Simons is just a sore place in his soul that won't go away. He feels responsible for her death—but he didn't cause it. All I know about Kate Simons is what Dan's told me. He's never said anything about her dating Bell—and he would have if she had.''

"If he'd known."

She shrugged. "From what you've told me about Bell, I'd be surprised if she dated him.''

I laughed at her again. "You mean the Kate Simons you know from listening to Dan Sánchez, who loved her, wouldn't have dated the Russell Bell I know from listening to the people who claim to have known him, who disliked him!''

"That's right. Do you know any other Kate Simonses and Russell Bells?''

"No, not yet." I twirled pasta and sauce onto my fork and, closing my eyes, shoved the resultant festive mess into my mouth.

We put murder aside after dinner and talked instead of more pleasant things. I told her about Aunt Tess and the opening of the art museum, where the guests had to come dressed as characters from works of art.

When I told her I was going as Renoir's *Portrait of a Young Woman in a Blue Hat*, she said, "Don't know it. But Renoir was into light, wasn't he? And shimmering surfaces. Shouldn't you go as someone from a velvet painting that glows under black light?''

"Ha, ha."

"Just kidding."

She said she was flying home to Maryland the next morning to spend Christmas with her parents, then out to Los Angeles where a television company was making a made-for-television movie of one of her books. She'd be back for New Year's. She gave me a phone number where I could reach her in case I needed to.

I took the hint and went home early. My porch light was on, and I could see the porch was empty. The bushes in front of it, bright with holiday lights, weren't hiding anyone either.

Sixteen

Aunt Tess arrived the next day, Christmas Eve, in the little red 1957 Corvette that had belonged to my father when it was new. It had sat in Tess's garage until a few years ago, when my mother demanded that Tess sell it and send her the money. Tess bought it instead, then tried to give it to me. I refused since funny-looking sports cars aren't my style, so she decided to keep it for herself.

Because it had sat indoors for nearly forty years, the car has no rust, and Tess drives it only during the summer, except on special occasions such as car shows and Christmas. People often make her outrageous offers for it, which she refuses.

As she drove us over to Lillian and Gary's for Christmas Eve dinner, we discussed our costumes. Tess had already made her own: the farm wife in Grant Wood's *American Gothic*. I'd tried to talk her out of it, since looking that straitlaced and grim would be a real stretch for her, and anyway her hair's much too lush and lively, but she said one of her fellow museum patrons, a man named Elmer Dill she was hustling, had suggested they go as the couple in the painting, and she'd agreed. ''Hustling'' wasn't her word. She might have agreed to ''courting.''

For my costume, I'd rented a gown from the University's costume shop and a large blue hat, and Tess was going to sew on the necessary additions for me, using a book of Renoir's paintings I'd checked out of the library as a guide.

I told her about how I'd met Thomas Fowler's wife and their children.

"Thomas's *second* wife," she said, looking suddenly flinty and disapproving, a little like the woman in *American Gothic*, as she wove the Corvette expertly in and out of traffic. "She has one of those fashion names— Chelsie or Tanya or Kimbra," she added.

"Kendra."

"That's not a name, it's a whim. Thomas's parents were unhappy when he dumped his first wife, Kathleen— a nice woman, I understand, although I never met her." She sighed and glanced over at me. "What's your impression of the new Mrs. Fowler?"

"She seemed okay," I said, in the spirit of the season. "Wears fur, though."

Tess shook her head. "Thomas was a good student but different. Held himself above his classmates, insisted on being called Thomas, not Tom, and he couldn't wait to get out of that little town. I don't blame him for any of that, though," she added. As she hunched over the wheel, she looked uncertain, as though she blamed Fowler for something but just couldn't put her finger on what.

"So what's the problem?" I asked.

"I don't know. I guess I was a little disappointed that he never came back to the school to visit me. He always seemed so grateful for the things I did for him and the other kids. The field trips down here on my own time— and my own money, often enough—to go to plays and concerts and museums and such."

"But he's invited us to sit with him at the banquet," I reminded her.

She brightened up. "I know. And last month he seemed genuinely pleased to see me. He's looking forward to meeting you too, Peggy, because of course I told him all about you. But I wanted him to come back and tell me all the things he'd done in the world and how much he appreciated the small part I played in his success." She laughed. "I'm just greedy, I suppose—one of those nasty women who's always saying, 'After all I've done for you!' ''

"Try not to rear-end that truck up ahead," I said, "or make me laugh."

Ginny Raines, who's my oldest friend in the campus cops, was already at Lillian's when we arrived, a can of beer in her paw. Christmas music was coming from Lillian's old stereo, mostly Lawrence Welk stuff and the Mormon Tabernacle Choir.

They'd made oyster stew—a bizarre tradition Lillian and Gary have in common, even though they're separated in age by nearly half a century. Neither Ginny nor I care much for mollusks floating in warm buttery milk, so I'd brought a large frozen pizza for us, half sausage, half pepperoni, with green olives and mushrooms over all of it. I figured that watching me eat pizza on Christmas Eve would take out whatever residual sting there was for Gary over no longer living with me. He's always had a problem with my taste in food, just as I've always had a problem with his, so in a way it was a gift of the Magi kind of thing.

After we'd eaten, we repaired to the living room and opened presents, then had coffee and the pumpkin and minced pies Ginny had baked. It was the nicest Christmas Eve I could remember, and I occasionally caught myself with the unfamiliar feeling of a fatuous smile on my face as I watched my friends laughing and talking in the glow of the Christmas-tree lights that I'd managed to rearrange when nobody was looking.

Ginny asked Tess how long she'd be staying in town, and Tess told her she'd be here through the New Year and explained about being a patron of the new museum and taking me to the opening.

"Ugh," Ginny exclaimed, "that monstrosity!"

Tess fixed her with a very un-Christmassy glare. She loves the new museum as much as I do, and she has a lot of modern art in her home. She even owns an original Warhol painting of a can of something that she bought in New York before he was famous and you could buy his stuff for next to nothing.

"The old museum was humorless and stodgy, Ms. Raines," she lectured Ginny. "In addition to being small, old and dark, it took itself much too seriously, like a small-town library. Art museums aren't supposed to be like that. Art is supposed to upset you or disturb you or make you laugh or even feel some kind of reverence, not put you in the mood to read a novel by Henry James!"

"It could get pretty noisy in a place like that," Ginny said, unfazed by Aunt Tess's passion. "Some people clutching their throats in horror, others crying their eyes out, others cracking up and rolling around on the floor."

"Better than pretending you're in church," Tess retorted. "And speaking of which, you shouldn't have to wear your Sunday best to come into a museum either. After all, the artists didn't wear theirs when they were making the art, did they? If the artists can belch, scratch, and fart while they're working, you and I ought to be able to laugh and carry on when we're admiring the result."

"Bravo!" Lillian exclaimed, petting Rufus, curled up in her lap, as she rocked vigorously.

"Something between a carnival and a church," Gary suggested solemnly.

"That's right!" Aunt Tess agreed.

Gary was thumbing through the big coffee table book of Renoir's paintings that Tess was using to put my costume together. "How come you're not going to the opening as *Dancing Girl with Castanets*?" he asked me. "A costume like this would probably add fire to your tango."

Ginny looked over his shoulder at the painting and said, "Peggy isn't plump enough. She needs more pie."

Tess and I said our good-byes around ten o'clock and went home in time for me to get my own car and drive to work.

You have lots of time to think on the dog watch on Christmas Eve and in the early hours of Christmas morning. I could have thought about my mother in Los Angeles and how she'd be spending Christmas with her surviving brother and sister and whomever among their kids they could still trick into spending it with them—Judgment Day I call it since Christmas in my family is always a time of reckoning.

I chose to think about murder instead.

If Dan Sánchez hadn't killed Russell Bell, who had? Bell had isolated himself from the Studio Arts Department for years. He'd been a pain in the ass at departmental meetings, and he'd put all his energies into the art museum.

He'd apparently had an affair with Blair McFarlane's wife. McFarlane was the only person I'd been able to turn up so far, other than Sánchez, who had a reason to hate Bell. If Sánchez could nurse a grudge into murder over two decades, so could McFarlane.

I thought of him, the tall, pipe-smoking printmaker who specialized in children's book illustration. He looked the gentlest of men. Osmond had told me his wife spent time at the Factory while McFarlane stayed home and baby-sat. A nice reversal of the traditional gender roles but probably not one Blair McFarlane took any pride in.

According to Buck, he'd tried to implicate Bell in Kate Simons's murder—before he was supposed to have known about Bell's affair with his wife. Could he have gone just as quietly about his business for twenty-three years, brooding on his humiliation, plotting revenge? And just before Bell was about to retire, could he have come up behind him and garroted him with a clay cutter? He was tall and strong enough, and could have got behind Bell a lot more easily than Sánchez could.

He'd witnessed Sánchez's verbal attack on Bell in the department meeting. It wouldn't take much to learn Sánchez's schedule and how easy it would be to steal one of his clay cutters. He knew Russell Bell's schedule, and he also had access to the building, whereas Sánchez had to count on the front door being left unlocked. The only thing in McFarlane's favor was that his wife insisted he was home the night of Bell's murder. Not the most iron-clad of alibis.

I thought it would be worthwhile to see if I could get Sally McFarlane to talk to me, tell me a little about the way things were back when she was going to the Factory, and—

"Hey, Peggy!" It was Ron, his dispatcher's metallic voice breaking into my reverie. "Where are you?"

I told him. He said Jesse Porter was cold and lonely and wanted company in the dining room in Adamson Hall. Would I like to join him for coffee?

"Sure," I said, and headed in the direction of Adamson. It was one A.M.

As I came around the side of the art museum, I heard music. A dark, heavily bundled figure was leaning up against one of the lampposts on the plaza, a boom box at his feet.

Gary.

"May I have this dance?" he called, and came swaying through the falling snow toward me, his arms spread wide, looking ridiculous.

"You idiot!" I said, laughing. "Where's Jesse?"

"Jesse who?" he asked, and took me in his arms. "One-two-three, *rock* back," he chanted, "one-two-three, *rock* back," and he flung me away from him at the exact right moment. I twirled beneath his arm, scuffing new snow, and even managed to get back into his arms in time for the next count of "one." We were improving.

He'd put in a tape we'd practiced to called *Holiday Ball*, and when the swing piece was over, a tango began. We'd practiced the tango a lot, so I think we looked pretty good out there in front of the museum: me in my cop's uniform complete with pistol, club, and portable radio; Gary in his overcoat and old wool cap. It was silly, but so what? There was nobody to see us.

We broke down laughing as the tango came to an end, then held each other in the silent night, our breath mixing with the falling snow around us—into a kind of passion freeze, I suppose. Over Gary's shoulder, I could see into the museum. Both O'Keeffes were up now, the University's and the one that Russell Bell had somehow got for the opening—why, I couldn't imagine. I pulled Gary over to the window.

"You like O'Keeffe?"

He looked at me. "No. Was that a test?"

"Sort of."

"Did I pass?"

"Sort of."

"Do you have a key to the museum?"

"No."

"You must know someplace warm around here with a soft, horizontal surface," he said huskily. Like most men, he enjoys making love in dangerous places, which wouldn't bother me all that much, except that most dangerous places are also uncomfortable places that don't encourage fore- and afterplay. Which may be why men like places like that.

"I'll see you when I get home," I whispered, equally huskily. "Maybe under the bed. It's horizontal and uncomfortable, and dangerous on account of the dust bunnies."

He groaned, still more huskily. "You won't wake up until after noon, your aunt'll be there—and I have to get over to Lillian's to fix the turkey!"

"We'll skip the turkey," I breathed into his ear. "We'll send Tess over to Lillian's. You and I—"

"Skip the turkey! You don't know what you're saying!"

"Well, then," I said smugly, "I'll just have to wake you up when I get home won't I? So you'd better get over to my place and get some sleep right now."

He trudged off through the snow, muttering. Humming carols, I headed over to Adamson Hall and down to the dining room and the coffee machine. Jesse joined me a few minutes later.

"Did Gary find you?" he asked innocently.

"Merry Christmas, Jesse."

Seventeen

Paula and Lawrence, who'd spent Christmas Eve with her family, were with us for dinner that afternoon. So was Elmer Dill, Aunt Tess's love interest and the other half of *American Gothic*. I didn't know there were any men left named Elmer outside of a cartoon—but then, I'd never heard of Dill as a last name, either. Tess had met him at the old museum a few years ago. He was tall and slightly stooped, a widower and a wheat farmer who looked a little more like the farmer in Grant Wood's painting than Tess did the farmer's wife, although there wasn't anything grim about Elmer.

After Gary's turkey and dressing, sweet potato pie with marshmallows, and my cream puffs—I do make a decent cream puff—we did the dishes and then Paula and Lawrence, Gary and I went skiing in Nichols Park to work off some of the calories. Gary dropped me off at home around nine and came in to make sure it was only Tess inside waiting for me. Tess was looking pleased with herself. Elmer was showing her around his farm the next day, and she might not be home when I woke up that afternoon.

"Going to get to know the cows and pigs?" I asked her.

"The children," she replied with a sniff, "the grandchildren, and the horses."

"I just hope your intentions are honorable," I said. "I'm not worried about his."

It was a little after ten and snowing lightly when I left

for the University. As I reached the end of my block, headlights came on behind me. I turned the corner and drove down the hill toward Lake Eleanor. A few moments later, headlights appeared in my rearview mirror again. I noticed them because it was Christmas night, and because there aren't many cars out that late in my neighborhood on any night, and because the driver had his high beams on.

I turned left on Lake Eleanor Drive, which winds along the shore of the lake. There's an ice-skating rink just off the shore near where I live. I can see a piece of it from my living-room window, and I often skate there myself, alone or with friends.

The headlights behind me had come closer and grown bigger and brighter, their reflection in my rearview mirror hurting my eyes. I hate it when people don't lower their beams when there's a car right in front of them.

I reached up to flick on the nonglare mirror but left it alone when I saw that the vehicle behind me was closing the distance between us much too fast. I was going about twenty-five miles an hour, as fast as you can drive safely on that road under snowy conditions, and it had to be traveling much faster than that. Before I had time to become even more indignant, I realized that it was going to try to pass me—either that or rear-end me.

In even the best of weather, only morons try to pass on Lake Eleanor Drive because it curves too much. To try to pass at night, with snow falling, is suicidal.

In a crisis, my first thought is that it must be my fault—a habit you can never entirely wean yourself from; you can only try to silence it with reason, if you have the time. So I wondered if maybe my taillights weren't working and the other vehicle's driver couldn't see me. Except that there wasn't that much snow, and I could see him.

"Damn it," I whispered, mad and afraid in equal measure. "I'm going to be killed by a drunk driver on Christmas night!"

I couldn't pull any farther over to the right without

jumping the curb. Just as I thought he was going to ram me, he swerved to the left into the oncoming lane. I started to slow to give him a better chance to pass before we reached the next curve. As he came abreast, I glanced over and saw that it was a panel truck and the driver was wearing a ski mask. He turned suddenly and our eyes met—stray light flickered on glasses under his mask—and then he jerked the steering wheel hard to the right, sending the truck into the front end of my car with a jarring, grinding shudder that knocked the Rabbit up over the curb and onto the parkway.

Our two vehicles separated for a moment, still moving parallel, and then the truck swerved to the right again, bounced up over the curb, and smashed back into my car hard, forcing it onto the embankment that sloped steeply down to the bike and walking paths on the lake shore.

The Rabbit started to tip over. I turned the wheel to the right, into the direction of the roll, and the car came back down on all four tires, but now sliding and bouncing down the embankment through the thin layer of snow. A large oak tree rushed at me through the glare of my headlights. I twisted the wheel and slammed down hard on the gas pedal, trying to get some traction and control, and the car raced past the tree, scraping the trunk with a shrill, angry howl.

Now the only thing between me and the lake was a wooden bench, one I'd probably sat on many times on summer walks to watch the sailboats and windsurfers.

I tried to put on the brakes, but the Rabbit began to swerve out of control, so I took my foot off the pedal, braced myself, and smashed through the bench as if it were balsa wood, and then I was on the lake, and alive, the car sliding slowly across the ice and snow. I took a deep breath and blew it out, then glanced back to see what had become of the truck.

It had come down the embankment about a hundred yards ahead of where I'd gone down and was out on the ice too. I thought it had gone out of control, but then it straightened out and began slowly curving around into my path, its headlights blazing, trying to head me off as I sped across the lake.

Some cops, I whispered angrily to myself, take their pistols to and from work, even cops—dumb cops—with small kids in the house. I don't have kids, but I always leave my pistol, along with my uniform, in my locker at police headquarters. I'd have given anything to have it now. I could stay where I was and shoot the driver. And to hell with all the people in the big mansions around the lake, digesting their dinners like Nativity-scene cattle in front of their fireplaces and Christmas trees. And I'd sing carols at the top of my lungs as I fired away!

I accelerated carefully so as not to spin my tires on the ice, and urged the Rabbit on toward the opposite shore about a quarter of a mile away, across the surreal lake with little fish houses clustered on it here and there. I watched the truck's headlights pass across my car. It seemed to have better traction than the Rabbit, and I could see that it was going to cut me off before I reached the opposite shore. The shore on that side was a narrow strip of rocky beach that ended in a stone retaining wall about waist high, so I turned the wheel—slowly, slowly—angling towards the swimming beach at the end of the lake to my right, knowing that any sharp change of direction would send the car sliding out of control. The truck's driver saw what I intended to do and turned to cut me off.

Now it was just a race like the sailing races I'd watched on the lake in the summer: a question of whether the tack I was on would let me reach the beach before the truck, coming faster and at an angle, got to me.

I wasn't going to make it. The truck was speeding at me at an angle that meant he would broadside me about a hundred yards before I got to the shore. That would knock me up onto the shore to the right of the beach, and I would hit the stone retaining wall either broadside or head-on. It wouldn't make much difference at the speed I was going.

Seconds before the truck was about to hit me, I did

the only thing I could—turned the wheel hard to the left and jammed on the brakes. The car skidded, not slowing, and began to revolve counterclockwise. As it did, the truck flashed past, inches in front of me. When the Rabbit had done almost a complete 360, I turned the wheel sharply to the right, took my foot off the brake, and stomped down on the gas pedal. For a long moment, nothing happened. The car just continued its revolution as it slid toward the shore and the stone wall to the left of the beach. Then the tires bit into the ice, and I turned the wheel—slowly, slowly—to the right, swearing and muttering prayers at the same time, trying to point the car onto the beach without going into a skid.

If I'd had another twenty, twenty-five feet, I would have made it. Instead, my left fender struck the stone wall with a loud metallic scream, and the car turned on its axis and rolled over on its side. Then it rolled over again, onto the roof, and slid to a grinding stop with me hanging from my seat belt upside down, facing the lake and the way I'd come.

Silence. And no movement. I opened my eyes and stared out my window. The snow was falling upward—rising, I mean. I'd never seen that before, except in one of those paperweights with winter scenes, when you shake it and the snowflakes float up.

I've had worse experiences, I thought as I hung there—an amusement-park ride with Gary a couple of years ago, for example. Except there you knew you were probably going to walk away alive and not seriously hurt because there was a line of people waiting to do it after you, and you'd seen other people do it while you waited your turn, and they'd survived, nauseated and happy and, unlike you, ready to do it again.

There hadn't been such a strong smell of gasoline then, I thought. In fact, there hadn't been any—

"Hey, lady, you okay?" I looked out the window again and saw a strange sight: a torso and face, upside down, framed in the window and peering at me through the glass. I was kind of like the figure in the paperweight. Someone had turned me over.

"How 'bout can you unlock the door?" A tinny voice, coming from far away.

I like looking at faces upside down—Gary's, for example, most recently—because you see their features the way you must have seen people as a newborn baby, before habit took away their weirdness: a slit like a knife wound in flesh that expands and contracts like a thick, pink rubber band, two holes on the end of a silly piece of protruding flesh, two glittery, moist puddles that stare at you like the eyes of something from outer space, two hairy caterpillars. I started to laugh.

"Hey—later, okay? There's gasoline leaking out all over the place. This thing could go up any second. C'mon, you can have hysterics after I get you outta there, okay?"

I became my usual sober-sided self at once. I reached up and pulled on the lock. Is this what astronauts do? The guy who looked like he was floating upside down outside the car tried to open the door.

"Jammed," he hollered. "Try to open the window."

"You bet!" I said, all business now and eager to please. I reached for the handle and cranked it, using all the strength I had, hoping it wouldn't break off. The window opened, cold air blowing into the car.

I didn't waste any more time. I hooked my legs under the seat, released my belt, quickly slid down onto the ceiling of my car, and climbed awkwardly through the window, pulled by the Good Samaritan.

"Can you run by yourself?"

I showed him, made it clear of the car before he did, fell down on a bench breathlessly, and looked out at the pathetic heap that had been my beloved Rabbit, on the lake, on its back, the snow falling around it like a winding sheet. I started to laugh at the inappropriateness of the image, then decided to cry instead. This was no way to end Christmas night.

"Go ahead," the man said, sitting down next to me

and reading my mind or, more likely, my quivering chin.
"It'll do you good." He threw a down-jacketed arm
around my sheepskin-jacketed shoulders.

"Thanks," I said, and gave him a grateful smile and
told him my name. His was Bill something—I didn't
catch the last part. "Did you see what happened?"

"Uh-uh. I just heard the noise your car was makin' as
I come down the bike path on my skis, then saw the truck
come barreling up the beach and onto the parkway like
a bat outta hell. When I got here, there you was."

"You didn't happen to get the license, did you?"

He shook his head. "Happened too fast."

I looked over my shoulder at the rich people's homes
across the parkway. Christmas lights glittered in their
windows and outlined the eaves of their roofs, but nobody had heard the crash or wanted to come out to see
what it was if they had.

I asked Bill if he'd mind going up to one of them and
calling the cops, and he did while I sat and waited, the
snow falling just as gently and as quietly as it had when
I'd first got in my car minutes before, minutes that now
seemed like hours.

Snow falls on the happy and the sad, I mused as I
contemplated my Rabbit lying out there on the ice, its
tires in the air. It falls on the living and the dying. It's
neither concerned nor unconcerned, its indifference is beyond our ability to comprehend. So to hell with it.

It's not the first time someone's tried to kill you, I
reminded myself, so there's no sense becoming an exis-
tentialist now. Why'd you think it would never happen
again—especially if you keep on getting involved in
other people's murders?

I'd been thinking of getting a new car for a long time
anyway. With its scabs of rust, and bumps and scratches,
the Rabbit had borne a strong resemblance to a lichen-
encrusted boulder at the best of times. But Jesse Porter,
who's good with cars, had been shocked at the idea of
my getting rid of one he could keep running perfectly for
years to come.

I doubted even he could fix it this time, though. Still, junking that Rabbit was going to be as hard as putting any other kind of pet to sleep. And Jesse wouldn't like it either.

Bill returned to say the cops were on their way.

"You probably cut the truck off in traffic," he said. "Some of those sons of bitches—you should excuse my French—get real pissed, you do something like that, even though you don't mean it. You're lucky he didn't have a gun, the way they do in California."

I didn't bother to tell him there hadn't been any traffic on Lake Eleanor Drive.

They were the same two cops I'd met at my place the previous Thursday, a woman and a man. They surveyed the damage, scratched their heads, and asked cautious questions. They didn't know what to make of me.

If Bill hadn't been there, they might have thought I'd lost control of the car, scraped an oak tree, demolished a park bench, flipped over, and totaled my Rabbit because I'd had too much holiday cheer, and had invented the truck. Or else I was in desperate need of attention and had made up the attempts on my life.

Instead, they asked me if I could describe the truck or its driver.

I told them the driver had been wearing a ski mask and had glasses on under it, and reminded them that I'd thought the intruder on the porch had been similarly disguised. Bill and I both agreed that the truck was light brown or tan. Neither of us could guess how old it might have been, just that it wasn't new. Bill thought he'd seen rust patches on it here and there, but that was just an impression. It was really too dark to see much, and it had taken him by surprise and been going awfully fast besides.

The woman cop gave me a concerned look. "You know anyone who's got a grudge against you?"

"Hey, she's a cop too," the other one said. "A campus cop, but still a cop. She might've arrested somebody for going up the down staircase, so he decided to get even." He guffawed, saw the look on my face and that of his partner, and stopped. "My point is," he added, deepening his voice to indicate he was now being serious, "a lotta people got it in for cops."

"Or it could've been someone whacked out on drugs," Bill stuck in helpfully, "and just out to raise some hell. He thought you were some sort of tin monster he had to get before you got him. That happens," he said knowledgeably.

"You didn't flip him the bird when he tried to pass you, did you?" the male cop asked. "No matter how stupid they behave, I always act like I don't notice. Unless I'm driving a squad car, of course."

I was sure someone had used the truck with the intention either to kill or maim me, and in my own mind I was sure the driver was the same person who'd waited for me on my porch the previous Thursday, but I didn't see much point in insisting on it to the cops. They said they would put out an APB for a panel truck as Bill and I had described it, with a right side that must look as though it had been in an accident.

I thanked Bill again and asked the cops to drive me home, which was only about a mile away as the crow flies across the lake. I hadn't got far that night on my way to work.

Tess came out of the guest bedroom in her flannel nightgown, and I explained to her what had happened. As a matter of principle, I try not to lie to people I love, especially when I need to borrow their car. After she'd expressed sufficient worry and wrung her hands helplessly for a moment or two, she asked me what I intended to do now.

"Go to work."

"You can't be walking around on that deserted campus in the middle of the night now, with people trying to murder you waiting in doorways and bushes!"

"That's right," I said, flaring suddenly, surprising myself, "it's much safer for me to just leave my house and drive to work, isn't it?"

"But Peggy—!"

"I've been walking around campus in the night for years, Tess," I said, more calmly, "and nobody's ever tried to kill me. But now I think somebody does want to hurt me—maybe kill me." I'd already told her about the intruder on the porch, of course. "But whoever they are, they aren't attacking me when I'm on patrol—probably because I'm armed."

"But they might!"

"Maybe, but I doubt it. I think they're amateurs. I'd be dead by now, if they weren't. They'd get a gun and wait behind a building for me to come strolling by, then blow me away. End of story. Amateurs don't do things like that because they don't know how—especially when their victim carries a pistol and knows how to use it." I hoped I knew what I was talking about. "Amateurs do what these people have done," I added. "And amateurs fail, as these people have—twice."

I laughed suddenly. "So I guess the playing field's even, Aunt Tess. I'm an amateur and so are they."

"Except they know who you are."

"Yeah, and I know they're after me, and that's going to make their task a little harder. Now, can I borrow your car?"

She winced, as she always does when I refer to her Corvette as a car. But she said of course and added, as I left the house, "Drive carefully."

I'd driven the 1957 college boy's dream car a few times before, but I always felt silly doing it—and uncomfortable too: it has the shocks of a lumber wagon and if you're not used to it, it takes a long runway to bring to a stop.

I took side streets and kept looking over my shoulder, anxious to get to the University and into my uniform, with the pistol strapped to my side.

"You're late, O'Neill," Bixler growled, feeling on safe intellectual ground.

"I was in an accident," I told him. "My car was totaled."

"I never knew a woman yet could drive in snow," he mumbled, almost, but not quite, inaudibly.

Eighteen

Tess was gone, off to visit Elmer Dill's farm, when I woke up the next afternoon. While the coffee was brewing, I made arrangements to have the Rabbit towed off the lake. Then I sat in the front window and stared out my corner of it and relived my night's adventure. It was a bright, sunny day, almost cloudless, perfect for skiing or skating, except I no longer had time for those pursuits and would not have felt safe doing them if I had. I had to try to catch whoever was trying to kill me first.

I didn't think last night's attempt on my life was the senseless act of an angry drunk or a psychopathic thrill-seeker. I was sure it was related to Russell Bell. Just as I was convinced the intruder on my porch the previous Thursday had been because of my involvement in Bell's murder too.

I'm not a great believer in bad guys who go to a lot of trouble to get rid of someone simply because she's playing busybody. That kind of thing happens in Sandra's thrillers, but I doubt it happens in real life. If I was right about that, it meant I was on to something. But what? I didn't know. And since I didn't know, I also didn't know if it would make any difference if I quit poking around in Bell's murder and started minding my own business instead. Would whoever was trying to kill me leave me alone then? How would I ever know or feel safe until I did?

The only suspect I had in addition to Sánchez was Blair McFarlane. But I couldn't see him driving that

truck, even though he wore glasses like the man on the
porch and the truck's driver—and like half the population. Of course, McFarlane could have had an accomplice.

Joel Osmond? He wore glasses too. But I hadn't talked
to him yet when the intruder waited for me on my porch.
Of course, that didn't exclude him from being the intruder if he was somebody's accomplice. I couldn't forget
the look of shock, then fear, on his face when I told him
my name. He'd known who I was and what I was doing
at his gallery—I was sure of that.

And the talk of Kate Simons had also stirred something
in him. He hadn't liked himself very much when he'd
suggested to me that she might have used sex to help her
get promoted.

I decided to talk to Dan Sánchez again, return to where
I'd started exactly a week earlier when I'd agreed to look
into Russell Bell's murder for Sandra. I wanted to know
more about Kate Simons. I didn't know if her murder
had any direct connection with Bell's, or if she was simply the catalyst that drove Sánchez to murder him. Whatever else she was, she was a mystery in her own right, a
shadow falling into the present. In a few days, I was
going to attend the opening of the University's art museum, and in a gallery off to one side, the faculty would
have a show of its own. If Kate Simons had been promoted twenty-three years ago, she might have had work
displayed in that gallery too. Instead, it was going to be
Lloyd Schaeffer's work hanging in her place—the man
who'd got the position she'd wanted, "a painter of spectacular mediocrity," Shannon Rider had called him.

Or had she lived, she might have created something so
good by now that the University would have bought it
for its permanent collection, and it would be out in the
main gallery with the other twentieth-century Americans
who'd made it nationally and internationally.

She'd been murdered instead, the victim of a burglary
that had turned violent. I fear random, senseless violence
more than planned violence because you can't anticipate

it, or explain it afterward. That's why I didn't want what had happened to me to be random and senseless too.

I rode my bike over to Sánchez's. The streets were clear because it had stopped snowing in the middle of the night and the snow removal crews had done their job long before I got up.

He came to the door and, without saying anything, let me in. I stomped snow off my boots and then followed him back into his studio.

"So, how's it going?" he asked awkwardly, when he'd handed me a lovely mug full of bad coffee.

"I don't suppose I should ask you if you had a good Christmas," I said. I noticed the bust of Kate Simons unwrapped on his worktable in the middle of the room.

His face darkened a little. "It's a children's holy day," he said. "I guess Elena and I carried it off okay. If I get out of this without going to prison . . ." He broke off, not wanting to think that far ahead. "You take my advice, talk to Joel Osmond?" When I nodded, he asked me if I'd learned anything interesting.

"Not much." I didn't want to tell him I suspected Osmond had held out on me and that he'd known who I was. For one thing, Osmond seemed like the sort of person who holds back just as a matter of principle. For another, I wasn't sure what Sánchez would do, if he decided Osmond knew something about Bell's murder that he wasn't telling the police or me.

"I have found someone at the University who might have wanted to kill Russell Bell as much as you did—"

"I didn't want to kill the son of a bitch," he flared. "I told you—" He broke off when he heard the anger in his voice. "Who'd you hear might want to kill him?"

"I don't think it'd be a good idea to give you the name," I said. "Did Kate ever mention Bell having an affair with another faculty member's wife?"

He frowned, thought about it, finally shook his head.

He turned to the clay bust. "She tried to stay out of stuff like that," he said. "If she knew Bell was playin' around with a faculty member's wife, she didn't tell me about it, or I don't remember if she did. She didn't usually bring gossip home.''

"When did you and Kate break up?"

He thought for a minute. "January, 1972—late January, I guess. Why?"

"And you didn't see her after that?"

"Not really. I mean, I'd catch little glimpses of her, you know, here and there. I'd go to places I knew she sometimes went to, hopin' to see her.''

"The last time we talked, you told me she sold a piece of sculpture to a rich woman in town just before she was killed. How'd you know that?"

He looked down at his hands. "I called her sometimes, just to say hello, find out how she was doin'.''

"Did she ever call you?"

He shook his head.

"So you really don't know if she dated Russell Bell after you, do you?"

"No! I told you—the cops asked me that back then. Far as I know, she didn't date nobody.''

"She was a grown woman, Dan. Her social life didn't end when she dumped you. She must have known other men.''

His face darkened around the scar, and his knuckles turned white as he clenched his fingers around his coffee mug. He noticed what he was doing, made a disgusted noise, and put the mug down as though it had burned him. "If she did," he said, "I didn't know.''

He laughed suddenly. "I remember there was a guy— a skinny, blond college kid who worked for Osmond. He was always making eyes at Kate. You could tell he couldn't figure what she saw in a loser like me—a short Mexican who never went to college! I offered to punch his lights out for her if he bothered her, but she said he didn't. She said she knew him from when he'd been an art student a couple years before.''

It was a little worrisome that Dan Sánchez seemed partial to the simpler problem-solving techniques.

"That was before I went through treatment, of

course," he added, as though reading my mind.

"Do you remember his name?"

He shook his head. "Just a kid Osmond had helpin' him in the gallery. Ask him about it. Jeez," he added, shaking his head in resignation, "you're really desperate, ain't you—trying to find somebody who took a second look at Kate twenty-three years ago?"

He was right. I suddenly felt overwhelmed by the impossibility of what I was trying to accomplish, and silently cursed Sandra Carr, now basking in the southern California smog, watching them make a movie from one of her simple-minded thrillers. I wondered how much thought she was giving to us here. Sandra had a way of setting things in motion and then getting out of the way, just in case they tried to run her over.

"So you called Kate sometimes, after you split up in January," I plowed on. "And she was killed in May, not long after she'd learned she wasn't going to get promoted. How'd she feel about not getting promoted?"

He looked up from what he was doing. "She sounded like she didn't care, but I knew better'n that. When we were still together, she talked sometimes about how the stuff she was makin' was so good, they'd really have to go some to turn her down! She was on a roll, she said, an' gettin' great evaluations from her students—the best in the department."

He laughed sarcastically. "Bein' stupid, I told her she was a shoo-in, but she said uh-uh, on account of teaching doesn't count for shit at the U and besides, she was a woman. They hadn't promoted a woman in the art department since the Second World War, when they'd had to hire one because all the guys were in the service. She retired ten, maybe twenty years before Kate came along."

"What about Kate's family? Were they as angry as you about her not getting tenure?"

He looked puzzled. "You think someone in her family might've killed Bell and is trying to blame it on me?"

"I don't know. You tell me. If you're telling the truth,

somebody's trying to pin Bell's murder on you.''

"I guess it's possible, but it's crazy too." He shook his head. "She had parents, and a brother 'n sister. They lived in Wisconsin. We visited 'em once together, an' I went to the funeral—they weren't too happy to see me, though. The parents are probably dead now. But why would they wait twenty-three years to get their revenge on Bell?''

"The police think that's what you did," I reminded him.

"Yeah, but I live here. I got reminders of Kate everywhere I go.''

I laughed in spite of myself. "That's exactly what the prosecutor's going to tell the jury.''

"I know.''

He traced Kate's clay mouth gently with a finger, as if trying to bring it to life.

"Joel Osmond told me her sculpture was a little like Louise Nevelson's," I said.

"Yeah, Kate liked Nevelson's work a lot," Sánchez replied absently. "Nevelson never got married. According to Kate, she didn't think serious artists should." He stared into the bust's blind eyes and added, "I think maybe she was tryin' to tell me somethin'.''

I liked Nevelson's sculpture too—big rectangular frames divided into boxes that she filled with all kinds of objects. She reminds me of Georgia O'Keeffe, although their work doesn't look at all alike. But they both took things that were considered "women's things"— flowers in O'Keeffe's case, homely, domestic objects like table legs and newel posts in Nevelson's—and made great art out of it. O'Keeffe liked living alone too—even when she was physically and emotionally involved with Alfred Stieglitz.

I also like Nevelson's stabiles, those huge steel constructions that seem to muscle their way into the places where they're standing. You don't see much sculpture by women, and the stuff you do see is rarely as big and assertive as Nevelson's. I'd like to be able to occupy a space the way her sculpture does.

I asked Dan if there was any of Kate's work still around.

He shrugged. "I dunno. She sold some of her smaller stuff to local people through Osmond, but I don't remember who, and that big piece just before she died I told you about. She sold it through Osmond, so maybe he's still got the records."

Maybe I'd use that as an excuse to go see Osmond again, I thought.

"What do people do with art they buy from people who die young, I wonder?" Sánchez asked. "It's kind of like"—he groped for words—"the work they've already done stops growing, you know? Because people stop talking about it, stop writing about it, stop looking at it."

He laughed tonelessly. "It's kinda funny, ain't it? You'd think that if somebody did one thing that was perfect, that's all they'd need to do. But that's wrong, I guess, 'cause nobody can do that one perfect thing. Artists just keep working towards it all their lives." He laughed again, with a little more humor. "Even me, I'm still tryin' to make the perfect coffee mug!"

I thought that was a worthy goal too.

"What about friends?" I asked him. "Are any of them still around?"

"I don't know. They were my friends too—as long as we were together." He rewrapped the bust, then went over to another table, took a huge slab of clay and began kneading it with his big hands. "I guess you could say," he added, more to himself than to me, "I lost 'em in the divorce, and I don't know where they are now."

"Who found her body?"

He gave me a puzzled look, as though wondering why I was asking so much about Kate Simons. I wasn't sure I knew myself.

"The caretaker of her building," he answered. "When she didn't show up at the U for a couple of days, the secretary got worried and called him. Kate'd been in her place, alone an' dead, all weekend.'' He started crying, and kneading the clay for all it was worth with his powerful hands.

Nineteen

I left Sánchez's studio and crossed his showroom to the front door. His wife, Elena, was standing by one of the display tables, running a dust cloth over the pottery. She'd obviously been waiting for me.

"How's your investigation going?" she asked.

I shrugged and made noncommittal noises, uncomfortable under her unblinking gaze.

I asked her how long she'd known Dan.

"Always," she said matter-of-factly. "Since I was eight and he was fifteen. And that's when I fell in love with him too. I thought we'd get married when we were old enough—until Kate Simons came along and he fell in love with her." She leaned across the table, her dark hair falling down around her face. "It is a reason to kill," she said, speaking with an exaggerated Spanish accent and flashing her white teeth menacingly, "if your name is Elena Ramos."

"You've convinced me," I said.

She straightened up, glaring at me. "How would killing Kate Simons have made Dan Sánchez love me again, I wonder."

"People in love don't always think clearly," I replied, "even people with torpid Norwegian blood."

"It wasn't her fault Dan fell in love with her."

"Did you ever meet her?"

She nodded, a little smile playing around her mouth. "Oh, yes, and I didn't like her at all. Of course that was because Dan forgot all about me when he met her. But also because I knew she wasn't right for him."

"How could you know that?"

"Because of the way she talked and the way she treated him. I knew that she would have to get rid of him someday. It was just a matter of time. Dan's drug use and drinking were just her excuse."

"A good excuse, in my opinion," I said.

She shrugged. "Of course, but an excuse anyway. I also think Dan would have broken the engagement sooner or later himself if she hadn't. Kate Simons didn't want to get married and have a family, you see. But those things were important to him—*are* important to him. He's a good father, and he's a good husband too."

"You sound like you knew Kate Simons pretty well."

"No. But Dan would bring her to his family gatherings sometimes—a wedding, a funeral once, birthdays—and I would be there too. The Chicano community is a small one here, you realize. It was obvious Kate felt uncomfortable in such situations."

"Tell me about her."

"I'll tell you what Dan has told me about her," she replied, "and what I observed myself. Dan said he put a lot of pressure on her to marry him. She went round and round about that. She sometimes said she thought she wanted a family too; sometimes she said she didn't. She had big plans for sculptures—in steel, in concrete, in parks, and in front of big buildings. I didn't like what she made much. It left me cold, but other people liked it. She was very ambitious and needed to work hard on her art, so she could get the kind of money she needed to make such large sculptures. Dan was not ambitious in the same way. He thought you could combine being an artist with having a happy family." She smiled, glancing toward her husband's studio. "Instead of great big sculptures, he makes pottery that families can use."

"And he's working on a bust of her now," I said.

Elena Sánchez shrugged. "I think that when he finishes it, he will be finished with her. Kate was very selfish, I think. But it was her choice, what she did with her life. I hated her for giving Dan hope that maybe she would be what he wanted. I wanted her to make up her mind once and for all, and let him go.''

"And then she did.''

"Did she?'' Elena's dark eyes seemed to stare through me. "Did she? She threw him out, but with the promise that she might reconsider if he proved to her that he had quit using drugs forever.''

"And did he?''

She stuck out her chin defiantly. "He entered a treatment program. He hasn't touched alcohol or drugs since.''

"Did he ask her to take him back, once he'd quit using?''

She shook her head. "He says he didn't. He didn't want to ask her because not enough time had passed—and because he was afraid she'd say no. And then she was killed. It makes me angry that he blames himself for that. He thinks she would not have been murdered if he hadn't been using drugs. But I think she would have found some other reason to get rid of him, and she would have been alone when her killer arrived anyway.''

I wondered if Dan had kept a key to Kate Simons's apartment and if Elena Ramos, who wanted to be Elena Sánchez, had known that and knew how to get hold of it. I don't like the way my mind works sometimes.

I'd known a few women who were the way Elena Sánchez had described Kate Simons. Sandra Carr was one of them: too involved in her writing and in pushing her career to want the distraction of a husband and children. Men don't have to face choices like that; they can walk away from the distractions every morning when they go to their offices or studios if they want to. And most do, even today.

I'd known a few women who'd begun to enjoy success in their chosen fields but then felt the pressure to become full-time mothers and wives too heavy to bear, and ended up turning their promising careers into hobbies or abandoning them altogether. I can't understand how men are able to live comfortably with such women.

I asked Elena if she'd known Kate Simons well enough to know if she had an affair with Russell Bell before or after she dumped Dan.

"Not before!" she said quickly. "She wasn't that kind of woman, who would cheat on her fiancé."

How fast she rushed to the defense of her rival, I thought, when she felt her husband was threatened.

"How about afterward?"

She shrugged. "I didn't know her well enough to say. But maybe—to influence Bell to help her get the promotion? I don't know. If she wanted the position badly enough . . . Women have gone to bed with men for less, haven't they? Only the men who have denied them other ways of achieving what they want find that so terrible."

She walked me to the front door and held it open. "I'm not a hot-blooded Spanish woman who would kill my rival," she said scornfully, "if that's what you're thinking. And Dan is not a hot-blooded, macho Spanish male who would kill a woman who spurned him either. I know the police suspected him at the time, but they were wrong. You've seen how powerful his arms are from lifting and kneading the clay and throwing big pots. He's never hit me—not once—in our entire relationship. And he's never hit the children either—not even come close. He's afraid of his anger and his strength."

"Then who did kill her, Elena? Was it just a burglar?"

She shrugged. "Who knows? It was so long ago. Her killer is probably dead now too."

Twenty

I left the Sánchez's home and biked over to the Studio Arts Building to see if I could get Gloria Williams to talk to me. She'd been the department's secretary for a long time and must know most of its dirty secrets, even though she'd insisted, maybe a little too loudly, that she paid no attention to gossip.

I parked my bike in the rack next to the entrance, took a deep breath, and went in. I wasn't looking forward to trying to get anything out of her. She hadn't liked me from the start, and when she'd discovered I wasn't investigating Bell's murder officially she'd enjoyed blowing my cover to the Emeriti.

She greeted me with a smile that contained all the joy of a Christmas tree in July. "Everybody's gone home for the night, Miss O'Neill."

"Not everyone," I said, and gave her my best smile, hoping to set an example. "You're still here."

She grimaced again. "And busy. I don't have time to help you play detective."

"Somebody told me Kate Simons was a slut," I said, "willing to sleep her way into that promotion twenty-three years ago."

That got her attention. Her head jerked up. "That's not true! Who could have told you any such thing?"

"I didn't think it was true either," I said, pleased with her reaction, "but I thought I should run it by you just in case. After all, you were here at the time she was killed, weren't you? Didn't you even find her body?"

She stared at me a long time, as though wishing I'd never been born or, if that was wanting too much, had never set foot in her office. Then she sighed and said, "No, Miss O'Neill, I didn't find her body. I was the reason it took as long as it did to find her."

I gave her an expectant look. She sighed again and then began: "You see, the Monday following the weekend the police said she was killed, Professor Simons didn't come in, and she didn't call to tell me she wasn't coming in. That was unlike her. She was a very organized person, always where she said she would be. If something came up and she wasn't able to meet a commitment, she would let you know, unlike most of the faculty. And she almost never missed a day of work either. If she did, I knew it was because she was really sick, and she would always call in so I could cancel her classes and appointments.

"When she hadn't come in by noon that Monday, I called her at her apartment, but there was no answer. Of course not, since she was dead." Her screen saver came on, sending colorful fish across the computer screen behind her. "I should have known something was wrong; I should have done something right then."

"It wouldn't have made any difference, though, would it? She'd been killed sometime during the weekend?"

She nodded. "Yes. Friday night, the police thought. But maybe it would have helped them find her killer if I'd shown more courage—hadn't been so afraid of what people would think! By the time they found her body, the trail was cold. I've always blamed myself. And the thought of her, alone in her apartment like that for so long . . ."

She shook herself. "When she didn't come in Tuesday morning and didn't answer her phone, I finally called the caretaker and persuaded him to go in. He didn't want to do it, but I insisted—all the time feeling I was meddling in her affairs and making a fool of myself."

"But you did it," I pointed out.

She gave me a quick grateful smile. "You know how

it is. You don't think awful things happen to people you know—only to other people. Or, at least, back then we did. Things are different now. Bad things happen to people we know all the time. But it wasn't like that then.''

She was silent for a long time. I asked her to tell me about Kate Simons's last days in the department.

She gave me a puzzled look. ''Why? What does her death have to do with Professor Bell's murder?''

''I don't like unsolved murders,'' I replied.

''I don't either,'' she said, and echoing Elena Sánchez, added, ''But it was so long ago. I really don't remember very much about that time.''

''How did she seem, the last time you saw her?''

Her eyes went out of focus, as mine do when I'm staring into the past. ''Friday, that would have been. She behaved the way she usually did, as far as I could see. I didn't see much of her after she learned she wasn't going to be promoted. She came in, taught her classes, and buried herself in her studio. If I remember correctly from the newspaper account, she went out to dinner with a friend Friday night. The friend was the last person who saw her alive—except the murderer, of course.

''Her murder was a terrible shock to everyone,'' she went on after a moment. ''The faculty, of course, felt guilty because they'd denied her promotion.'' Her voice turned suddenly acid. ''They were probably wishing they'd voted to promote her—since she was going to get murdered soon anyway, what difference would it have made?''

''Do you know if the vote against her was unanimous?''

''I counted the ballots. I always do. There was one vote for her—probably Professor Sweeney's. He made no secret of his support.''

She stared at me, her eyes angry. ''I know nothing about art, Miss O'Neill, and I could care less. I didn't understand Kate Simons's sculpture and didn't care for it much either. But from what I could see, it was no better or worse than anyone else's art. And none of the tenured faculty was setting attendance records with shows, here or in New York! I typed up their annual activity forms, so I know they weren't getting many reviews in the best places. Professor Simons's teaching was excellent—her students all liked her—but teaching never was and never will be a priority at this university.''

"You don't think she was having an affair with Russell Bell?''

"To try to get tenure?'' She shook her head in disgust. "Who told you that? Professor Bright?'' When I didn't answer, she shrugged and said, "Whoever it was didn't know what he was talking about. Professor Simons would not have stooped to that.''

She considered something for a moment, then continued. "I think she had the chance but passed it up.'' She paused and waited until I asked her what she'd meant by that.

She lowered her voice conspiratorially. "I have eyes and ears, Officer O'Neill, and the faculty isn't always careful about what they say and do around the secretary. After she'd dumped her fiancé, Sánchez, Professor Simons was a little down in the dumps. Professor Bell noticed and began to 'befriend' her. He was the chairman, of course, and pretended to take a fatherly interest in her well-being. But I knew it for what it was—I'd seen him in action before,'' she added bitterly.

"He made a pass at her?''

"Oh, yes. I think at first she thought he was only interested in her as a friend, and for a time I would notice them talking and chatting together quite pleasantly. And then came a period during which things seemed very cool between them. And then it seemed to blow over.''

"And this was after she'd broken up with Sánchez? Can you remember when, exactly?''

She shook her head. "It was so long ago. Late January, perhaps. Early February.''

"And when did she learn she wasn't getting promoted?''

"They always make those decisions in April.''

"She showed courage," I said, "turning down a date with the chairman of the department a few months before she was coming up for promotion."

"I don't think Professor Simons chose whom she went out with according to what would serve her best interests as an artist."

That was nicely put. "Did you tell the police about it after she was murdered?"

"No, of course not. Professor Bell was in Chicago at the time she was killed, and it was so obviously a burglar who killed her—or your Mr. Sánchez."

"Someone told me they heard Professor Bell and Simons quarreling a short time before she was killed."

She looked interested. "Really? I don't know anything about that. And it doesn't matter anyway, since Professor Bell couldn't have killed her."

"You must have known him pretty well at that time," I said, "since he had that office behind you as chairman. Do you think he was capable of killing her?"

"I don't know about that. I do know he wouldn't have killed a woman just because she'd turned him down. Professor Simons wasn't the only fish in the sea."

"And then," I said, "he had to step down as chairman."

The expression in Gloria Williams's eyes modulated into secretarial blank; her voice became suddenly neutral again. "Professor Bright became chairman after Professor Bell, yes."

"I've heard there was a big scandal. Professor Bell and the wife of one of the faculty members."

"Did you?" She looked me squarely in the eye. "I don't stick my nose in things like that."

I wondered what made her dry up all of a sudden, revert to her old stonewalling self. To protect Blair McFarlane?

"After Bell stepped down as chairman, he retreated into himself," I went on. "Became a recluse. Do you know why?"

"No."

"Have any ideas?"

"No."

"Okay," I said, and smiled, hoping to get back in her good graces.

"You realize, of course," she went on coldly, "that if that man Sánchez knew about Professor Bell pestering Kate Simons for a date, it would have enraged him even more and given him an even stronger motive to kill him."

I didn't need her to remind me of that. I asked her how long she'd been in the department.

"Almost thirty years," she said. "Why?"

"Did you have to fend off Russell Bell too?"

"Of course—and some of the others back then as well. Men with power often seem to confuse the tops of their desks with nuptial beds," she added with a grim smile. "But they can be trained, and after I got married and my daughter was born, they lost interest in me as a woman. I hope you haven't wasted any of your time imagining I might have murdered Professor Bell! My husband and I played bridge until well past midnight the night he was murdered."

She touched a key on her computer, and the fish vanished and a spreadsheet came up. She seemed to find it fascinating.

I couldn't think of anything else to ask her, and she'd reverted to her old veteran secretary self anyway, so I thanked her for her time and help and left.

Twenty-One

As I started out of the building, a man came in, stomped snow off his boots, and pulled off his broad-brimmed leather hat and the scarf covering his face. It was Herb Sweeney, the retired potter. He tried to see who I was through fogged glasses, then peered over the top of them.

"Maggie MacNeil!" he exclaimed, giving me his wide, gap-toothed grin. "Back again, are you? Well, we're quite used to the police snooping around, trying to pin murders on us—now that Studio Arts is getting a reputation for being an abattoir. You know what an abattoir is, of course?"

"A slaughterhouse."

"Exactly! It was the same thing twenty-three years ago. 'Where were you on the night of . . . ?' Etc., etc. The police were very offensive about it, even though it was quite clear that poor Kate was the victim of a housebreaker. And now it's déjà vu all over again, as the Bard of Avon put it—except that this time it's you, passing yourself off as a real cop officially investigating Russ's horrible death. Who're you pretending to be today, Maggie?"

"Peggy O'Neill," I said, "amateur sleuth."

He laughed, finding something in there funny. "Why not? At least that has a certain Nancy Drewish coziness about it." He lowered his voice conspiratorially, looking all around. "I loved Nancy Drew as a kid. Don't let it get out, though—it'd ruin my macho image."

As we talked, he continued through the swinging

154

doors, down the hall past the studios, and into the big ceramics area in back, with me hard on his heels. He hung his hat and coat on a peg and said, "You still don't think that fellow Sánchez murdered Russ, huh?"

"I don't know," I said. "I've picked up a lot of gossip, skirted around the edges of some secrets. I don't know what it adds up to yet."

"Not much, probably." He straddled his electric wheel and turned on the power. "Everybody has secrets." He looked around the studio. "We're a big family, Maggie—utterly, utterly dysfunctional, but still a family. If an outsider like you digs deep enough, you're going to turn up some ugly things. Haven't you learned that yet?"

"Sure. But usually not in connection with two murders."

"Two murders separated by twenty-three years," he reminded me. He removed a ball of clay from plastic and slammed it down squarely in the center of his wheel.

"When I talked to you and the other Emeriti last week, Professor McFarlane said he thought Kate Simons was hustling Bell in an effort to improve her chances of getting promotion."

Sweeney's dwarfish face turned mournful as he centered the clay, opened it, and pulled it up into a somewhat wobbly cylinder, all in one motion. "That wasn't very nice of Mac," he said, "even though she's dead and no longer gives a hoot what anybody says about her. Kate wouldn't've stooped to that. For one thing, she had too much pride."

"And for another?"

"She didn't really care if she got promoted or not." He gave a mirthless laugh, cut the cylinder off the wheel, and put it with a lot of others on the table next to him. "That's the tragedy of your Mr. Sánchez, you see, Maggie," he went on. "If he did kill Russ because he thought Russ stood in Kate's way, he was sadly misguided. Kate was almost relieved when she didn't get promoted."

"She was? Why?"

He slapped another ball of clay on the wheel and

started it spinning. "Because she wasn't sure she wanted to stay here. She once told me she thought getting tenure—which means lifetime security—might make it harder for her to up and leave."

"Leave for where?"

"New York, New York!" he replied, belting it out. "New York was where it was at back then and, unfortunately, still is for American artists. That's where the national newspapers and magazines are and, therefore, the most influential critics and galleries.

"I hate doing this," he said, nodding at a new cylinder sprouting from the spinning wheel under his hands, "but I need a lot of cylinders for a big sculpture I'm doing, the latest in my *Vat* series. You've probably heard of it," he added hopefully.

When I said I hadn't, his face fell, and I was a little sorry I hadn't lied about it. "You were saying about Kate . . ."

"Yes, where was I? I got the impression she lived frugally, was saving her money so she could survive in New York for a while without starving any more than would look good in her autobiography. She also sold a big piece of sculpture to Dulcie Farr right after she learned she didn't get promoted. I suspect she got a nice piece of change for it too."

He chuckled, rubbing his hands together. "God, how Russ and Charlie bitched and moaned about that! They'd been here a hell of a lot longer than she had, you see, but they couldn't interest Dulcie in buying any of *their* crap. Charlie, I remembered, pooh-poohed it by saying Dulcie was just an ex-whorehouse madam who didn't know anything about art. She'd buy anything."

Dulcie Farr must have been the rich woman who'd bought a big sculpture by Simons through Osmond's old gallery, according to Sánchez. Her name had a familiar sound to it. I asked Sweeney who she was.

"You've never heard of Dulcie Tyler Farr, Maggie? Well, she never actually *owned* a whorehouse—Charlie was wrong about that—but she played the piano in one.

In fact, that's how she met her husband, although you won't find that bit of information in the official Farr family hagiography. Maurice D. Farr the Third inherited his fortune from Maurice D. Farr Junior, whose father owned railroads and land and mines and miners.

"The Farr genetic material had weakened considerably by the time Three came alone, and he squandered what he could of the fortune he'd inherited from Junior in the same low places where he met his devoted wife Dulcie. Dulcie—after Three's untimely death and after she'd paid off her worthless children—now squanders what's left on Good Works and High Art. The wings of hospitals bear her name, as do symphony halls, charitable foundations, endowed chairs, scholarships, and a variety of churches across the denominational spectrum."

"And she buys art," I said, hastening Sweeney along.

"Purchases. She *purchases* art, Maggie. You buy socks, you purchase art. Indeed she does—or did. I understand that she's unloading her private collection little by little. She even owns one of my early pieces," he added proudly.

I suddenly remembered where I'd heard her name before. Laura Price, the associate director of the museum, had told me that Russell Bell talked Dulcie Tyler Farr into lending the museum her Georgia O'Keeffe flower painting! I felt the little hairs on the back of my neck tingling: Kate Simons had sold a large piece of sculpture to Dulcie Farr and was murdered soon after. Russell Bell was murdered soon after he'd met with her too.

When I told Sweeney about that, he looked up from his wheel and exclaimed, "Good grief—will wonders never cease! That does *not* sound like the Russ Bell I knew! He was not—to put it gently—a friend of women artists. I think I mentioned to you the last time we talked that he was outraged when Miss O'Keeffe was invited here to receive an honorary degree and give a lecture on art."

He centered another ball of clay, made another cylinder. "But perhaps I'm being unfair to the poor man. People can change. And Russ hardly spoke to any of us after he was forced to step down as chairman of the department, so how would any of us know if he'd changed too?''

"Something's been bothering me, Professor Sweeney, ever since I talked to you and the other Emeriti last week."

"Herb, Maggie, please," he said graciously. "And what's that?"

"Professor Bright started to talk about a Georgia O'Keeffe Bell had painted himself. You said it was a parody of O'Keeffe and then changed the subject."

He smiled glumly and said, "You don't miss much, do you?" He counted the cylinders on the table next to him, all sagging in one direction or another, then began a new one. "What we were talking about," he said firmly, "had nothing to do with Russ Bell's murder. Or with Kate Simons's. It was just a bit of nastiness that Charlie Bright had no right bringing up in front of you."

"It's nastiness I'm looking for," I said.

"That's too bad. You could do so much better for yourself."

I could see I wasn't going to get any further with that approach, so I said, "I just talked to Gloria. She wouldn't tell me anything about Bell's affair with Professor McFarlane's wife."

He looked up at me with inexplicable agony in his eyes. "You would have found out about that, wouldn't you? I suppose Mr. Sánchez's lawyer will drag that whole sordid business into court to try to instill a reasonable doubt in a jury. Mac had a motive and perhaps he had the means and opportunity too—I wouldn't know. The only difficulty I have with that is that I've known Mac for over thirty years, and he wouldn't hurt a fly. And I'd hate to see all the dirt from such a long time ago surface again now. It wasn't Mac's fault, what happened between Russ Bell and his wife."

"I've heard that he and Bell got in a fight, and they both landed in jail."

The cylinder of wet clay he was pulling up collapsed, and he scraped it angrily off the wheel. "I suppose it was Charlie Bright who told you that."

Bright seemed to get blamed for giving me every bit of nasty gossip I'd picked up so far. "No, I haven't talked to him since last Thursday when I talked to all three of you."

"Gloria, then."

I shook my head. "She's as closed-mouthed about it as you are. She also seems to want to protect Professor McFarlane."

"Good!" He slapped a new ball of clay onto his wheel.

"Listen," I said, "Herb. Somebody's tried to kill me."

He stared up at me, a shocked look on his face.

"At least once," I went on. "Probably twice, and I don't know why. Maybe the attempts on my life aren't related to Bell's murder, but I don't know and I can't stop now. I've got to find out who killed him if Sánchez didn't. Or maybe it's because I've stumbled onto something about Kate Simons that I don't know I know, and her killer feels threatened by it. Help me, will you? I think the two murders are connected, and I think I'm in danger too."

He shook his head. "Blair McFarlane isn't trying to kill you. I'm sorry I don't know anything that could help you. What happened between Sally and Russ Bell has nothing to do with Russ's murder. That's all I know."

"Why did Russell Bell become a recluse after he had to step down as chairman?"

"I don't know, Maggie. Maybe it was because of the scandal." His heavy lips twisted into a melancholy smile. "I'd like to believe so—wouldn't you? Believe that when he saw through the glare of scandal what he and Sally had done, he felt ashamed. After all, the Mc-Farlanes had children!"

"Do you think Russell Bell cared?"

Sweeney threw out his wet, clay-streaked hands in a helpless gesture. "I don't know."

"What did Kate Simons think about it? You knew her."

"I'm not even sure she knew about Sally and Russ. She didn't socialize much—she was the only woman in the department, you know, and it was a little hard for her among all the men. She was dead by the time the scandal broke anyway."

"She was?" That came as a surprise to me. "When did it break?"

"A week, maybe two weeks after she was killed."

"Things were quite hectic around here at that time, weren't they? Murder, a sex scandal."

"Yes, they were. But we had no reason to connect Kate's murder with the affair between Russ and Sally. We still don't," he added pointedly.

Before I left, I asked him what he knew about the Factory. He made a face, then said, "All those flagrantly heterosexual artists were a bit too much for me, I'm afraid. I didn't spent much time there."

"How about Joel Osmond? What can you tell me about him?"

"The gallery owner? It wasn't nice of me, but my heart flew up in my breast like a pheasant when I heard he'd gone to jail for cheating on his taxes. He wouldn't handle my work, so needless to say I didn't spend much time in his gallery."

He chuckled. "Have you seen his gallery today? Thronging with yuppies who've graduated from posters asking, 'Can I get five yards of paintings in the style of Picasso's pink period by Wednesday?' It serves him right!"

"He also handled Russ Bell's work, and somebody told me they were friends."

"I suppose they must've been since Osmond seemed to take an inordinate—and totally incomprehensible—interest in Russ's art. What other reason could there have been for that?"

Twenty-Two

It was getting dark when I left Sweeney. I made sure I wasn't followed as I biked down to the River Road, then took it to Riverview Mall, where I retraced my steps up to Osmond's gallery. I wanted to see if I could stir him up a little, under the pretense of asking him if he still had a record of the people who'd bought—excuse me, purchased—Kate Simons's sculpture from him. That wasn't only a pretense, either. I really wanted to see some of her work.

I also wanted to ask him about the skinny blond college kid he'd had working for him that Dan Sánchez told me about, the one Kate Simons had known who'd seemed interested in her. It was a very slight lead, but since I wasn't exactly rolling in leads, I couldn't afford to be picky.

It was almost five, and the brightly lit shops were mostly empty of customers. The salespeople glanced up hopefully as I walked by, then went back to studying their fingernails or rearranging merchandise as they recognized me as a member of the working poor who'd made a wrong turn somewhere on my way to K-mart.

The saleswoman wasn't the same one I'd seen the last time I'd talked to Osmond. Although this one was dressed in an expensive sweater and skirt, she was short, plump and gray-haired. The discreet tag on her sweater said she was Dorothy Haverford and that she was an art consultant.

161

I asked to speak to Osmond. She told me he wasn't in and asked if she could be of assistance.

"It's a personal matter," I replied, disappointed. "Will he be back tonight?"

"Oh, no. The poor man's home in bed with pneumonia. Isn't that terrible? He pushed himself too hard during the Christmas shopping frenzy, which must have weakened his resistance. Is it something Mrs. Naylor, our senior art consultant, can help you with? She'll be in tomorrow morning."

I told her I wasn't sure and started to leave. On an impulse, I asked her if Osmond owned a panel truck. She said he owned some kind of truck—he delivered art to customers within certain geographic limits—but she didn't know what kind it was. She'd never seen it, she was only working at the gallery part-time during the holidays, for pin money.

Tess, looking none the worse for her bucolic adventure with the dashing wheat farmer, was there when I got home. She told me Buck had left a message on my machine. I called him, and without preliminaries he said, "I saw the report on what happened to you yesterday."

"Have they found the truck?"

"No, and it hasn't been reported stolen yet either. Tell me about it, Peggy."

When I did, he said, "What do you know that has somebody frightened enough to want to scare you off?"

I shook my head at him over the phone. "Not just scare me off. Kill me, or at least put me in the hospital for a long time. And this wasn't the first attack on me since I started investigating Bell's murder." I told him about the intruder on my porch before Christmas.

"All I've done is ask questions," I went on. "The only real liar I've met, as far as I know, is a guy named Joel Osmond." I told Buck about him, and how I'd thought he'd known who I was and what I was up to.

Buck asked who could have tipped him off.

"Anybody. He was an important figure in the local art

community before he went to jail, and maybe he's kept some of his old friends." I went through the names of the people I'd talked to about Bell: his studio mate, Shannon Rider; McFarlane, Sweeney, Bright; the department chairman, Lloyd Schaeffer; the secretary, Gloria Williams. "Not to mention Laura Price, the associate director of the U's art museum," I added. "And even the museum's incoming director, Thomas Fowler, might know about me. I haven't talked to him yet, but I've spoken to his wife. He studied painting with Bell."

"That certainly narrows the field," Buck remarked dryly.

"If somebody's slipped up and told me something that makes me a danger," I said with a pathetic attempt at humor, "I wish they'd tell me what it is."

"Why don't you quit what you're doing, Peggy?"

"You know I can't do that, Buck. Now it's just a question of who gets who first—or whom," I corrected myself, although it didn't sound as punchy as who gets who.

"The least you can do is ask to be reassigned to an inside job. You shouldn't be walking around that campus in the middle of the night, under the circumstances."

I told him what I'd told Tess: that whoever was trying to kill me wasn't trying to do it when I was armed, which probably meant that he, or she, wasn't carrying a firearm.

Before we hung up, I asked him if he'd do me a favor.

"If I can."

"Check to see if Joel Osmond owns an old panel truck—brown or tan."

He said he would.

Aunt Tess and I worked on my costume for the museum opening until it was time for me to go to work. As I stood there while she hemmed the gown around me, I thumbed through an expensively printed brochure the museum had published about itself, complete with a tear-out postcard for anybody interested in becoming a patron at a price I couldn't afford. I paused when I reached a short biographical sketch of Thomas Fowler, the new director.

He'd received his B.A. in English from the University in 1966 and his Ph.D. in art history in 1973. His dissertation was a catalogue raisonné of George Bellows.

"What's a catalogue raisonné?" I asked Tess.

"A list of every known work of art an artist has produced, and when he produced it, plus what the artist and others had to say about it, if anything, and who's owned it over the years," she replied through a mouthful of pins.

"It must be very tedious, putting one of those together."

"I suppose so."

I told her I'd never heard of George Bellows, and she explained that he was an early-twentieth-century American realist.

"He did that violent boxing painting that gets reproduced in every coffee table book on art, *Stag at Sharkeys*," she added. "You can almost smell the cigars and sweat and blood."

"That's what I want hanging on *my* wall!" I muttered, and continued reading. Armed with his doctorate, Fowler had taught art history at several private colleges in the East before accepting a joint position as professor of art history and museum director at one of them. Now he was looking forward to the challenge of being a full-time museum director, free to develop new community outreach programs, build the museum's already extensive holdings, and spread the word about our magnificent museum through his national and international contacts. Etc., etc.

The studio portrait of Fowler showed a man of about fifty with a high forehead and a full head of well-groomed hair graying at the temples. He was looking at something off to his left, one eyebrow raised. His thin lips hinted at a bemused smile; his chin rested in the V created by his thumb and forefinger. He looked familiar, the way everybody who poses like that does, giving the impression that profound ideas frolic in their heads like kittens with a ball of yarn. The camera lens must have been dipped in Vaseline.

"Doesn't look like the sort of guy who'd spend his time grubbing around in libraries with a stack of three-by-five cards," I said, "putting together catalogues raisonnés."

Tess squinted at the photograph. "It doesn't, does it? I thought he would become an artist or an actor. Thomas always wanted to be 'his own star,' you see."

I gave her a questioning look.

" 'Man is his own star,' " she quoted, " 'and the soul that can render an honest and a perfect man commands all light, all influence, all fate.' That's from a play by Beaumont and Fletcher," she added in her normal voice. "They came right after Shakespeare. I remember Thomas standing up in front of the class and declaiming that poem in a deep rich voice, deeper and richer than his own. I always have my students memorize worthy poetry, you know—it builds character. The other kids cracked up laughing, partly because they didn't have any idea what the speech meant and partly because it was rolling out of this skinny, tow-headed kid with buck teeth and glasses. When I saw him last month, I noticed he'd had his teeth straightened and had put on weight too. And I suppose he wears contact lenses now."

She stood up and stretched, her bones creaking, then went over and sat down on the couch and picked up the blue hat I was going to wear at the opening. She was going to sew roses on it to match those in Renoir's painting.

"He tried his hand at being a painter," I said. "According to his wife, he gave it up because he didn't think he had the talent to be a great one."

Tess gave a short laugh. "Maybe so. Besides, it takes a long time to make any real money as an artist, if you ever do. I don't think Thomas had the temperament to wait long for success or to gamble on his future. What he wanted, he wanted now. Anyway," she added, "being a first-rate museum director's nothing to sneeze at. And they're necessary too."

Twenty-Three

When I got off duty the next morning, I thawed out with a cup of hideously burned coffee in the squad room, changed into jeans and a wool Pendleton shirt I'd stolen from Gary, and drove over to Blair McFarlane's home in Tess's Corvette. He lived in Faculty Grove, a few miles north of the University. I thought I might try to talk to his wife while her husband was at the Studio Arts Building with the other Emeriti, fortifying himself with doughnuts and coffee before setting off to wrestle with his muse. If he'd stayed home that day, I'd just have to play it by ear. All they could do was throw me out, and I'd been thrown out of classier places than Faculty Grove before—more culturally and intellectually stimulating too.

The house came as a surprise, not because it was a fifties-style split-level rambler with a lamp in the bay window—that was par for the course in the Grove, where most of the inhabitants have the taste of shoe-store clerks. It was the cedar wheelchair ramp that led up to the front door that was out of character and gave the place interest.

I rang the doorbell. A few minutes later, a woman's face peered up at me from the little slit of a window on the left side of the door. I pulled out my shield and showed it to her. She looked from the picture to me and back at the picture again, then nodded and vanished from the window. The door opened, and she wheeled back in her chair to allow me to step inside.

"Nothing to do with Mac, is it?" she demanded, looking concerned.

"No," I said. "Are you Sally McFarlane?"

"Who else would I be?"

I told her my name and gave her my story about investigating the murder of Russell Bell.

"On your own time too," she snapped. "Mac told me about you. What do you want with me?"

"Somebody mentioned that you used to spend a lot of time at the Factory. Professor Bell spent time there too. I was hoping maybe you could tell me a little about what went on there."

"Bullshit. You want to find out if Mac killed Russ because I had an affair with him two decades ago. To tell you the truth, that was my first thought too, when I heard that Russ had been murdered. C'mon in."

Sally McFarlane was wearing dark wool slacks and a heavy wool shirt. Although it was quite warm in the house, she also had a white crocheted sweater over her shoulders. She looked younger than her husband—about sixty, with curly gray hair piled carelessly on top of her head. The years and whatever had put her in the wheelchair hadn't been able to obliterate the traces of a once beautiful woman.

I slipped off my shoes and padded after her as she wheeled herself down a ramp into a sunken living room that looked out on a neighbor's backyard and smelled of cigarettes, her husband's pipe tobacco, and pine. Flames licked around a fake log in a white brick fireplace, and prints, mostly her husband's book illustrations, hung everywhere on the walls. A small, neatly trimmed Christmas tree, a real one, stood in a corner.

"I'm not here because I think your husband killed Bell," I said, not entirely truthfully. "I just assume you could tell me a lot about Bell if you wanted to. But I am kind of interested in what you just said," I added with a smile, "that your first thought was that your husband killed him."

"I'll bet you are! I considered Mac a suspect for about

ten seconds. He's not capable of hating anybody as much as whoever murdered Russ must've hated him. Maybe at first, when he found out about us, Mac hated Russ—what red-blooded male wouldn't hate the man who'd put horns on him? Except I don't think hate's the word. Rage, maybe, fueled by shame.''

She sighed. ''If Mac was going to kill Russ, he would've done it at the time, and probably by accident— tripping over him, maybe, with his big feet. 'Oops, sorry, Russ!' He wouldn't wait twenty-some years and then sneak up behind him with a clay cutter in the middle of the night.'' She cocked her head at me and said, ''I'll bet it was that nasty little shit Charlie Bright who told you about me and Russ, wasn't it?''

I told her no, I'd heard it from more than one source.

She sighed. ''They're all hypocrites—well, most of 'em, anyway. I could tell you a few things about what goes on in that department—went on, I should say, since most of 'em are dead now, or as good as, the ones I knew!''

She picked up a pack of cigarettes and a lighter from a little glass-topped table. ''You mind?'' Without waiting for my answer, she fumbled the lighter into flame and lit the cigarette.

''I know, I know,'' she went on, waving the smoldering thing around in the air in front of her face, ''it was a terrible thing I did—a cliché too, having an affair with one of my husband's friends. But damn it, how's a woman, especially back then, ever going to get to know her husband's enemies well enough to have affairs with 'em, eh?''

She chuckled at that and then her face fell. ''It *was* a terrible thing I did, and Mac didn't deserve what I put him through either. I didn't even have youth to justify it—I was almost forty. Although,'' she added on a lighter note, ''a damned young forty, if I do say so myself.''

''When it came out,'' I said, ''Bell had to resign as chairman.''

"Yeah," she said with a happy little sigh. "So I guess he lost something on the deal too."

I told her I'd heard that he seemed to go into a shell after that and his art dried up. "He even stopped hanging out at the Factory."

She gave a scornful laugh and fanned smoke away from her face. "I wouldn't know anything about going into a shell. I can't think that losing his semiweekly rendezvous with me was that big a deal to him. But it's true; I never saw him at the Factory again after our affair ended. Who would've guessed he'd care what other people thought of him? I kept going to the Factory until Mac threatened to divorce me and go for custody of the kids. I didn't want that, so I gave staying home nights a chance and learned to crochet."

She shuddered. "Besides," she added, "the Factory wasn't the same after Russ. As far as his art drying up, I can't say anything about that either. He was a mediocre painter and according to Mac, a rotten teacher—although Mac's probably not the most objective judge of Russ. But he was a damned good lover. He—" She broke off. "Well, I don't suppose you came here to hear me talk about how Russ was in bed."

I asked her how long the affair had lasted.

She spun away from me, faced the picture window, and stared out, or at her reflection in it, or both. "It started in the fall," she said. "I remember that because whenever we met—always on Tuesdays and Thursdays, when Russ didn't have classes to teach—I'd forget how cold and miserable it was outside. The snow came early that year, but it always seemed like summer in Russ's house—he rented a little house back then. We drank wine and pushed cheese and fruit into each other's mouths— and laughed and fucked, laughed and fucked."

She inhaled smoke, let out what her lungs couldn't absorb, and looked to see how I reacted to the f-word. I've always liked it when properly used, so I smiled encouragingly.

"And then it was time for me to leave," she went on.

"I had to be there for the kids, you know, when they got home from school, and get them started on their homework. And tidy up the house and start dinner, too, of course. I'd walk out of Russ's little house and it would be—cold." She came down hard on the word.

"What year was that?" I asked, more interested in the nuts and bolts than the poetry.

She thought about it. "Seventy-one, seventy-two. The affair lasted all winter and ended in spring, in May— with all the flowers bursting out and the birds singing their heads off. I wanted to wring their lousy little necks!"

She pointed a gnarled yellow finger at me, shook it, and said, "Never start an affair in the fall! Start 'em in the spring, when everything's greening and growing. Let 'em wither in the fall, and die and be buried in the cold and snow of winter."

She glared out at the season she was talking about, one of my favorites.

"It wasn't the season of the year that ended the affair," I said. "It was when your husband found out about it."

She wheeled back to me. "Was it?" She thought about it a minute, then shook her head. "I don't know. Everything happened so fast. Herb Sweeney—he's a potter, you know him?"

I nodded.

"He and Mac and some of the other guys in the department had gone to lunch at a little café somewhere near campus. Herb had a couple of beers too many—he bashed the bottle a bit back in those days, as he used to say—and spilled the beans. He didn't mean to."

Laughter and smoke. "Mac lost it for the first and only time in all the years I've known him." She shook her head. "Poor man! He tried to beat Russ up—he had to since his colleagues were sitting there watching. He and Russ thrashed about, destroying everything but each other, until the cops finally arrived and hauled 'em both off to jail. It got in the papers—even got picked up by some gossip columnist desperate for scandal in this nice, dull state. Russ quit as chairman as soon as he made bail.''

That explained why Herb Sweeney had been so protective of McFarlane and wouldn't tell me anything about what had happened back then.

''And that was in May nineteen seventy-two,'' I said.

She nodded indifferently.

''But the affair didn't end then?''

''Didn't it?''

''You said you weren't sure.''

She thought a while. ''I think Russ wanted to end it before that,'' she said finally. ''He missed a date . . . a Tuesday . . .''

''How can you remember that?''

''Because it was the first time—the first time he'd missed a date that entire fall and winter and spring—and he didn't even call me to cancel. You see, I'd drive straight over to his place every Tuesday and Thursday, as soon as I got Mac off to the University and the children off to school, and he'd be there waiting for me, with wine and cheese and fruit. But not that day! I rang his doorbell and he didn't answer. Then I pounded on the door. I felt like a fool, but I couldn't help it.''

''Did he ever explain why he wasn't there?''

She stubbed out her cigarette in a big glass ashtray on her lap. ''Just said he was sorry, that something'd come up and he forgot all about us!''

''Did he say what it was?''

''Probably, but I don't remember. I'm not sure it was worth remembering.''

''Did you believe him?''

''No.''

''Was there another woman?''

She shrugged, staring listlessly out the window.

''What about Thursday? Did you meet then?''

''No, on account of he had to fly to Chicago—family business, he said. That's why I was so mad we'd missed Tuesday, 'cause I knew we wouldn't be meeting again for a whole week. I would've been even angrier if I'd known we'd never meet again!''

My pulse jumped as I realized what was going to happen next—twenty-three years ago. "Go on," I said quietly.

"What do you mean?"

"Bell missed Tuesday—you don't know why. He flew to Chicago on Thursday. What next?" I held my breath.

"Kate Simons got murdered," she said indifferently. "That's what happened next."

Twenty-Four

"She was murdered sometime that weekend," she continued. "They said it was a burglar, but they never caught him. That's all anybody could talk about for weeks afterward—poor Kate this and poor Kate that! You'd think they'd all loved her in the department, the way they talked about her, and were really going to miss her. They were just feeling guilty because they'd turned her down for promotion."

"And you never saw Bell again?"

"Not with my clothes off."

"Why?"

"Everybody was pretty upset over Kate's murder. I called Russ Monday morning, when I knew he'd be back from Chicago, but he told me he didn't want me to come over on Tuesday."

"Did he say why?"

She looked at me as though she thought I was a little slow. "I suppose it was on account of Kate," she said. "It's not every day someone you know is murdered, is it?"

"No," I replied, shaking my head, "that couldn't have been why. Her body wasn't found until Tuesday sometime."

"Oh." She looked at me blankly.

"*Why* didn't he want you to come over? Try to remember!"

She shook her head, bewildered. "I can't. It was so long ago, and I've got it all mixed up with Kate's murder now."

"Did he say you could come over on Thursday?"

She struggled to remember. "I think he said he'd call me—he'd let me know. But he didn't call on Tuesday either. I think that's when I figured out something was wrong. Then, on Wednesday, the whole department was in an uproar over Kate, so I wasn't surprised when I didn't hear from him."

She lit another cigarette. "I left him alone after that, waited for him to call. It felt awful when he didn't. And then, a week or so later, Herb got drunk and spilled the beans. Mac and Russ wrecked a café and ended up in jail. And that was that."

It's amazing how fast tragedy can turn to farce sometimes.

"If Herb hadn't blabbed," she went on, "maybe Russ and I would've gotten back together again, when the murder blew over. And we'd still be seeing each other now—or at least until last week," she added, and laughed, perhaps at the unlikely possibility that they would have continued their affair into old age and infirmity.

"I know you think I'm cold-blooded and selfish," she said, glancing at me. "A mother of two children cheating on her husband and feeling sorry only for herself when a young woman had just been brutally murdered. But damn it—I didn't know Kate well, and I didn't murder her either! Life goes on, and I needed Russ—or thought I did." She sighed noisily. "Mac's twelve years older than me, but back then it sometimes felt more like thirty! I'm older than him, now."

A little smile played around her mouth. "I give remorse a try every now and then. But it's hard trying to regret a choice you made more than twenty years ago while remembering how much laughter and pleasure you got out of it at the time."

I couldn't be too judgmental about Sally McFarlane since I've been in love—if that's the word for it—like that once or twice myself, where you don't give a damn about anything or anyone. I even took a man away from another woman once, without considering her feelings at all. Of course, they weren't married, and no children were involved, and her name *was* Deirdre, which is almost unforgivable. They got back together later, and they're married now. I sometimes see them together, pushing a double stroller along the walking path on Lake Eleanor.

For Sally McFarlane, Bell's behavior right before and after Kate Simons had been killed only spelled the end of their affair. But was that all it was? Something had happened to upset Bell's usual routine, and after Kate Simons's murder, he'd apparently never been the same again.

"Your husband told the police he thought Bell was having an affair with Kate. Could that have been why your affair was cooling down?"

"It wasn't cooling down," she snapped. "It just stopped. Boom! Like that. Mac would think that, but he's wrong." She laughed. "Russ did make a pass at Kate, though. He told me about it, made a joke out of it, didn't think I'd mind. I did, though—but of course I didn't let him see it."

"When was that?"

"Sometime that winter—after Christmas. January, early February. I don't think it was serious. I liked Kate Simons, what I saw of her, but if you ask me, she was a pretty plain Jane—very serious-minded, very committed to her work, no time for small talk. But she'd just broken up with the Mexican, and she was a little down at the mouth—or so Russ thought. So he asked her to dinner. He was chairman of the department, you see, and the chairman's supposed to hold the faculty's hands when they're having personal problems.

"So he took her out to eat somewhere and then to a jazz club. She liked jazz, he said. Russ didn't, but he pretended to, the scoundrel! It was all very nice and civilized—so nice and civilized that he invited her over to his place a few weeks later. He fed her dinner that he'd fixed himself. They sat around and listened to some jazz records he'd bought for the occasion and talked.''

She took a drag off her cigarette. "And then the idiot had to ruin it by making a pass at her!" She shook her head in disbelief—still, after all these years. " 'Oh, Russ! Why?' I asked.

"He just laughed and answered, 'I thought it was expected of me!' Men!''

"How'd she take it?''

"He said she was very nice about it—just said no and that was that. She stayed a little longer and then drove home.''

"And he wasn't upset about it?''

"Russ? Hell no! He made a pass at her only because she'd come over for dinner—two unmarried adults alone in his house. He thought it was the gallant thing to do, like holding a door for a woman or complimenting her on her hair. Nothing personal. He told me he admired her for turning him down.''

I told her that her husband had told me—and the police too, apparently—that he'd overheard Bell and Kate Simons quarreling a few days before she was killed.

Sally McFarlane nodded. "Mac got a certain amount of satisfaction out of telling me the same thing back then. Well, Russ never gave *me* any indication he was having trouble with Kate. Even if he did, what of it? He was in Chicago when she was killed.''

"And your husband was home in bed the night Bell was murdered.''

She tilted her head back, blew smoke at me, and said, "Of course he was—where else would he be? If he didn't do anything at the time except make an idiot of himself trying to beat Russ up, he never would.''

"Maybe twenty-three years ago he was concerned about the kids. But they're grown up now. Gone.''

There were family portraits on the mantle over the fireplace: two couples, four kids, eight smiles.

She looked at me, amusement in her dark eyes. "And

so you think he might have done last week what he didn't do almost a quarter of a century ago on account of the kids? You just don't know Mac. For one thing, he's still concerned about his kids, and the grandkids too.''

"Daniel Sánchez nursed a grudge for twenty-three years, and the police think it finally erupted into murder. And he's also got two kids.''

She didn't say anything to that—just shrugged, smiled, smoked.

I asked her what she remembered about Joel Osmond.

"My, you do get around, don't you! I haven't thought of that man in years—not since I read that he'd had to pay the piper for trying to cheat on his income tax.''

I told her he had a gallery in Riverview Mall now.

"In the old days,'' she said, "he had one of the best galleries in town. All the artists sucked up to him, hoping he'd represent their work and give them shows. He was quite the little rooster.''

"I've been told that he and Russell Bell were close friends,'' I said, "but he denied it.''

She chuckled. "I'd deny it too, if I were an ex-jailbird being asked about my friendship with someone who'd just been murdered! But they were friends, all right. Always with their heads together. Sometimes, when I was at Russ's house, there'd be notes reminding him to call Joel or meet Joel for lunch. Russ even had art from Osmond's gallery on his walls, things he could never have afforded to buy that Osmond loaned him. Russ was always interested in good art, even if he couldn't create it himself, which must've been why he got involved with the art museum. Mac told me he was a guide or something.''

She looked at me and said, "Russ Bell was a good man at heart but terribly frustrated. He'd enjoyed a little success in New York, and he was a friend of a lot of the artists—at least, so he said, but I didn't see any expressions of sorrow over his death in the obituary from any of 'em, did you? He claimed he'd painted with them, got drunk with them, even starved with them. Then he took the job at the University and left all that behind.

"He told me he regretted leaving New York and the struggle, settling for the security of a tenured position in the Midwest. He said it poisoned everything he did."

Violins up and out. "You'd think," I said, "that he'd be supportive of somebody like Kate Simons, who apparently really did have talent. And yet he saw to it that somebody else got the position she should have got."

"Lloyd Schaeffer, you mean? Russ told me they'd known each other in New York. Schaeffer had come highly recommended by some of Russ's artist buddies there. Maybe he thought he was making a responsible decision—or just doing a favor for his friends in the hopes of getting a show in New York out of it. He wanted to get back East badly, you know. He said his creativity had gone underground here in the boonies."

She smiled suddenly. "But he did paint one wonderful picture. It was of me." She got a dreamy look on her face. "You see, he was very good at figure drawing—he taught the life drawing classes his whole career. He liked drawing me sometimes, after we'd made love. And I liked it too. It was a nice break from sex, and sexy in its own way."

She thought about that a moment, a smile playing around her lips. "Anyway," she went on, "one day when I got to his house, there on the easel in his studio was a painting he'd done of me from some of the drawings! It was very beautiful—erotic and realistic—and on the wall behind me was a Georgia O'Keeffe flower painting!"

"O'Keeffe?"

"Yes—you know, the flower painter. Russ didn't like her work, actually, but he knew how much I like flowers, so he thought it would be amusing to paint an O'Keeffe on the wall above the bed behind me. It was a hibiscus—all pinks and reds and yellows—just like me, then. Russ would have made a very successful art forger," she added.

Somebody else had said that about Bell, I remembered:

one of the Emeriti. I wondered if this explained Charlie Bright's allusion to an O'Keeffe that Bell had painted himself, and Herb Sweeney's quick change of subject that had puzzled me when I'd talked to them. Sweeney had assured me it meant nothing. Once again he seemed to be trying to save Blair McFarlane some embarrassment.

"Several months before we broke up I asked Russ for that painting as a birthday present," Sally McFarlane went on. "I wanted it partly because I knew our affair would end someday, but also because I was afraid Russ might put it in a show or something. The portrait was *quite* a good likeness of me, and he had it hanging over his fireplace, where anybody who came in could see it!"

"He *gave* you the painting? Your husband's seen it?"

"God, no! Russ took it out of the frame for me. I keep it rolled up on a shelf in my closet, where Mac would never think to look. I used to take it out sometimes and look at it, but I can't reach it anymore." She looked down at her legs in disgust.

An idea struck her. "Would you like to see it? You could get it down for me."

"No," I said. "I guess not."

"At your age," she said wistfully, "I'd have wanted to see it. You're either a hypocrite or a prude."

I felt myself blush, and she laughed. "Never mind! I'll just have to ask my daughter to get it down for me some day. I won't tell her what it is, of course—she'd pretend to be shocked too. I'll wait until she leaves before I look at it. Of course," she added, "then I'll have to find some other place to hide it from Mac."

I wondered if it was possible to hide something from one's mate as long as Sally McFarlane thought she'd hidden that painting from her husband.

We talked a while longer. Belatedly she offered me coffee or tea, but I said I had to go—it was way past my bedtime. I thanked her for her help, and she said it'd been her pleasure.

I mustn't think too hard of her, she added, as she

wheeled herself along beside me up to the front door. She and Mac had gone to marriage counseling together after the big blowup, and they'd grown closer than they'd been before it happened.

"And I got some wonderful memories out of it too," she said. "And I learned to crochet."

Twenty-Five

I drove Tess's wretched little sports car home, longing for my Rabbit and wondering if I should break down and rent a real car until I had time to shop for a new one. A note from Tess on my bed told me Sandra Carr had called from L.A. and wanted me to call her back—collect, of course—when I'd got my beauty sleep. Tess was out on the town with Elmer, but she said she'd be back by the time I woke up.

I slept late, and when I got up and staggered out to make coffee, Tess was on the couch reading. Leaning against the wall next to her was a pitchfork.

"What's that for?" I asked suspiciously, since I don't keep hay-eating animals.

"It's Elmer's," she replied. "He's going to carry it at the opening Friday night, the way the farmer does in *American Gothic*. I didn't think they'd allow it in the museum, so this morning I called Thomas to ask. And I was right; he said no."

"Fowler thinks Elmer might have one glass of sherry too many and start forking art he doesn't like through a window?"

"If they let Elmer in with a pitchfork," Tess said piously, "they'd have to let people in with all kinds of sharp things on long handles—spears and swords and hoes and such. Accidents do happen, Peggy. I told Thomas I'd replace the real tines with cardboard ones, and he said that would be fine. Do you have a hammer and a screwdriver?"

I did, and she got to work dismantling the pitchfork.

I called Sandra. Tess had already told her about the attempt on my life on Monday. Now she wanted me to stop investigating Bell's murder. She was going to hire a professional as soon as she got back in town.

"Too late," I said. "It's only in the kind of novels you write that people go to the trouble of trying to kill a person just because she's nosing around. I must know something already that's a real threat to someone. What should I do, Sandra, put an ad in the paper announcing that Peggy O'Neill, after having a frontal lobotomy, plans to devote her life to macramé?"

"People sometimes base their behavior on what they read in books," she replied, hurt.

"That's a scary thought too."

"I'll buy you a new car, Peggy," she said. "Even if you quit now."

"We'll see if I need one," I said somberly, and we hung up.

I called Buck and asked him if I could come downtown and look at homicide's file on Kate Simons.

"Sure. It's on microfilm, and I've got a microfilm reader in my office. Why?"

"I think whoever killed Russell Bell also killed her."

"Oh? And do you have any evidence of that?"

"No. Not yet," I added stubbornly.

I wrestled the Corvette downtown and parked in the underground lot under the Justice Building, recalling the last time I'd parked there almost two weeks before, when I'd picked Dan Sánchez out of a lineup.

The name on the wall outside Buck's office says his first name is Mansell, but nobody who knows him well enough to call him by his first name would do it. I knocked and went into the cluttered, oddly comfortable room.

The first thing I noticed was a painting on an easel in a corner. Buck wasn't a Sunday painter as far as I knew.

I went over and stood in front of it. "Bell's?"

"Right, the one he was working on when he was killed. The prosecutor plans to set it up in the courtroom to recreate the murder scene for the jury. He was in looking at it this morning."

It showed the profile of a man on the left side of the canvas, staring dully across it at something off the right edge or, more likely, at nothing. The background, what there was of it, was a series of horizontal planes in dullish reds, yellows, and browns, abstract but desertlike too. To me it added up to something lifeless, but I couldn't tell if that had been Bell's intention or not.

I said I supposed it was a self-portrait since the man in it resembled the old photo of Bell I'd seen in the newspaper.

"Yeah," Buck replied without a lot of enthusiasm. He thinks the creation of great art stopped around the time Picasso started art school.

"Where's the blood?"

He pointed to some dark spots that seemed to work okay with the painting's abstract background, and I could see a smudge of it on Bell's face too that added a certain morbid interest. "There, and there. And there, on the easel."

I wondered if an expert on Russell Bell's work, not knowing the origin of those spots, could tell they didn't belong. Except there were no experts on Russell Bell's work.

"Why isn't it smeared?" I asked. "The painting was lying face down when I saw it."

"It's acrylic," Buck replied. "Acrylic dries fast, so it wouldn't smear the way oil would, if Bell hadn't added anything to it for fifteen or twenty minutes before it fell."

He brought me a cup of coffee—since Buck loves coffee as much as I do, it was excellent—and gestured to the microfilm reader on a table against a wall. "I've already threaded it on for you," he said. "Help yourself."

I went over and started cranking the first microfilmed documents onto the illuminated screen.

"Looking for anything in particular?" Buck asked, his curiosity getting the better of him.

"No, I just want to get a sense of how it was back at the time of Kate Simons's murder."

I've looked through the files of what homicide cops call "Whodunit" cases before, the cases whose solutions aren't obvious fairly quickly. The longer it takes to solve them, the more they start to read like nineteenth-century Russian novels: more and more characters appear whose stories lead to more and more characters, so that after about a hundred pages, it's hard to remember who said what when. And weaving in and out of the narrative, like the old-fashioned omniscient author, are the comments of the detectives: their thoughts and feelings about the characters, their warnings and guesses and opinions. There was some of that in the case of Kate Simons's murder, but it was obvious that the investigators back then concluded it was the work of a burglar fairly quickly.

I was sure there'd be even less of a story for Russell Bell's murder if I asked to see that file.

Gloria Williams's story of how she'd persuaded the caretaker to go into Simons's apartment checked out. He'd noticed the newspapers in front of her door but assumed she'd gone out of town for a few days. At Williams's insistence, he'd opened her door. He claimed he didn't cross the threshold—he didn't have to—he'd been in Korea and knew what humans smelled like when they'd been dead a while.

Kate Simons had had dinner with a friend, a woman, Friday night. The friend had dropped her off at her apartment at around eleven and waited until she'd entered the building before driving away. She was the last person to see her alive—the last person who would come forward and admit it, at least.

Simons had been hit over the head with a piece of sculpture, a piece by a friend of hers for which she'd traded one of her own. It looked as though she'd crossed the living room to her bedroom, gone in, and surprised the burglar. She'd put up a struggle and been hit several times.

A note from the homicide cop in charge, heavily underlined in red, indicated that all information about where she'd been killed, the fact that she was still wearing her raincoat and the nature of the murder weapon, had been withheld from the public, the usual procedure for trying to weed out the weirdos who come forward and confess to murder as an attention-getting device.

Her body had been found on Tuesday, and the medical examiner's best estimate placed the time of death as late Friday night or early Saturday morning. The murderer had entered by climbing the fire escape and breaking the glass on her bedroom window to reach the latch. It was an old building; security wasn't as good back then as it is now.

Jewelry her sister and parents knew she'd owned was missing, and an expensive camera too, but not much else. She didn't have a lot that a burglar would find attractive anyway—mostly just art, her own and her friends'. Although she'd had a good stereo, speakers, and a TV, things burglars usually take, they'd been left behind. The police speculated that the burglar or burglars, after killing her, had panicked and left with only what they'd collected before she came home. None of the stolen items had ever turned up. That was unusual but not unheard of.

An inventory sheet enclosed in the file indicated that dried blood under the fingernails of the victim wasn't Kate Simons's and was presumed to be her killer's.

I asked Buck if the blood had been saved and he said it had. "It'll also still be valid for DNA testing," he added, anticipating my next question, "if we ever find a suspect."

Many of the names were of people I hadn't heard of—neighbors, family, a few friends. I read their interviews carefully, gradually building up a picture of a private woman, ambitious, energetic, deeply committed to her art, with not a very rich social life.

A lot of them mentioned Dan Sánchez. Everyone

who'd known them seemed to agree that Kate had been strongly attracted to him. She apparently hadn't known many men before him and found him exciting—his tenderness, his passion, his obvious devotion to her—but his drug and alcohol use had worried her a lot, as well as her own doubts about wanting to get married and have children. She'd found it hard to break off with him, however, because she felt sorry for him and worried about what he might do if she did.

The police asked them if they'd thought she meant she was afraid for herself if she broke their engagement. They all agreed that she'd made it clear she was afraid of what he might do to himself, not her.

The police interviewed Sánchez several times. It was clear that the detective in charge of the investigation wasn't happy about the burglary theory and considered Sánchez a strong suspect. He didn't have an alibi for the times during which she must have been killed. He'd voluntarily let the police see that there were no scratches or bruises on his body, or other evidence that he'd been in a struggle with her, but that didn't rule out an accomplice.

He'd told them that after Simons threw him out, he'd gone through drug and alcohol treatment, and he insisted he'd been sober and clean for almost three months. He made no secret of his hope that they'd get back together someday.

They'd kept in touch by telephone, but the detective noted that the telephone contact between them seemed to have become less and less, and he suspected that Kate Simons was trying to unload Sánchez as gently as possible.

I was especially interested in the interview with Blair McFarlane. He'd stated, asking for confidentiality, that he believed there'd been something going on between Russell Bell and Simons. In early February he'd overheard them discussing having dinner together and then going to a nightclub afterward. Simons had told Bell she liked jazz and Bell had said he did too. According to the detective who'd conducted the interview, McFarlane had snorted and said, "Russ hated jazz!"

McFarlane's office was next to Simons's, and two days before she was killed, he claimed he'd overheard them quarreling in there. Their voices were muffled, so he hadn't been able to hear the words, he said, but it sounded as though she was reading Bell the riot act. He sounded like he was pleading with her for something.

Good old Charlie Bright had let slip to the detective who'd interviewed him that Bell had been having an affair with McFarlane's wife for months. The detective speculated that McFarlane had probably known about it, and that had colored his testimony against Bell.

I tsked and shook my head, and Buck looked up at me from his desk with a questioning smile. "Sodom and Gomorrah," I said, and ducked back into the dead past, to a time when McFarlane wouldn't officially know about the affair for a few weeks yet.

Russell Bell was outraged when the detective confronted him with McFarlane's testimony, although he didn't mention McFarlane by name and Bell assumed it was Charlie Bright who'd told the detective the story. Apparently Charlie had a reputation for spreading dissension even back then.

Bell said there'd been nothing between him and Kate. He'd noticed that she seemed a little depressed, asked her about it and learned that she'd broken up with her fiancé. He felt it was his duty, as chairman, to do what he could to lift her spirits. They'd gone out to dinner and a nightclub once and he'd had her over for dinner once, and that was all there was to it. He expressed indignation that an adult male couldn't have a relationship with an adult female without small-minded people assuming sex was involved.

I glanced over at Bell's self-portrait and gave it a disgusted look. Instead of staring across the bleak canvas at something beyond it, or at nothing, he should have painted himself full-face, the way so many great artists had done in their self-portraits. He probably didn't have the guts.

He denied that he and Kate had ever quarreled in his office and reminded the detective that he had a cast-iron alibi for the time of her murder.

It took me over an hour to read through all the reports, badly typed on old typewriters, full of typos and grammatical errors and misspellings, with coffee stains and surly editorial comments in the margins that spoke of late nights and little sleep. It wasn't exactly like having been there in May of 1972, but it was close enough for me.

I sat back, noted the manila envelope on the table next to the microfilm reader, turned it over and saw that it was marked Crime Lab Photos.

I took a deep breath, opened it and slid out a stack of eight-by-ten color photographs of the murder scene.

In all of them Kate Simons lay sprawled on the floor of her bedroom, still wearing her raincoat, an umbrella beside her where it had fallen, both bright red. Her head was lying in a puddle that wasn't spring rain. Her eyes were blank under half-closed lids. She had short hair, dark and curly, matted to her head in places. I remembered the snapshot I'd seen of her with Sánchez at the beach, laughing into the sun. In these pictures she looked more like the clay bust of her that Sánchez was working on.

Another photograph showed the murder weapon, a piece of shiny chrome in the shape of a stylized bird about to take flight. It was sitting on a dresser where the murderer had put it when he'd finished with it. I wondered why he hadn't just dropped it.

As I slid the photos back into their envelope, I wondered who had created that scene, who had contemplated it for the first time—and how he, or she, could go on living with the memory of it. But maybe, as Elena Sánchez had said, the killer was dead now too.

I sighed deeply and got up to go. Buck asked me if I'd found anything useful, and I said I'd just confirmed some stories I'd already heard but didn't think I'd learned anything new.

"What now?" he asked.

I told him about the apparent coincidence of Kate Simons having sold Dulcie Farr a piece of sculpture just before she was murdered and Russell Bell approaching Mrs. Farr about the O'Keeffe just before he was murdered. And I told him I'd tried to talk to Joel Osmond, but he was home in bed with pneumonia.

I asked him if he'd had a chance to check to see if Osmond owned a truck that matched the one that had attacked my Rabbit.

"He's got two panel trucks registered in his name," Buck said. "One's new, cream-colored with brown trim. It's parked in the garage under the mall and doesn't have a scratch on it. The other one fits your description—it's old and brown. Osmond hasn't renewed the registration on it in five years, which could mean he sold it when he went upscale about three years ago and the title never got transferred."

"Or it's still in his garage," I said. "I suppose you'd need a search warrant to check it out, wouldn't you?"

"That's right, Peggy," he said levelly. "And it *should* go without saying that we don't have enough evidence to ask for one."

I knew that too. "But it would be nice to see if the driver's side is bashed in and streaked with my Rabbit's paint, wouldn't it?"

"I'll see what I can do," he said.

I drove home with the window down, letting the cold winter afternoon air clear my mind of the images of murder I'd seen in Buck's office.

Twenty-Six

I wanted to talk to Dulcie Tyler Farr, who'd played a role in the lives of both Kate Simons and Russell Bell just before they'd died violently. She wasn't listed in the phone book, so I called the University art museum and asked to talk to Laura Price, who I thought would have her address.

The receptionist told me she'd left for the day and asked if I wanted her to return my call. I reminded her of when we'd met before and told her I was hoping Doctor Price could give me Mrs. Farr's telephone number.

"Why don't you try again tomorrow," she asked, not taking the hint.

"Could you get it for me?"

She laughed indulgently, appreciating a good joke when she heard one. "I don't think so," she replied politely. "I like my job here and want to keep it. Perhaps you'd like to talk to Doctor Fowler. He's here this afternoon."

I said that would be fine.

She put me on hold, and after about forty-five seconds a man's voice said, "This is Thomas Fowler."

I told him who I was and that I was investigating the murder of Russell Bell.

"Oh, yes," he said briskly, "Tess O'Neill's niece." His voice was light, pleasant. "It's nice to finally speak with you in person, after hearing so much about you from your aunt and my wife. But if you're part of an official investigation," he went on, sounding puzzled, "as I believe you told my wife you were, you surely don't need me to give you Mrs. Farr's telephone number.''

Oops. "I'm sorry if I gave your wife the impression I was working on the case in an official capacity," I said. "I'm not. I'm doing this for a friend who thinks Daniel Sánchez is innocent.''

"Really? Are you experienced at investigating murders? Your aunt didn't mention that among your talents.''

I pretended not to notice the tinge of sarcasm in his voice and said I thought I was pretty good at it. Tenacious anyway, I added hopefully.

He chuckled humorlessly. "And may I ask what connection you think there could be between Mrs. Farr and Professor Bell?''

I told him how Bell had talked Mrs. Farr into letting the museum have her O'Keeffe on permanent loan, and why I thought that was strange. "I'd like to know what he might have told her about his interest in O'Keeffe.''

"Well," he said, after a pregnant silence, "that's not really much of a reason to pester Mrs. Farr, is it? My friendship with Russ Bell goes back a long way, Peggy— I hope I may call you Peggy." He didn't say anything about me calling him Thomas. "He was my teacher for a time, and I considered him a friend too. I also know that he had something to do with my getting the directorship here, for which I'm grateful.

"I want whoever killed him to pay for the crime," he went on, "and I'll do anything I can, within reason, to help in that endeavor. But as far as I can tell, the police seem to be satisfied that they have their man. My guess is—and please don't take this amiss, Peggy—that you're acting on behalf of the accused man, looking for evidence that will allow him to escape through a loophole. Am I right?''

"No," I protested, "that's not true. I don't think loophole law is justice.''

"Nor do I. Well, I'm sorry if I appear unhelpful, but as you know I'm new here. I only arrived Christmas Eve, and I don't know the terrain yet, politically speaking. Mrs. Farr is among the museum's wealthiest patrons, and I'm sure I don't need to tell you what that means. I'd hate to start off my tenure here by giving her telephone number to somebody whom she might feel has no business having it.''

As he spoke, I could almost hear him playing with the card with Dulcie Tyler Farr's telephone number on it. I wondered whatever happened to ''Man is his own star,'' the speech Tess told me he'd declaimed in high school. Maybe he got tired of being laughed at for it.

Switching into a heavily jocular tone, he went on: ''I'm sure your aunt will take me to task for saying no to her beloved niece, but I'm just going to have to risk that. It wouldn't be the first time! This morning I had to tell her she couldn't bring a pitchfork into the museum tomorrow night!''

''The O'Neills are real pests, all right,'' I said, trying to nudge a little heartiness into my words.

He laughed. ''I'm so looking forward to meeting you. Your aunt was one of those teachers the good student never forgets. She invested long hours in us, both during and after school. The first art museum I was ever in was this one, in fact, in its old location—your aunt drove us down in an old bus they probably wouldn't allow students on today! So in a very real sense I'm returning home now. It will be fitting to have Tess O'Neill beside me at the banquet tomorrow night.''

Nice words; generous too. I suspected he planned to use them in his banquet speech.

''Something just occurred to me,'' he went on. ''Mrs. Farr is going to be at the opening. Why don't I introduce you? You can make your case to her in person. What's one more day?''

I told him that I guessed that would have to do, and added that I'd also like to talk to him, since he'd been Russell Bell's student.

He chuckled. ''I was his student very briefly. I soon realized I didn't have what it takes to be an artist. I switched into art history after one year. Smartest decision I ever made.''

The penny suddenly dropped: from Tess's museum brochure, I remembered that he'd got his Ph.D. in 1973. ''You were a student here when Kate Simons was murdered, weren't you?''

''Yes—but I didn't know her except to nod to, of course. I had even less talent for sculpture than for painting. She was killed several years after I'd left Studio Arts.''

''Still, I'd like to talk to you about Bell.''

''Certainly, certainly.'' His voice had acquired a slight edge, and deepened, and sounded like one I'd heard somewhere before, but I didn't have time to try to remember where or when. ''But it'll have to be sometime after the New Year,'' he went on. ''Why don't you make an appointment with my secretary for the first or second week in January?''

I said that would be fine, and we hung up.

I had no intention of waiting until the next night to see Dulcie Tyler Farr if I could help it, so the next morning I hung around the squad room until Ginny Raines came in. As a detective, I figured she could find out anything she wanted to.

''My, we're coming up in the world, aren't we?'' she exclaimed. ''And what does a lowly campus cop want with Dulcie Tyler Farr's address?'' She was stirring nonfat dairy substitute into a Styrofoam cup of coffee, holding a chocolate doughnut in the other hand.

''I'll tell you sometime, Ginny,'' I said. ''Can you get it for me?''

She shook her head, making her curls dance. ''Uh-uh. If it's not available to the general public, what makes you think I'd have it? You think the police have secret directories of private citizens?''

''We don't?''

''Of course not. The newspaper probably does, though.

Don't you have a long-suffering boyfriend who's a big-time journalist?''

"Thank you, Ginny."

I called Gary at the paper when I got home, told him what I wanted and, after asking me why, etc., he said he didn't know Mrs. Farr's address.

"Damn!" I said. "Damn, damn, damn," I elaborated.

"I can tell you how to find her home, though," he said when I'd finished.

"How?"

"You know where Summit is? You take it as far up as you can. At the top, there's an ugly old mansion that looks like a charity hospital, except you can't see it right now because it's hidden behind over a million Christmas lights. That's it. You can't miss it."

"How do you know this?"

"Because every year Dulcie Farr's neighbors take her to court for creating a hazard and a nuisance with her holiday display. And every year she wins. And the following year she adds something new to the display. If you read the paper or watched television news, you'd know this."

Twenty-Seven

Summit is a wide street paved with old money all the way to the top and down the other side, and Gary was right: I couldn't miss Dulcie Tyler Farr's mansion.

A Santa, one arm waving drunkenly and about to crash his sleigh and reindeer into the red tile roof, seemed caught in the glare of anti-aircraft searchlights. Strings of lights outlined the mansion and every tree and bush in the vast yard, turning the place into a garish one-dimensional cartoon. Elves made toys in Santa's workshop in illuminated upstairs windows, and a life-size crèche on one side of the lawn was so brilliantly lit that its inhabitants should have been wearing sunglasses. I could understand why the neighbors might complain: in the event of another star of Bethlehem appearing in the sky, they'd be the last to know.

I drove through the open gate and up the long sweeping drive, parked in an area of inlaid brick next to the front door and went up and rang the bell. Nothing happened for a long time, and then the door was opened by a very tall, very thin, very stooped old man. He was wearing a butler's uniform somewhat the worse for wear, and lacked only the salver balanced on the tips of his fingers. Behind him in the house somewhere, I could hear the faint tinkle of ragtime piano music.

Shielding his eyes against the glare behind me, he looked me up and down. "Yes?" he asked, with a small expectant smile.

I asked him if I could speak with Mrs. Farr.

"On what subject, may I ask?"

"Murder."

"In general, or in particular? I'm sorry if I seem unduly curious, but Mrs. Farr will want to know before she decides whether to admit you or not."

"I'm investigating the murders of Kate Simons and Russell Bell," I told him. "I think Mrs. Farr knew them both. I'd like to talk to her about them."

"Yes, that might pique her interest," he said. He stood back, gestured me into a small, circular anteroom and took my name. "Please wait here. I should be back in a moment. Don't sit on that chair. It needs glue."

He returned a few minutes later and announced that Mrs. Farr would be delighted to talk to me. "Please take off your boots, though—I'm afraid some of the rugs are in rather fragile condition. I'm Butler, by the way. Not the *butler*, you understand, just Butler. It's Dulcie's little joke." Without further explanation, he led the way down a long hall, the piano music getting louder.

The living room was dim and cavernous, quite a contrast to the front yard, with large windows in one wall that offered a view of the city's skyline far in the distance, just visible in the failing afternoon light. The walls were hung with prints and paintings from all periods ranging from the eighteenth to the late-twentieth century, in no particular order.

A scrawny Christmas tree in a corner leaned slightly and made Jesse's in the squad room seem almost lush by comparison. Next to it was an upright piano. A woman was playing it, her back to me, a mass of impossibly silver hair piled high on her head like a messy nest of tinsel. Her feet barely reached the piano's pedals.

"It's Joplin's 'Maple Leaf Rag,' of course," Butler whispered. "You might want to compliment her on how well she plays it when she's finished—but don't request an encore, since the 'Maple Leaf Rag' is all she has left of her repertoire now. Can I get you something to drink?"

"Coffee?"

"Cream and sugar?"

"Black."

He disappeared, and I stood and listened to Dulcie Farr play, her thin wrinkled arms flapping up and down the keys, the many rings on her bony fingers flickering in the dim glow of the Christmas tree.

She finished with a flourish and immediately spun around on the stool, throwing her arms out as if to embrace an enthralled audience. "Not bad for ninety-two, wouldn't you say?" She was panting slightly.

"Wonderful at any age," I said, clapping enthusiastically.

"But no more, please, that's quite enough for one set."

"It certainly is," I agreed.

"Sit down, sit down." She gestured to a sofa in the middle of the room. "And how did you like the Christmas display?"

"It's dazzling."

"I suppose so. I'm not much into holiday folderol myself anymore, but the neighbors expect it, and I don't like to disappoint them."

She came over and sprawled in one corner of the sofa and peered at me inquisitively through bright hooded eyes. She was wearing a gold lamé pantsuit that went well with her hair and shimmered along with the stones in her rings. Bright lipstick had given her a little heart-shaped mouth that perched on her face like a valentine and bled into the wrinkles around it.

"I used to know 'Peggy O'Neil,' " she went on, wistfully. "It was one of my signature pieces in fact, back in the twenties. The men adored it."

She asked me if I played the piano and knew the song I was more or less named after, and I said that once I'd known how to do both, but no longer. As a kid I'd played the piano, and I'd also played "Peggy O'Neil." My father insisted on it, making me play it as he and his friends stood around the old upright and sang the damned thing in their drunken voices. Which is why I used to play the piano.

Butler came in with a silver coffee service on a tray and poured me a cup of coffee. He looked at Mrs. Farr and asked, "Dulcie?"

"The usual, Butler," she told him, waving him away. He nodded and left the room. She turned to me and asked me why I was interested in Kate Simons and Russell Bell.

I told her how I'd been asked by Sandra Carr to try to find evidence that somebody other than her friend Daniel Sánchez had killed Bell. "So far," I said, "I haven't found any reason why anybody would want to kill him— at least, not now. All I've discovered is that there was another murder in his background, one that was never solved—Kate Simons."

She nodded thoughtfully. "And you think there's a connection."

"I don't know. But I do know that you're connected with both of them through your art collection. You own the O'Keeffe, and you also own a piece by Simons."

Butler came back in with another tray, this time with a cut glass goblet on it full of something dark and green.

"Thank you, Butler," she said, taking the glass and sipping.

"What's that?" I asked.

"Spinach juice—full of iron. Want some?"

"No, thanks," I said. The coffee was excellent. "Did you know Russell Bell well?"

"I hardly knew him at all," she answered. "But four months ago he telephoned me out of the blue and asked if he could come over and discuss my lending the O'Keeffe to the museum. 'Sure, c'mon over,' I told him." She lowered her voice. "Between you, me, and the fence post, I'm a lonely old woman—it's just me and Butler now. I rarely go out anymore. I've been to enough parties to last me a lifetime. So I'll talk to just about anybody—even a half-baked talent like Russell Bell. You've seen his work?"

I said I'd seen a little of it.

"Thirty, thirty-five years ago, he was said to be promising. I was buying contemporary art back then—investmentwise it's a crapshoot, but that wasn't why I bought it. I bought what I liked. Couldn't stand his stuff and told him so. 'As a retired whorehouse pianist, Professor Bell,' I said, 'I know when someone's hitting all the notes but missing the music. Why don't you consider going into some other line of work—commercial art, for example?' I have no patience with mediocrities."

She sipped spinach juice. "So I was a little surprised when he called me up and wanted to discuss borrowing the O'Keeffe. Turns out he'd taken my advice and gone into another line of work—part-time anyway. He was working for the U's museum as a guide."

She nodded her approval. "I told him to come on over. I've grown more tolerant with the passing of the years. He couldn't help being what he was, and it must hurt like the dickens, having some talent but not enough. Neither of us mentioned what I'd said to him those many years ago, of course, and to make a long story short, I let him persuade me to give the O'Keeffe to the University on permanent loan."

She shrugged. "Why not? I've got more paintings than I can shake a stick at. Hell, I'd half forgotten I had the O'Keeffe until he called and reminded me. I have a vault in the basement where I keep my paintings. It's the right temperature and humidity, so there's no danger of rot or anything of that kind."

"Did he say why he wanted the painting?"

"Said he'd learned to appreciate Georgia O'Keeffe's art over the years he'd been a tour guide. And he said he thought more women should be represented in the collection too. I'm a sucker for that argument, of course, so I said fine, take it. They've got it up for the opening tomorrow night, I hear, right next to the O'Keeffe they already own. I'm going," she added. "You'll never guess as what."

The first thought that came to mind was Whistler's

mother, but I bit it back and said, "*Nude Descending a Staircase*?"

"Who told you? *Butler*!" She glared at him, hovering in the shadows over by the entryway. He shrugged, looked helpless.

"It was just a guess," I said. "That's going to be a hard costume to make, isn't it?"

"Butler spent a lifetime in the theatre designing costumes." She looked me up and down. "You'd make a good Vermeer *Laughing Girl*. At least, you would if you didn't have such deep frown lines between your eyes. Do they ever go away?"

"What's bothering me," I said, ignoring the question and returning to the business at hand, "is that back in the early seventies, Bell didn't like Georgia O'Keeffe— he even did a parody of one of her paintings. And as far as I've been able to find out, he wasn't much of a feminist either. Yet suddenly here he is, going to a great deal of trouble to get you to donate your O'Keeffe to the museum."

She said the same thing that Herb Sweeney had said. "Well, people change, don't they? It sounded to me like Bell genuinely loved O'Keeffe's work and wanted mine very much. I asked him what was so special about my O'Keeffe. His answer was that mine was the only O'Keeffe he knew about in private hands in town."

Her face darkened, and her painted mouth became a little biomorph of sorrow. "Professor Bell was a lousy painter, but I don't think he should have died quite so horribly! The only other artist I've ever had in my home, you know, was Kate Simons. She died horribly too. You don't think my house is cursed, do you?"

"Kate Simons was *here*?"

"Of course. I thought you said you knew that."

"I only knew you'd purchased one of her pieces."

"That's why she was here, of course, to supervise the installation—I made that a condition of the sale. She came and we had a lovely time. I looked forward to seeing her again.''

"Installation where?''

"In the garden in back. But it's not there now. It didn't weather well, alas, and sometime in the eighties I had it dismantled. It was steel—not large, but quite monumental anyway. Swooping, wouldn't you say, Butler? Had she lived, she could perhaps have advised me on how to save it, but—'' She shrugged. "It's in the basement somewhere.''

I went over to the big windows and looked down into the garden, a large formal garden of paths defined by low hedges. Snow-capped sculptures of various sizes and shapes were scattered here and there throughout it. I wondered where Kate Simons's had stood.

I remembered Dan Sánchez's question about what happens to the art of artists who don't live long enough to fulfill their promise. Now I knew part of the answer: Some of it ends up in the basements of ex-whorehouse pianists.

"I liked Kate Simons,'' Dulcie Farr went on, when I'd returned to the sofa. "She had definite ideas about art and she seemed determined to pursue her vision come hell or high water. She'd just received bad news from the University—the sons of bitches decided not to rehire her. But although she was royally pissed off about it, she wasn't deterred. She told me she'd probably move to New York when the school year ended. But three or four days later, she was dead.''

"Three or four days later?''

She nodded solemnly.

Butler, in the shadows by the entrance, cleared his throat discreetly.

"Yes, Butler, what is it?''

"If I remember correctly, Dulcie,'' he said, "Miss Simons even commented on the O'Keeffe. You'll recall that you had it on the wall over there where the Stella is hanging now. Among other questions, she asked you where you'd acquired it.''

Dulcie Farr thought for a moment, her long fingers massaging her temples. "Yes, I do remember that," she said doubtfully. "And what did I tell her?"

"That you'd purchased it at the same place you'd found her sculpture: Mr. Osmond's gallery."

"Osmond's!" I almost leapt from my chair.

She looked at me curiously. "Joel Osmond, yes. He was a big name in the local art community back then. Later, I believe he got into some trouble with the IRS and had to spend time reducing rock to rubble at a correctional institution for the good of his soul. I wonder if it worked. He was very knowledgeable about art though, and before the Feds got him, he sold me some lovely things."

"Not long before she was murdered," I said, "Kate Simons was here—in your house, sitting where I'm sitting—and interested in the same Georgia O'Keeffe I'm interested in. *Why* was she interested in it?"

"I have no idea," she replied. "Butler?"

"I'm sure I couldn't say," he answered. "She asked how much you'd paid for it. I think she even asked if you'd checked its provenance. After she left, you observed that for a struggling young artist Miss Simons was a tad impertinent."

"What's provenance?" I asked.

"Its history," Mrs. Farr replied. "Who'd first bought it from O'Keeffe and when, and who'd owned it after that, if anyone, and so forth."

"And had you checked the provenance?" I asked.

"Butler?"

He sighed. "Most likely not, Dulcie."

"Well, not personally," she said, giving him a hurt look. "But Mr. Osmond was a very reputable dealer, after all, and I'm not exactly a novice in the art collecting game myself. I know when a work of art's the genuine article—I get that frisson, if you know what I mean, in the presence of the real thing."

I knew what she meant. I was getting a frisson now myself.

"Anyway," she went on, "there couldn't have been

much of a provenance, since the painting was only thirty-five, forty years old when I bought it."

"Did Kate Simons like it—the O'Keeffe?"

"Butler?"

"I have no idea," he replied. "If I recall correctly—it's been a very long time, you know, and I only remember it because it was so soon before she was murdered—she noticed it, went over and stood in front of it, studied it a while without saying anything, and then began questioning Mrs. Farr about it."

"How'd you happen to buy it from Osmond?"

Butler said, "I believe that's one of the questions Miss Simons asked Mrs. Farr."

"And what did you tell her?" I asked her and waited for Butler to answer.

"You told her that you'd seen an O'Keeffe at the home of a friend while vacationing in Maine," he prompted her.

Recollection dawned on her painted old face. "That's right! Of course! It was gorgeous—quite sexy, I thought—and I vowed I was going to own an O'Keeffe too. So when I returned here, I told Mr. Osmond that I had to have one, and he said he'd arrange it. A few months later, he called to say he'd just purchased an O'Keeffe and was I still interested? Well, of course I was, so I drove straight down to his gallery and—there it was! I thought it was lovelier even than my friend's, and I absolutely had to have it. I didn't even haggle over the price, did I, Butler? I simply bought it on the spot, and we carted it home ourselves!"

Butler picked up the story from the shadows. "You were so elated, Dulcie, that you floated about the gallery. You felt like buying everything you saw that day. Fortunately, I was able to dissuade you from that. You bought only Kate Simons's piece."

"Yes, exactly—I do remember that! And it didn't come cheap, either! She was not well established, but she set a very high price on her work nonetheless."

"When he was here four months ago," I asked Mrs.

Farr, "did Bell tell you how he knew you owned an O'Keeffe?"

She nodded. "He said Joel Osmond had mentioned it to him."

"When? At the time you bought it, or recently?"

"Butler?"

"I don't believe he said."

"Have you ever had the O'Keeffe out on loan before?"

"I've never lent my art out before," she replied.

"So when's the last time Bell could have seen your O'Keeffe?"

"It would have to have been before Mr. Osmond delivered it to my home, of course."

I glanced over at Butler, who nodded in agreement.

"And he didn't see it when he was here?"

"Of course not!" she answered. "How could he? It was in the basement. He didn't want to see it, he only wanted to know if I still owned it and would I be willing to lend it to the University museum."

If he'd never seen Mrs. Farr's O'Keeffe, then how did Bell know it would be a nice match for the O'Keeffe in the museum's collection?

I got up to go, thanked Ms. Farr and Butler for their time.

"I've helped you, haven't I?" she asked, hopping up, spry for her age.

"Yes," I said, "I think so."

Butler led the way, and Dulcie Farr followed me to the door.

"She thinks my O'Keeffe's a fake, doesn't she, Butler?" she said as he help me on with my coat. "That must be what Kate Simons thought too. I suppose Joel Osmond *could* have been into that sort of thing. D'you suppose he murdered her when she confronted him about it?"

"I don't know," I said. "I just think that your O'Keeffe is somehow at the bottom of the murder of both Kate Simons and Russell Bell."

She shook her head. "How terribly sad. It's such a beautiful painting, too. A hibiscus."

"Go back inside, Dulcie," Butler said to her. "It's much too cold for you to be standing in the draft."

"And I'm much too old to care," she said, and reached up and patted him on the cheek.

She noticed Aunt Tess's Corvette squatting in the glare of the holiday lights. "Oh, look, Butler!" she exclaimed "Is it yours, Peggy? Would you sell it?"

"It's my aunt's," I told her, "and I don't think it's for sale."

"I had a 'Vette once—you remember, Butler?"

"Yes, Dulcie. Vividly."

Twenty-Eight

It's not natural for a guest to ask the kinds of questions Kate Simons had asked Dulcie Farr about her O'Keeffe. It was just as unnatural as Russell Bell, twenty-three years later, going to Mrs. Farr and asking her to lend that same O'Keeffe to the museum for its opening.

According to Charlie Bright and Herb Sweeney, Bell had once done a parody of an O'Keeffe painting. And according to Sally McFarlane, he'd done a copy of an O'Keeffe flower painting in the nude painting he'd done of her. I wondered if they were all talking about the same O'Keeffe.

How did Russell Bell know that Dulcie Farr's painting would go well with the University's? When could he have seen it?

Then I remembered something else Sally McFarlane had told me: Bell sometimes had paintings from Osmond's gallery hanging on his walls when she'd been at his house. Possibly, then, he'd had the O'Keeffe there at one time too, before Osmond sold it to Mrs. Farr.

Except he didn't like O'Keeffe in those days! Well, maybe he just borrowed it from Osmond so he could copy it into the portrait he was doing of Sally McFarlane.

As soon as I came in from my patrol the next morning, I called Mrs. McFarlane and asked if I could come over again. "I've changed my mind," I said. "I'd like to see that painting Russell Bell did of you."

"Why?" She sounded wary.

"I think it may help me figure out who murdered him," I said.

"It wasn't Mac! He doesn't know anything about that painting."

"I don't think your husband had anything to do with Bell's murder either," I said. "Could I come over?"

"Well . . ." I could hear her thinking, and I knew how much she wanted to see the painting again herself. "I don't suppose it could do any harm. But you'll have to be quick. Mac's just out shopping."

I drove over and parked, and she let me in. "It's in my bedroom closet," she said, "way in back. You'll need to stand on a chair. Don't dawdle."

She rolled swiftly off down the hall and into a bedroom with twin beds, and pointed to the closet.

I used a chair to reach the shelf and had to remove dusty boxes and plastic sweater bags to reach the back. The dust flew, making me sneeze.

It was a heavy cardboard mailer, about seven inches wide and three feet long.

"We'll find some other place to hide it when we're through looking at it," Mrs. McFarlane whispered conspiratorially. "Take it out and put it on the bed. I haven't seen it in years."

I pulled the cap off the mailer, slid the canvas out, and unrolled it. It smelled of oil and turpentine.

"Yes," Sally McFarlane said, and sighed deeply. "Oh, yes!"

She was lying on a bed, naked on rumpled sheets, her fair hair curling around her face and across her forehead. Her body and the bed seemed to pick up the hues and shades of the O'Keeffe painting on the wall behind her— a hibiscus. Its delicate, shadowy folds and furrows were repeated in the bed sheets, and in Sally McFarlane too, and in places she seemed to dissolve into the hibiscus, or it into her.

"I was almost forty," she said, "but you'd never know it to look at me, would you."

I turned to the woman in the wheelchair, her eyes sparkling with tears. "No," I said, "it's lovely."

"Too bad the son of a bitch didn't have the courage to do more like it," she said gruffly, as if trying to break its spell over her. "I told him it was the best thing I'd ever seen off his brush, but he just laughed."

The hibiscus seemed to me to look a lot like the one Bell had talked Dulcie Farr into loaning the museum. I asked her if Bell had copied the hibiscus from an actual O'Keeffe painting.

"Not exactly," she said. "There's an O'Keeffe in the University museum they have up sometimes. Russ had a nifty little camera back then, a German thing that fitted in his shirt pocket. He snuck into the museum one day and took a slide of that O'Keeffe. It was against the rules, of course, but he didn't give a damn about the rules. The museum's O'Keeffe has a rose in it along with the hibiscus, but he only copied the hibiscus. I like this one better." She dabbed at her eyes with a pink lace hankie she'd pulled from her slacks.

Trying to keep the excitement out of my voice, I said, "You're sure he used the University's O'Keeffe—he didn't copy this one from a painting Joel Osmond lent him that's of only a hibiscus?"

She shook her head. "I never saw an O'Keeffe on Russ's walls. I told you, he didn't like her."

And that's how part of the answer finally dawned on me. The last time I'd talked to her, Sally McFarlane had said Bell had a studio in his house. I would have bet anything that he'd created Dulcie Farr's O'Keeffe himself in that studio—probably on order from Joel Osmond, who'd been commissioned by Mrs. Farr to get her an O'Keeffe.

"You told me you used to see paintings from Osmond's gallery in Bell's house," I said.

She nodded, dabbing at her eyes.

"How'd you know they were from Osmond's?"

"Russ told me. Where else would he have got them? He couldn't have afforded to buy them—not on his salary!'' She blew her nose again, nodded at the painting. "Does this help?''

"I think it helps a lot.'' I got up from the bed. "Thank you.''

It told me why Kate Simons had died, at least.

She waited for me to explain, but when I didn't, she shrugged and sighed. "What the hell am I going to do with it now? What'll happen to it if I die before Mac?''

I thought the answer to that was fairly obvious.

"You can roll it back up now,'' she said.

As I picked it up, the front door opened.

"Oh, shit!'' Mrs. McFarlane's eyes widened in panic and she said, "Under the bed, quick! Don't worry about the mailer!''

Feeling like a lady's maidservant in an eighteenth-century farce, I lifted the bedspread and slid the painting under the bed just as Blair McFarlane strode into the room.

He looked at me, recognition dawning. "What the deuce are you doing here?''

"I just came to ask your wife—''

He spotted the cardboard mailer on the bed and his eyes widened and his mouth fell open. Then he glanced over at the closet and saw the boxes and sweaters piled on the floor. He looked back at me and laughed without music. "Russ Bell's masterpiece! Have you seen it?''

"Yes,'' I said. I know when the jig's up.

"I suppose it's enough to kill for,'' he said, "but not this long after the fact.'' He stuck his pipe in his mouth and began patting his pockets absently in search of matches. "Maybe, if I'd been more—or less—of a man, I would've killed Russ when I first found out about Sally and him. But I had too much else to think about: my kids, my marriage—and then Kate Simons's murder. Too much happening all at once.''

He lit his pipe. "That one time, in the cafe when Russ and I fought after poor Herb got drunk and told me something he didn't know I'd already guessed—that was enough violence for me.''

"Oh, Mac," his wife said, and buried her face in her soaked pink hankie.

"Later, when I came across that painting, I fantasized about killing him," he went on, nodding at the mailer on the bed, "but I could never figure out a foolproof way to do it. It's not so easy to murder someone, except in books." He smiled at me over the pipe in his mouth. "You think that painting's going to put me behind bars for killing Russ?"

I shook my head. "It doesn't have anything to do with you," I replied.

"You're right about that!"

"Do you think it's possible that Bell could have been forging paintings and selling them through a gallery, back around the time Kate Simons was killed?"

As he thought about it, his bushy eyebrows rose, and then he laughed. "Why not? Technically, he was a damn slick painter, and he must have tried his hand at every style, trend and fad going. I can't think of anybody more qualified to be an art forger than Russ, now that you mention it."

He puffed on his pipe for a few moments. "The problem would be in providing provenances for the fakes after he'd painted them," he went on. "You know what provenances are?"

"Sure."

He nodded. "But I suppose the gallery owner would've been able to do that." He laughed again, as something occurred to him. "That would explain something that's puzzled a lot of us who knew Russ—why Joel Osmond seemed to be such a pal of his."

"I think it's a little soon to be spreading that rumor around," I said.

McFarlane grinned around his pipe.

I had to talk to Buck. I asked them if I could use their phone.

"You can use the one in the living room, next to my easy chair," McFarlane said.

As I started down the hall to the front door, I heard

Sally ask her husband when he'd discovered the painting.

"A couple of years ago when I was dusting up there in your closet," he told her with a chuckle. "You can't expect an artist to see a mailer like that and not wonder what's in it, can you? It's the best thing Russ ever did."

"Damn you, Mac! Do you have to be so damned civilized?"

"Can't help it, Sal," he said. "But I won't have it hanging in my house!"

I found the phone next to McFarlane's easy chair, a contraption in burgundy leather that simultaneously leaned back and lifted your feet off the floor. I called Buck and told him I had something I thought he'd be interested in.

"I've got something I think you'll be interested in too," he replied. "Come on in."

"The truck?"

He hung up without answering.

The McFarlanes were still in the bedroom, talking quietly. They seemed to have forgotten me, so I let myself out.

Twenty-Nine

"You first," Buck said. He leaned his elbows on the desktop and rested his head in his hands and watched me with his chilly blue eyes with the laugh wrinkles at the corners that weren't laughing now.

I told him that a few days before she'd been murdered, Kate Simons had been in Dulcie Farr's mansion. She'd seen the Georgia O'Keeffe and questioned Mrs. Farr about its provenance.

"Pedigree."

"Right." I hate reverse snobbery. "That wasn't very tactful, was it—a young artist questioning the provenance of a work of art in the home of a wealthy woman who's just bought one of her sculptures?"

He shrugged and said, "It's your story, Peggy. Go on."

I told him how Russell Bell, a few months before he'd been murdered, had gone to Mrs. Farr and talked her into lending that same O'Keeffe to the museum for its opening.

"What's odd about that?"

"One, he didn't like O'Keeffe. Two, he didn't have a very high opinion of women's art, and yet he argued that the museum was underrepresented in that area. And three, how did he know Dulcie Farr owned that particular O'Keeffe?"

"You tell me."

"I'm going to," I assured him, "in a minute. Twenty-three years ago, Bell painted a portrait of his lover, Blair

McFarlane's wife, Sally. She was lying on a bed under a Georgia O'Keeffe painting—the same painting that, a few months later, Dulcie Farr bought from Joel Osmond's gallery.''

"I was wondering if Mr. Osmond would appear in your story," Buck said. I gave him a questioning look. "Keep going," he added grimly.

"Sally McFarlane never saw the original of that O'Keeffe in Bell's house," I continued, wondering what Buck had up his sleeve. "But she did see works of art by other famous artists that Bell told her were originals Osmond had lent him. Osmond, by the way, told me he and Bell weren't friends, but everybody else I've talked to insists they must have been. They couldn't understand why Osmond would have been such a strong supporter of Bell's art otherwise.''

"And you think those paintings Mrs. McFarlane saw on Bell's walls were originals—original Russell Bell fakes, that is?''

"Right. Bell painted them in the studio he had in his home. He'd known most of the New York artists in the fifties and sixties, knew how they worked, knew their tricks—and was a very facile painter himself. You couldn't ask for a more perfect forger of their art. He painted the fakes; Osmond sold them.''

"And how did Kate Simons catch on that the O'Keeffe in Dulcie Farr's mansion was one of Bell's fakes?''

"She broke up with Dan Sánchez. She was feeling down about it and Bell, the chairman of the department, took it upon himself to offer her emotional support. He took her out one night and, a few weeks later, invited her over to his house.''

"To look at his etchings," Buck said dryly.

"Except that what she looked at was *The Naked Sally* above the fireplace—with the Georgia O'Keeffe behind her on the wall. I've seen the painting, Buck—it's gorgeous, in a slightly overblown way. But Bell must have been proud of it, to display it like that—or else he just wanted to show off his facility and maybe scandalize his colleagues too, since Mrs. McFarlane says she's quite recognizable in the painting. And anyone seeing it would have been struck by the O'Keeffe, too, because it's such a big part of the composition.''

''And so,'' Buck finished for me, ''a couple of months later, Kate Simons sees an O'Keeffe in Dulcie Farr's mansion that she recognizes as the same one she'd seen in Bell's painting—and guesses it was a fake.''

''Yes. And at that moment she probably understood why Osmond and Bell were such good friends too,'' I added.

''She confronted Bell about it and threatened to go to the police.''

''Right. According to McFarlane's testimony in that microfilm file over there, he overheard Bell and Simons quarreling in her office a few days before she was killed.''

''But Bell couldn't have killed her,'' Buck reminded me. ''He was in Chicago at the time she died. So it must have been Osmond, after Bell had created an ironclad alibi for himself.''

''Yes. And listen, Buck, everyone I've talked to who knew Bell back then has told me his personality changed after that. He went into a shell, becoming a recluse, a nasty and destructive influence in the department. Some people think it was because he had to step down as chairman in disgrace, others because his career was going nowhere. But his career had never gone anywhere, and it couldn't have been all that much of a disgrace to get caught having an affair with a colleague's wife—not in those circles, anyway. I think it was because he was horrified by what he'd been a part of doing to Kate Simons.''

''Or terrified he'd get caught,'' Buck said. ''It's amazing the role terror can play in the creation of remorse.''

''Unless he didn't realize Osmond was going to kill her, and when he returned from Chicago, it was done and he couldn't tell the police without implicating himself.''

''You would think that, Peggy,'' Buck said with a smile. ''And now you're going to tell me Osmond had to kill Bell because Bell was about to break down and confess.''

''I don't know what Bell planned to do. All I know is he wanted his O'Keeffe in the museum's opening show. Maybe it was because he was a failed artist, and that was his way of getting revenge on the so-called art experts who don't know a fake when they see one. In any case, he was obviously behaving irrationally, to work so hard to get the fake O'Keeffe in the show, where it would be seen by art critics and scholars from all over the country. I'm sure Osmond would have preferred that it stay buried in Mrs. Farr's private collection. It must have made him nervous, Bell suddenly acting up after all those years.''

''Osmond wouldn't have had to worry about going to jail for selling a fake O'Keeffe twenty-three years ago, though,'' Buck said. ''The statute of limitations on art fraud is only five years.''

''You're kidding! You mean, if I sell you a genuine *Mona Lisa* I painted myself, I only have to fool you for five years, and then I can laugh in your face?''

''The system rewards the skillful forgers,'' he said, ''and punishes the incompetent. Don't you wish more occupations worked that way?''

''I supose. But Osmond has a high-class gallery now, and a well-heeled clientele. He's worked his way back up. If it got out that he'd ever been involved in selling forgeries, his reputation would be ruined and it would be back into the gutter for him. Also, of course, he may be up to his old tricks.''

I poured more coffee from Buck's pot, then went back and sat down. ''It's possible Bell planned to wait until the art community had oohed and aahed over the fake O'Keeffe for a while, then announce that he'd painted it himself,'' I continued. ''And he might have been planning to confess to his other forgeries too. He didn't have anything to lose, after all. He was about to retire, and the statute of limitations would also have run out for him.''

''He might even have thought it would give his reputation as an artist a boost,'' Buck agreed. ''He could go on the talk show circuit and describe how he fooled all the experts. Moral sleazeballs become cultural heroes in that sewer."

He stared out his window into the weak winter morning sunlight. "If your theory's correct, Peggy," he went on after a minute, "Bell and Osmond must have been in touch recently. Osmond couldn't have found out Bell was getting the O'Keeffe for the museum opening otherwise."

"And Bell must've told him about Dan Sánchez breaking into the Studio Arts Department meeting," I said, "which gave Osmond the idea of framing Sánchez for his murder. That's probably how Osmond got into the Studio Arts Building too—his old friend Russ Bell let him in and let him get behind him."

"You're going awfully fast, Peggy," Buck said. "And, of course, your theory depends entirely on Mrs. Farr's O'Keeffe being a fake."

"It is," I said firmly. "I trust Kate Simons on that. And when you prove it, Buck, you'll know as well as I do that Osmond must have killed both her and Russell Bell."

"If he killed her, we could probably pin it on him, since we still have the blood and skin samples found under her fingernails. But we don't have that kind of evidence in Bell's murder. Also," he went on, "if your friend Sánchez somehow suspected what you suspect, that Bell was involved in Kate Simons's murder, that gives him even more reason to want to kill Bell, doesn't it?"

"Yes," I retorted, "but if he knew that much, he'd know Osmond was the actual killer, wouldn't he? And he'd want to kill him too."

I walked right into it.

"That's the news I had for you, Peggy," he said. "Osmond's dead. He was murdered."

I sat back in the chair and stared at him. "How? When?"

"He was shot. We found him in his garage underneath

his apartment. He was sitting behind the wheel of the panel truck that was used to attack you. He's been dead at least three days—probably since he got home from trying to kill you on Christmas night."

"You mean he just drove into the garage and somebody was waiting for him and shot him?"

"That's what it looks like."

Buck told me that, according to Sophie Naylor, Osmond's assistant, a man claiming to be a friend of Osmond's called her at home early Tuesday, the day after Christmas. He told her Osmond had pneumonia and wouldn't be in the rest of the week.

I asked Buck how they'd discovered the body. He said he'd decided to follow up on my interest in Osmond's old panel truck. He'd sent a detective over to Osmond's house that morning to ask him if he still had the truck and if the detective could take a look at it. Nobody answered the door, and there were three days' worth of newspapers on the porch and a lot of mail jammed in his mailbox. With pneumonia, of course, Osmond could have been in the hospital or staying with relatives or friends, but the detective decided to take a look around anyway.

Buck's eyes were as expressionless as his voice when he said, "The detective saw that the utility door to the garage was ajar and went in to investigate. He found Osmond's body."

"Careless of the killer," I remarked, "to leave the utility door ajar like that."

Buck shrugged, and looked out the window at the courtrooms across the way.

"At least now we know who tried to kill you," he said after a moment.

"But we don't know why."

This was ruining the ending I'd foreseen, in which Buck arrests Osmond, the DNA evidence shows he murdered Kate Simons, the O'Keeffe is proven to be a fake, the evidence is overwhelming that he killed Russell Bell, and Dan Sánchez is cleared. Sandra pays to have my Rabbit restored to life or buys me a new car, Gary and

I and Paula and Lawrence celebrate by dropping the dance class and trying something else—bowling, maybe.

And Osmond would have explained why he'd gone to so much trouble to try to kill me. Now he never would, and I had just as much to worry about as I'd had before he was killed.

"I suppose you didn't find the gun," I said.

"No, but the bullet came from a small-caliber weapon, probably a pistol—the kind you can buy on just about any street corner these days."

He called in Sergeant Burke to take it all down, and I told Buck everything I'd learned since starting to look into Russell Bell's murder. When I'd finished, I asked him how Osmond's murder and the forgery scam he'd been involved in with Bell would affect Dan Sánchez.

"First, of course, we have to prove Mrs. Farr's O'Keeffe a fake," he reminded me. "After that, I don't know."

As I got up to leave, Buck came over and stood next to me, closer than he had in a long time. He said, "You have more to worry about than Daniel Sánchez does, I think, because if Osmond was killed by someone involved with him and Bell, your theory that they don't have a gun has just gone out the window. Take care, Peggy. You ought to ask for time off, or an inside job, until we've solved Osmond's murder."

I needed to get to bed, get some sleep. I resisted the temptation to lean my weary head on his shoulder.

"I'll think about it," I said. "At least I won't be out patrolling the campus this weekend. Tonight's the opening of the museum, and I have the rest of the weekend off. I'll worry about someone armed and dangerous who's out to get me on Sunday."

"Worry about it now, Peggy."

Thirty

The museum looked like an ornament, a fantasy castle that had fallen from the Christmas tree and landed in the snow. Its glittering sides and battlements reflected all the colors of the city's lights in the distance and the stars in the clear sky, and light poured from its windows onto the snowy plaza in front of it too, where Gary and I had danced not so many nights before.

As Tess and I hurried across the plaza, we could see people in bright costumes through the big windows moving around in the main gallery as though they'd just stepped down from the paintings on the walls, and as we got closer, we could hear music.

"There should be a drawbridge!" Tess exclaimed breathlessly.

We checked our coats and pushed our way through the crowd into the women's lounge to make last-minute adjustments to our costumes. I'd brought the big blue hat with roses on it in a grocery bag, and Tess helped me adjust it and pinned it onto my hair, which I'd piled up on my head. It's too short to do that easily, but Tess has a way with a bobbypin. I thought I made a credible *Portrait of a Young Woman in a Blue Hat,* thanks to Tess and her skill with a needle and thread, but I told her that the high collar was chafing my neck.

"It's good to suffer for your art," she assured me.

"But I'm a character in a painting by Renoir," I protested. "What do I know of suffering?"

"Hurry up," she said. "There are people behind us waiting for the mirrors."

The crowd of art lovers, patrons, artists, and critics were dressed in a crazy mix of costumes inspired by art from all parts of the world. Impressionist characters jostled characters from African, Asian, medieval, Renaissance, and modern art. I recognized men in costumes straight out of Renoir's *Luncheon of the Boating Party*—I'd had a poster of it on my wall when I was a student—who wore straw boaters and undershirts that showed off their beefy arms. Toulouse-Lautrec can-can girls and other Parisian lowlife rubbed elbows with Degas ballet dancers in pink and blue tutus with fluffy ruffles, and Cubist characters stood chatting animatedly with people wearing the African masks that had inspired their creation.

A group of musicians in Renaissance costumes strolled through the museum, playing Latin American dance tunes.

I spotted two Saint Sebastians—men dressed in loincloths, arrows sticking out of their bodies in various places—an unfortunate choice of costume for such a crowded space, since people kept knocking off the arrows which, I assumed, were cardboard. Fair's fair, after all.

Within half an hour, I'd seen three Van Gogh self-portraits with the ear cut off—they looked more like men with a toothache, but then so did van Gogh—several Munch's *The Scream*—hard on the muscles around the mouth and eyes, I would have thought—but mercifully none of his *Puberty*.

There were plenty of Old Masters too, of course, including several Mona Lisas with smiles that ran the gamut from frosty to inane, and that *Man with the Golden Helmet* the experts used to think was by Rembrandt but don't any more. I never liked it anyway. There were several resplendent Gainsborough *Blue Boys* too, and Japanese Noh dancers and Chinese sages.

"That must be an Emil Nolde," Tess said, tugging at my heavy skirt and nodding in the direction of a tall, ungainly figure dressed in black and wearing a crayon-yellow beard and wig, his face a mask of lurid purple and orange, his lips bright red. "Nolde was nuttier than a fruitcake," she added in a hushed voice, as though he might be somewhere nearby.

Under the garish makeup, I recognized Herb Sweeney, the potter, who caught my glance and grinned hideously back. Nolde wouldn't have had to be a fruitcake if he'd used Sweeney as his model.

I gradually led Tess over to the two O'Keeffes—one O'Keeffe, actually, and one Russell Bell—but I was the only person there who knew that. I wanted to see them, to see if I could tell by looking at it that the one was a fake.

"Hello, Miss O'Neill; hello, Peggy." It was Laura Price, the museum's associate director. She looked me up and down and said, "Renoir would have loved to paint you, no question about it." She spun around, flaring her skirt—or rather, skirts, for there were three layers of material. "What do you think I am?"

"That hibiscus on the wall behind you," Tess said.

"Right," Doctor Price said with a smile. "In honor of a man who couldn't be here tonight but who got us the O'Keeffe *Hibiscus* for the museum opening."

I pointed to Dulcie Farr's O'Keeffe and asked her if she could tell if it was genuine or not just by looking at it.

Her smile faded. "Oh, dear!" she said. She lowered her voice, glanced uneasily around and asked me if I had a particular reason for wanting to know.

"I do," I said, "but I'll talk to you about that some other time."

She looked at the two paintings for a minute. "I can't tell just by looking at it if it's genuine, but I'll bet an O'Keeffe expert could, unless it's a remarkably good fake. It's not easy to fool someone who's spent a lifetime studying an artist's work."

She looked from the one painting to the other and frowned. "Mrs. Farr's hibiscus does seem to be an almost exact copy of the hibiscus in our painting, doesn't it? I wonder if Georgia O'Keeffe repeated her subjects quite so exactly.''

Playing devil's advocate, I said I thought Dulcie Farr's O'Keeffe was a very lovely painting. "So what if it turned out to be a fake? Would that make it less good?" I knew there were all kinds of answers to that question and wondered what Laura Price's would be.

"Well," she said after a moment, "all I can tell you is that when Georgia O'Keeffe painted something, she was taking a risk. She was creating something nobody had ever seen before—just as the architect of this building was doing, for example, when he designed it. Furthermore, O'Keeffe had been doing that for a long, long time, and it shows. A forger, or anybody who works in somebody else's shadow or tries to repeat what's been done before, is just hiding behind someone else's courage—and that will show too. Do you think such people should be rewarded?"

"Thomas—is that you?" Aunt Tess exclaimed, her face lighting up as she turned to a man who'd come up and stood next to us.

"I wondered when you'd notice me," he said with a grin.

Grabbing both his arms and pushing him a little away, Tess looked him up and down and then laughed. "Doctor Nicolaes Tulp, I believe."

"You must have known I'd come as something from Rembrandt," he said. "After all, Miss O'Neill, it was you who showed me my first genuine Rembrandt and taught me to love his paintings."

"Don't you think it's time you started calling me Tess?" she asked.

"Tess, then," he said with a little formal bow that went well with his costume. He was wearing a Vandyke beard and moustache, a white lace collar over a dark coat, and a dark, wide-brimmed hat pulled down over his eyes that gave him a slightly sinister appearance.

She turned to me and explained that *The Anatomy Les-*

son of Dr. Nicolaes Tulp had established Rembrandt's reputation in his own time. I knew that already from the art history survey course I'd taken. I didn't like the painting at all.

"So you're Peggy," Fowler said. "It's nice to meet you at last. No hard feelings, I hope?"

"None," I lied, smiling.

"And who are you supposed to be?" When I told him, he said, "Ah yes—of course! The hair, if I remember correctly, wasn't quite so red, but you have the eyes, I think, and something of the mouth. I think you've already met my wife, Kendra."

Kendra Fowler was wearing the costume she'd told me about, John Singer Sargent's *Madame X*. I had to admit that she wore it well.

Fowler introduced her to Tess. The contrast between them—Tess in her homely farm wife's outfit, her normally curly gray hair parted in the middle and pulled severely back in a tight bun, Mrs. Fowler in a black, low-cut dress, with white makeup and her mahogany hair swept elegantly up on her aristocratic head—was stark.

"I do so want you to meet our children, Miss O'Neill," Mrs. Fowler said to Tess. "They're such barbarians, but perhaps you could civilize them the way you civilized Thomas." She gave Tess a sunny smile that I could see Tess struggling not to rain on.

We talked for a few minutes and then the Fowlers were dragged away by other art lovers wanting some of their time. Fowler called after us that he was looking forward to talking more at the banquet, and disappeared into the crowd.

Aunt Tess snatched a glass of wine from a passing waiter, muttered something about "trophy wives," and then spotted her friend Elmer Dill, the other half of *American Gothic*. He was carrying the pitchfork Tess had rendered harmless.

They posed together, and I used a little pocket camera to take their picture while other people, looking equally ridiculous, paused to point and laugh.

"I'm going to give Elmer the grand tour," Tess said after a while. "He missed the open house last month for the patrons."

We agreed to meet back at the O'Keeffes at ten, if we didn't bump into one another before that, so we could go in to dinner together.

Thirty-One

I wandered around the crowded, noisy museum, looking at the art and wondering how much of it was fake—not my usual thoughts in a museum, but understandable under the circumstances.

"There you are, Peggy O'Neill!" a voice shrilled. I didn't need to turn to see who it was.

"Hello, Mrs. Farr," I said.

She attempted a pirouette, and the overlapping cloth panels fluttered away from the body stocking she was wearing under them. Butler caught her before she could fall. "Like it?" she asked breathlessly.

"Duchamp would be ecstatic," I assured her.

"I met him once," she replied. "Seemed like a pleasant enough fellow, for a Frenchman. Butler, here, sewed the costume for me. He's a genius."

Butler nodded solemnly. He was wearing the same moth-eaten butler's outfit he'd worn when he let me into the mansion the day before. "I *am* a work of art," he explained suavely.

We chatted a while and then drifted apart. The museum was getting hot, and I began wishing I'd worn a cooler outfit. It was also hard to walk with the swirling gown, and the high collar was rubbing my neck raw.

I spotted Herb Sweeney again—not hard to do, with his height and wig and makeup—and went over and said hello. He asked me if I'd seen the faculty show yet and when I said I hadn't, he dragged me through the museum and into one of the smaller side galleries.

Paintings, prints, photographs and collages lined the walls, and sculptures in the various styles of yesterday, today, and perhaps tomorrow were scattered around the gallery floor. People in costumes stood contemplating the art or reading the descriptions of it on the walls, their hands clasped behind their backs in the solemn pose of museum goers everywhere.

"That is mine," Sweeney announced.

It was a large bowl-shaped sculpture about four feet tall and three feet across, its sides composed of hand-thrown cylinders of all sizes and shapes, and brightly glazed. It was, like Sweeney himself, a real eyesore, one that might grow on you with time.

"In this one," he explained, "I combined the wheel work of my beginning students to form the walls. Saved me a lot of time and effort, and it's the only immortality some of these kids are ever going to get."

"What's it called?"

"Don't remember. Titles are the hardest things to come up with for an artist, but people expect 'em." He bent over, squinted at a little card on the wall. "Ah, yes: *Vat Three*. Very early in my *Vat* series." Against museum rules, he caressed its rough sides—but it was his own work, after all, so perhaps that was all right.

"I've matured greatly since doing this one," he assured me, "but I can glimpse in it the seed of my later more mature work."

He spotted somebody out in the main gallery. Giving my arm a squeeze, he said, "Would you excuse me? I see a potential buyer." He dashed out of the gallery on his long legs.

In a corner of the gallery, old children's toys—a fire engine, a crane, a cap pistol, tin soldiers, alphabet blocks—stuck out of a mound of dirt or lay scattered on top of it. The card on the wall next to it told me that it represented aspects of the artist's childhood, some of which had been happy, some sad, and some not yet uncovered: there were still treasures buried in the dirt!

"Notice how the shape suggests an ancient burial

mound," a lean gray-haired woman with an intense, hawkish look on her face said to me.

"Or a landfill," I mused.

"Exactly," she exclaimed through thin lips. "The burial ground of the late twentieth century. It trembles on the knife edge of the ambiguity!"

"Can't make up its mind," I agreed.

A tall figure wearing an African mask of black ebony entered the gallery, glanced at me through slitted eyes, then stopped in front of a room divider and appeared to study the art hanging on it.

I went looking for the Russell Bell painting that Shannon Rider told me she'd selected for the show from the canvases she'd found on his side of the studio they'd shared. I spotted a couple of Blair McFarlane lithographs that reminded me of things I'd seen before and spent a few moments with a depressing cityscape by Charlie Bright in shades of glittering black, all squares and sharp angles.

I stopped at a painting by Shannon Rider. It was as striking as the painting I'd seen of her mother when we'd first met in her studio. This one showed Shannon herself standing by an easel. She was wearing an artist's beret tilted at a jaunty angle and holding a brush in one hand, a palette in the other. She was glancing solemnly over her shoulder at the viewer as if just interrupted in putting the finishing touches on a laughing self-portrait.

I laughed too.

"Huh! In the presence of art, she laughs."

I turned to find the real Shannon standing next to me. That made three of them, except this one was dressed in a straw hat with a floppy brim, a sheer white summer dress with a tight-fitting bodice, and high-heeled pumps. She looked cool and comfortable and as though she'd just stepped out of the 1940s. I remembered that the last time we'd talked, she'd said she was coming as a woman in a painting by Edward Hopper called *Summertime*.

"Pleasure makes me laugh," I told her.

"Must cause problems during sex."

"Not if he's laughing too."

I asked her where Russell Bell's painting was, and she said, "Over here," and led the way to a divider in the center of the gallery, where a big abstract expressionist painting hung.

I looked at it for a few moments.

"Well?" Shannon asked, watching me.

"Kind of boring," I said with a shrug. "I guess I've seen too many that look just like it, painted a long time ago."

"I know. The painting he was working on when he was killed was more interesting, but the cops wanted it for evidence or something—and anyway, it wasn't finished."

"It looked finished to me," I said.

"Really? The last time I saw it, he was having trouble with one of the figures. He'd paint, and then scrape it off and paint some more—all the while muttering angrily under his breath. He seemed quite frustrated."

Her words didn't register for a moment. When they did, I turned to her and said: "*One* of the figures?"

"Yeah, the woman."

"I wonder if we're talking about the same painting."

"I'm talking about the painting he was working on the day he was killed. What are you talking about?"

"The painting the cops found lying in Bell's blood under the overturned easel," I said. "It was a self-portrait. He's staring across the canvas, sort of out at nothing."

She shook her head. "That wasn't what he was working on the last time I saw him. Russ didn't like it when I looked at his paintings while they were still unfinished, but that Friday, when he left the studio to pee or whatever, I went over and took a look to see what was causing him so much trouble."

"And what did you see?"

"An interior: two figures standing in a bedroom. A bed in the background, just sketched in in pencil. One of the figures was a young man, the other a woman without a face. It was her face Russ was having trouble with, that he kept scraping down and repainting. Her hair was reddish brown—auburn. She was wearing a raincoat and holding an umbrella.''

I could feel the blood draining out of my face. The noise of the other people in the museum faded away, the pulsating Latin rhythms of the strolling band grew louder. The man in the African mask, who'd also been looking at Bell's painting, moved down to the painting next to it and seemed to be studying it intently.

"What's the matter, Peggy?" That was Shannon's voice. "You look like you've seen a ghost."

"Was it—did it look like a violent scene?" I found it hard to get the words out.

"That's not how I saw it," she answered. She laughed quietly, adding, "Knowing Russ's history, I thought it was two lovers."

"Why?"

"Well, the bed helped, of course. But mostly on account of the color. Both the woman's raincoat and her umbrella were a vivid red, glittering like fresh blood, the color of passion."

The color of murder, too.

Thirty-Two

Shannon Rider had seen the ghost; I'd only heard her tell about it.

Where was the painting she'd described now? Bell could have painted over it and then put it aside, of course, and put the self-portrait up on the easel before he was killed. But why would he do that? Even if he'd given up on it, why paint over it and then put an older, finished painting on his easel?

No, Bell's killer had taken the painting away because it described the murder scene at Kate Simons's apartment twenty-three years ago, and he'd replaced it with one of Bell's already finished paintings.

I asked Shannon what the man in the painting had looked like.

"He was tall," she said, "and young, with long, straw-colored hair. Glasses. He was holding something in his hand that looked like a bird. That's what made me think it was a love scene too," she added. "Birds often symbolize love."

This one hadn't.

"How long would it take to get a painting like that off the stretcher," I asked her, "if you were in a hurry and didn't care what happened to it?"

She looked at me as though I'd lost my marbles. "Well, if I was really disgusted and angry with it, I suppose I could tear it away from the staples in about thirty seconds. Once you'd done one corner, the rest would be easy."

I thought about that for a moment, imagining the killer in the studio doing it, Bell's freshly killed body at his feet.

"And what if you wanted to get it out of the building without anybody you might meet noticing you were carrying a painting?"

I knew the answer before she gave it, and should have known it even sooner.

"Roll it up," she said. "Stick it under your coat, if it's small enough."

"Or, if you had one, put it in a cardboard mailing tube?"

"Sure."

"You have those in your studio?"

"I think there are some in the supply closet."

Sally McFarlane had kept the painting Bell had done of her in a cardboard mailer for twenty-three years, and I'd handled that mailer this morning—was it only this morning?—without remembering that, half an hour before I'd found Russell Bell's body, I'd handled a mailer like that too.

And someone had tried to kill me twice since then.

I pulled Shannon away from the people in the gallery and told her why I thought what she'd told me was important: her testimony, and mine, would almost certainly get Sánchez off the hook.

This couldn't wait, I decided. I had to find a phone and call Buck. I told Shannon I'd see her later and walked back out into the main gallery, now noisier and more crowded than before.

Straw-colored hair. Tall. Glasses. The words ran through my mind. Aunt Tess had described the young Thomas Fowler like that, and when that finally clicked into my mind, just about everything else began to make sense too.

Dan Sánchez had mentioned someone who'd worked for Osmond—a blond college kid, skinny. Kate Simons had told him she knew him from when he'd been a student. Fowler had been Bell's student.

"We meet again! What's your hurry now, Peggy?"

It was Sally McFarlane in her wheelchair, dressed as Whistler's mother. She misunderstood the look I gave her, which wasn't about her at all. "Well, what else could I be, damn it?" she demanded. "I suppose it's a form of penance."

Blair McFarlane was wearing a clown face. "Rouault," he explained morosely. "It seemed appropriate."

"I've got to make a phone call," I told them. "I'm sorry. I'll talk to you later." I rushed away.

I knew there was a phone at the information counter at the museum's entrance. I threaded my way through the crowded room, the guests feeding canapés into their grotesque mouths, laughing and talking into each other's costumed faces. I reached the counter and started to slip behind it. As I did, a hand came down on my shoulder.

I spun around and stared into the African mask I'd seen in the faculty gallery and the chilly eyes behind it.

"Look down," the voice within it said. I did and saw the pistol pointed at me, shielded from the crowd by the counter. "I'll shoot you if you scream or do anything to attract attention."

It was Thomas Fowler's voice.

I said the stupid thing, the thing they always say, "You'll never get away with it."

"I don't know about that," he said softly. "But I've a better chance if you don't use the phone than if you do." He brought the mask closer to my face, whispering, "I'll shoot you, and I'll shoot anyone who gets in my way. And in the panic, I should be able to unload this mask and become Dr. Tulp again. You can't save yourself; you can only harm others now."

"All right," I said.

"We have to get through the crowd to the stairs and up to my office. Act as though you're enjoying my company. If anyone stops you, be pleasant and brief. If anyone seems to catch on, I'll shoot you and then them. I mean it. I have nothing to lose."

He backed away and let me go past him, back into the

crowded museum. He bumped me casually, and I felt the hard barrel of the pistol in my ribs.

"Have you seen Thomas Fowler, Peggy?" It was Laura Price. "Mrs. Farr wants to talk to him. She gave Fowler a curious look.

I said I hadn't seen him.

Fowler said, in the deep Bostonian voice I'd heard when I'd first met him, totally unlike his own, "I think I saw him by the Warhol a few minutes ago."

"Thanks. You'll never guess what she wants to do, Peggy," she went on to me. "Donate a big Kate Simons sculpture she owns to the museum. She wants us to install it on the plaza. She's talking about a retrospective of her work too."

Fowler dug the pistol into my side. "I'm sure Doctor Fowler will love the idea," I said. "I'll see you later, Laura."

"Okay." She looked again at Fowler, then smiled and walked away.

I paused at the foot of the stairs and then started up them slowly when Fowler whispered for me to hurry. People were standing at the balcony at the top, looking down over the crowd in the gallery below. They hardly glanced at us as we passed them.

The administrative office lights were on behind the glass walls at the end of the hall and the door was ajar.

"Inside," Fowler said.

I pulled the door open and went inside with him behind me. The room was empty.

"Over there!" he said, and backed me around a corner where we couldn't be seen from the hall. He took out the pistol, pointed it at my belly, and said, "I've only fired a pistol once before in my life—this one—but I can't miss at this range. Press that button on the wall. Now!"

It was a fire exit door, with a red-painted bar across it with the words *Alarm Will Sound* on it. I pressed the button on the wall that disconnected the alarm. I had no room to move left or right, and straight ahead, just inches away, was the barrel of the pistol. There'd be time enough to commit suicide when there were no more options.

"Turn around and open it," he said, and I did, and the alarm didn't sound. "Down the stairs. Hurry! Hurry!"

I hesitated. Fowler poked the barrel of the pistol into my back hard. "Hurry," he said again, his voice rising slightly, and I could hear the edge in it. I went down the stairs slowly, against the pressure of the pistol, into the basement's watery light. Off to the sides were doors that opened into carpentry and framing shops, and vaults for storing fragile works of art. They were closed now, but I knew that because Aunt Tess, along with Fowler and some of the other patrons, had been given a tour of the entire museum in November, and she'd given me a full report.

The pistol nudged me down one of the aisles created by tall shelves that held small sculptures and ceramic pieces. At the end of the aisle was a door in the wall. It was open, and the room beyond it was small, dark and cluttered.

I stopped and turned to face Fowler halfway down the aisle. If I had to die now, it wouldn't be in that room, it would be here, surrounded by art, dressed as one of the happiest artist's loveliest creations, and where I could hear the faint sounds of music coming from the museum over my head—where, maybe, somebody might hear the shots too, I thought on a more practical note.

"Turn around!" Fowler ordered, taking a step back, the knuckle of his finger on the trigger white. He removed the African mask, set it on a shelf, became Rembrandt's Nicolaes Tulp again, at the anatomy lesson, with a piece of human meat in front of him. In Rembrandt's time they used executed criminals for lessons like that, and the public was invited to sit in, for a price.

"You're going to have to shoot me here," I said, "while I watch."

"Turn around!" he said again, his face pale and his eyes wide, and I knew I was only seconds away from death.

I was about to dive for the pistol, an arm's length,

an eternity, away, when out of the corner of my eye I spotted movement several aisles over and behind Fowler, or thought I did.

It looked like Aunt Tess, gliding out of a steel-gray door, holding the pitchfork in front of her like a crucifix! I couldn't be sure because I kept my eyes rigidly on Fowler. I wondered if this was a common experience for people about to be killed, to see someone they loved coming to save them—in costume?

I took a step back and threw out my hands slowly. "All right," I said. "All right."

"Turn around," he repeated, like the stuck record he was.

"Yes, I will," I assured him, and took another step back. "But first I've got to know why you killed Kate Simons. You had so much less to lose than Bell or Osmond. You were only a student. How could you have done it? Just for kicks?"

"*Less* to lose?" He was outraged, he looked at me as though I were insane. "Kate Simons was going to destroy my career before it even began! I could never have gotten a position in an art history department, much less a museum, if I'd gone to jail for art forgery! Can't you see that?"

He held up his free hand. "Listen, Peggy! Do you hear it—the music? And can you see the people, laughing and talking as they move elegantly around in those beautiful galleries, surrounded by all that magnificent art? I'm the director of all that—of all this," he added, gesturing around at the shelves of art. "Do you think I'd be here now if I hadn't killed Kate Simons? For kicks, you say? No—necessity made me do it!"

Had I just imagined Tess—and was it Tess anyway? Maybe it *was* the farm woman from *American Gothic*, haunting the museum. I couldn't see her back there in the shadows now. It had just been a hallucination.

Fowler must have misunderstood the look of sorrow on my face. "I know," he said, "it's unfair that you should have to die like this—but what happened to me was unfair too."

"It was?"

"Of course it was! If I had it to do over, do you think I would have risked my entire future by getting involved with Joel Osmond? I was young and foolish."

"We all do things when we're young that we regret later in life," I said, sounding a little like Aunt Tess. Where was she?

"Yes!" he agreed eagerly. "And should we have to pay today for the terrible choices we made then? Would that be fair?"

Fairer than others having to pay for those choices, I thought, but I asked, "What choices?"

Again something moved in the next aisle over, near where we'd come in, and I wondered if it was just a scrap of my life passing before my eyes as I was about to die.

"Getting involved with Osmond," he said. "I worked for him while I was getting my Ph.D., part-time. I cleaned the gallery, delivered art, helped with framing, even assisted him in putting together his catalogs. It was good experience for me, but then I found out he was selling fakes. He was doing the provenances himself and they weren't very good, which was why I caught on to what he was up to."

He sighed—and almost, but not quite, looked down— as he thought about the step he'd taken over two decades before that had brought us down here tonight. "I offered to help," he said. "Why?" He shook his head, as though stumped for an answer. "Who can say now? Because I was good at that kind of thing, because it was a challenge and a little dangerous."

"And because you wanted the money you knew he'd have to pay you to keep quiet," I added.

"Yes," he agreed sadly, "that too, of course. I was greedy and impatient. Youth!"

I said I thought Russell Bell must have got him involved with Osmond.

"No, no—just the opposite. I knew Bell could paint

in the styles of the forties, fifties, and sixties—God knows, I'd seen enough of his crap when he was my teacher! We had dinner together once—the teacher and his former student—and I dropped a few hints, and he jumped at the chance to earn money faking the work of his successful New York buddies. It was as if he'd been preparing himself for that task his whole life!''

"And then Kate Simons discovered the fake O'Keeffe," I prompted him, for I wanted him to go on. I didn't want the silence, the loneliness of death in that dark little room behind me.

He grimaced under the false beard and moustache. "Her death was a tragedy, but it couldn't be helped. The irony is, I had almost nothing to do with the O'Keeffe. It was supposed to have been painted fairly recently, so faking the provenance was nothing. And yet, that's the one that's led to—this." He gestured with the pistol. "Turn around now. I have to go back upstairs. It's almost time for the banquet."

"I will," I said earnestly. "You've tried to kill me twice. The third time ought to be the charm."

"The first two times it was Osmond."

"And what did you give him the death penalty for? Failing to kill me?"

"You know about that, do you?" He looked at me thoughtfully, perhaps wondering how I knew about Osmond's murder, then shrugged it off. "No. When I killed him, I thought he *had* killed you, or at least hurt you badly enough so you couldn't come to the museum tonight. And he thought so too. I killed him because I thought he was the last link to my past—to Kate Simons and Russ Bell."

"At least he died thinking he'd achieved something," I said. "You must have been disappointed when you found out I was still alive and well."

"Yes, I was." He smiled wanly. "You have a lot of your Aunt Tess's spunkiness, you know, Peggy. If I were in your shoes, I'd be terrified. Now I've told you enough. Turn around and walk into that room, please. If I have to shoot you here, someone might hear the shots upstairs and come down to investigate. Then I'd have to shoot them too. You wouldn't want that on your conscience, would you?''

"All just to save your career," I said. I tried not to stare as Aunt Tess tiptoed down the aisle behind him, the pitchfork raised high above her head, the cardboard tines wiggling like fingers, as in a dream.

"More than just my career," he said. "I have children, remember, and a wife. You've met them—"

He broke off and started to turn when he heard the scrape of Tess's shoe behind him. She was still too far away. I crouched to leap. Then he froze, staring at something over my shoulder. A man's voice behind me grated, "Hold it right there, buster!"

It was Elmer, Aunt Tess's friend.

"Who—?"

Tess brought the pitchfork down on Fowler's head with all her strength and he dropped the pistol and I scooped it up as it hit the floor. He sagged to his knees and fell onto his hands. Then, slowly, blood streaming down into his eyes, he lifted his head and looked up to see what had hit him.

The sight of Tess glaring down at him, the pitchfork at her side like a rifle at parade rest, and Elmer next to her, must have been too much for the historian of American art. His eyes closed slowly, his elbows buckled, and he fell onto his face in a dead faint.

"Spunky!" Tess spat.

Epilogue

They say confession's good for the soul, so maybe that's why Fowler made a full one. It probably helped that the best defense attorney in the state would have had trouble sowing doubts in even the most brain-dead jury's head.

The pistol he was going to kill me with was the same weapon he'd used to kill Osmond, and the technicians at the state crime lab thought the DNA from the skin and blood found under Kate Simons's fingernails would still be good enough to show if it was Fowler's. Tess and her friend Elmer had heard Fowler tell me he'd killed Simons and Osmond, and I could place him near the scene at the time of Bell's murder too.

Russell Bell hadn't wanted Kate Simons killed. He'd wanted to make restitution to the people they'd cheated instead. He'd even persuaded Kate not to go to the police for a few days while he, Osmond, and Fowler came up with a plan to make restitution. Then he'd flown to Chicago on family business. When he returned, Fowler told him he'd killed her.

After the initial shock wore off, Bell tried to go on with his life. After all, he hadn't killed her, and he wouldn't have gone along with it if he'd known, would he? But he'd never be able to persuade the police of that. It didn't make any sense to confess, to throw his life away. What was done was done.

His small talent shrank even further, and he became bitter and reclusive, finally seeking solace in the art museum as a tour guide, where he discovered he had a talent for explaining other people's art to museum visitors. At the same time, he was aware of how Thomas Fowler's career was thriving.

When Fowler learned about our new museum, he wanted to be its director. He explained to Buck that he was convinced he'd been preparing for that his whole life. The old museum, after all, had been the first he'd ever been in, thanks to Aunt Tess. Surely he was the man for the new one!

Before applying for the position, though, he called Russell Bell and asked him if he would mind. Bell assured him he would be delighted—what was past was past, life goes on. With Bell's enthusiastic support, Fowler got the position.

And then Bell sprang his trap: *he* would be running the museum through Fowler, *he* would be calling the shots. If not, he would blow the whistle on the art fakes of the past and destroy Fowler's career. After all, since the statute of limitations had run out on the forgeries, only Fowler and Osmond would be ruined. Bell had nothing to lose.

Fowler had leaned across the table in the interrogation room and fixed Buck with his wide gray eyes and asked: "Can you imagine how it would feel, to be at the beck and call of a man like Russell Bell? To have to okay your every decision with him? To implement *his* dreams, instead of your own?"

He'd tried to back out of the directorship, but Bell wouldn't let him.

I asked Buck why Bell wanted Dulcie Farr's fake O'Keeffe in the museum's opening show.

"Fowler tried to talk him out of it," he answered, "but Bell laughed in his face. He told him it would hang there until they'd purchased a work by a woman artist of equivalent stature. He said Mrs. Farr had a sculpture by Kate Simons in her basement, and told Fowler they were going to acquire it from her and restore it. And they were going to scour the country to find every piece by Kate Simons they could and give her a retrospective."

"And what did Fowler say to that?"

"He agreed to every one of Bell's demands. But he asked me in an aggravated voice: 'How could I justify the expense to the museum board? Who's ever heard of Kate Simons?' "

The poor man! Dulcie Farr, with her money and her clout, and Laura Price, were going to try to realize Bell's plan to give Kate Simons a measure of the recognition she'd deserved. But it would be just as much a measure of loss.

Fowler kept coming back to the fact that it was unfair that Bell was making him pay now for a crime he'd committed almost a quarter of a century ago. "What responsibility do I—the museum director, the scholar, the father and husband—have for the folly done by the young Thomas Fowler?" he'd asked Buck.

"Folly!" I said. "Didn't he show any remorse for having killed Kate Simons?"

Buck shook his head. "None. He implied that the young Fowler was an embarrassment to him, and assured me he wasn't the same person anymore."

"Well, that's true," I replied. "Young Thomas only committed one murder. By the time I met him, the distinguished Doctor Fowler was up to two, and counting."

I asked Buck about Bell's painting of Kate Simons's murder scene.

"When he came to kill Bell that night, Fowler didn't know about that one. He only knew Bell would be working late on a painting for the faculty show. It wasn't until he was in the studio with Bell that he realized what the painting was about, and that he had to take it away with him and destroy it. He didn't ask Bell about it, but he thinks it was another sick joke, Bell twisting the knife a little more."

I said I supposed so, but I wondered if maybe Bell was also trying to work Kate Simons out of his system by painting that scene. According to Shannon Rider, he'd been having a lot of trouble getting the face right in acrylic, just as Dan Sánchez was in clay.

Fowler and Osmond agreed that Bell was becoming too unstable and had to die. And, of course, Fowler couldn't stand the thought of living with Bell pulling the strings at the museum.

"He wanted to be his own star," I told Buck, "in charge of his own fate. It's a speech from Beaumont and Fletcher," I added knowledgeably.

"*The Honest Man's Fortune*," Buck said, nodding.

"Yes," I gritted.

"Anyway," he went on, "Fowler decided he had to kill Bell before he officially moved here from New York. Once here, he'd be working with Bell at the museum and would be a suspect like everyone else if Bell was killed. He didn't want to risk us looking into his past. But if Bell was murdered before he arrived in town, nobody would think of him."

Bell had told Fowler over the phone about Sánchez's invasion of the departmental meeting and his angry tirade. Sánchez's comments on Bell's failure as an artist and his failure to promote Kate Simons had upset Bell even more and, in Fowler's eyes, made him even more unstable.

Fowler and Osmond agreed that they would try to frame Sánchez for Bell's murder. Osmond learned enough about Sánchez's habits to know he often worked far into the night in his potter's studio. He stole the clay cutter while pretending to be a potential customer who'd come in to browse. It had been twenty-three years since Sánchez had seen Osmond, so there was little danger of Sánchez recognizing him.

Fowler paid cash for his plane tickets. You can do that if you buy them from a travel agent and not at the airport. Osmond picked him up at the airport, drove him to the University, and waited for him in the old neighborhood behind the New Campus.

After killing Bell, Fowler crossed the park separating the Studio Arts Building from the Law School, went inside and down the hall to the public pay phones, and called Sánchez. They'd driven past his home on the way to murder Bell and seen the lights burning in the studio, but it didn't really matter if they lured Sánchez to the crime scene or not: it would just be frosting on the cake, if he went and left evidence behind.

Everything went according to plan—until Fowler slipped on the ice and I got a good look at his face. But he didn't think anything of that until, back in New York, he read the newspaper account of the murder that Osmond sent him. Osmond was ecstatic at how well things had gone: Sánchez had not only gone to Bell's studio, he'd even been seen by a campus cop!

A campus cop named Peggy O'Neal.

They'd misspelled my name, but that didn't fool Fowler.

Aunt Tess, of course, had told him all about me in November and what I did for a living. So he knew I'd be coming to the museum opening, and would sit with him at the banquet too. He couldn't be sure I wouldn't recognize him after we'd all unmasked, and wonder what he'd been doing so close to the scene of Bell's murder—especially if I learned he wasn't supposed to be in town at the time.

So I would have been killed even if I hadn't started investigating Bell's murder, and nobody would ever have known why. There's probably a moral in there somewhere.

I asked Buck how Fowler had been able to get into the Studio Arts Building.

"You won't believe this, Peggy," he said, "but he still had his key from when he was Bell's student over twenty-five years ago. He tried it when he was here in November, and when it slid into the lock and turned, and the door opened, he took it as a sign that he was going to get away with murder again."

"And he wanted to be his own star!" I said, disgusted. "People who are their own stars don't need signs. Did you tell him he might never have been caught, if I hadn't hung back that night to readjust the lights on the Christmas tree?"

"No, Peggy, I spared him that."

"I'm going to find a way to let him know," I said.

A couple of weeks after the museum's eventful opening, the Sánchezes were having a dinner party in Dan's studio. Sandra Carr was there, of course, looking very Hollywood, and Aunt Tess and Elmer, and Gary and I. One end of Dan's long worktable had been cleared to make room for dishes of meat, vegetables and sauces, with Elena's homemade tortillas to wrap them in, and things to drink in Dan's stoneware pitchers.

The Sánchezes hadn't heard the story of what Tess and Elmer had been doing in the museum's basement.

"Well," Tess began, "the museum had an open house for all the patrons in November. That's where I met Thomas—Fowler," she corrected herself, putting heavy emphasis on the first syllable, "after all those years. Doctor Price showed us over the building. It was most interesting and instructive—the carpentry shop, the humidity-controlled storage rooms, the . . ."

"But see," Elmer broke in, perhaps, being a man, more interested in moving the plot along than in atmosphere, "I couldn't make it down here for that—on account of one of my horses was sick."

"At the opening," Tess went on, "we were wandering around and Elmer was beginning to look more and more hot and bothered—"

"Hate crowds," he explained at length.

"And so I offered to show him what he'd missed at the open house—"

"I asked her how in Sam Hill she thought she could do that," he said. "Everything that's not open to the public's kept locked up tighter'n a drum."

"How in what?" Sandra asked through a mouthful of taco. She'd been following the story with wide eyes, as though finding the truth stranger than fiction, which was unusual for her.

"Sam Hill."

"Except when we got up to the second floor," Tess

crowed, "the door to the offices was unlocked! That murderous scoundrel must have unlocked it himself so he could get you inside quicker, Peggy. That's how Doctor Price took us to the basement at the open house after showing us the offices—she pressed the button that turns off the alarm on the fire exit door and we walked down."

"And then Peggy came down," Elmer said, leaping over a large chunk of time as he dumped hot sauce on a new tortilla piled high with chicken and chilis.

"We didn't know who you were for a few moments," Tess continued quickly. "We thought maybe you were down there for the same reason we were."

"And what reason was that again?" I asked innocently.

She glared at me, red-cheeked.

"Where were you?" Elena asked, looking from Tess to Elmer and back again.

"Carpentry shop," Elmer said, rolling up the taco with thick fingers, his tongue sticking out the corner of his mouth in concentration. My grandfather rolled cigarettes like that.

"Without light?" Elena pressed on, puzzled.

"We couldn't find the switch," Tess said.

"Then how could you see—?"

Dan poked a hot pepper into her mouth. She glanced at him, startled, and caught his wink.

"You want to know what happened or don't you?" Tess demanded huffily.

"Sure," Dan said.

"We heard Peggy tell Fowler he was going to have to shoot her while she watched," Tess continued.

"That got Tess's attention!" Elmer added with a bucolic chuckle. "She whispered for me to get ready to jump out and distract the man if he looked like he was gonna shoot Peggy, while she snuck around behind him with the pitchfork. I would've of done that part, of course, but there wasn't time to argue with her about it."

"Luckily," Tess went on, "Peggy kept the louse talking until I got into position to whack him over the head."

* * *

Later, I went down to the far end of the worktable to look over the first pieces of the dinnerware set, still in the greenware stage, that Dan was making for me. He came with me.

After we'd discussed what he wanted to do in the way of a glaze and showed me some samples, I asked him where the bust of Kate was.

"I'm no sculptor," he said. "Even if I was, I couldn't bring her to life again."

"No. But you weren't responsible for her death either. Thomas Fowler was. Even if you hadn't been an addict, the chances are you wouldn't have been there for her the night he came to kill her anyway."

He didn't say anything for a minute, just went on looking down at my dinnerware, his eyes glittering with tears, the scar a pale line on his swarthy cheek.

"I know," he said finally. "She talked a lot about what she wanted to do with her life, an' I knew it was gonna be hard for her to fit me in, no matter what I did." His mouth twisted into a wry grin. "I wish I'd made it harder for her though."

The back door opened then and Carlos and Luisa burst laughing into the studio, their snowsuits clotted with snow. They rushed across the room to their father, almost knocking him over. At the other end of the studio, Elena caught my eye and smiled.

Dan knelt in front of his kids and began helping Luisa out of her snowsuit. He glanced up at me and asked, "You wanna know where the bust of Kate is now?"

"Where?"

"It's in your dishes."

I thought back to the head he'd been struggling to bring to life for so long, and compared it to the raw clay dishes sitting on the table waiting to be glazed and fired and used.

"I hope you don't mind," he said.

I told him I didn't.

FAST-PACED MYSTERIES
BY J.A. JANCE

Featuring J.P. Beaumont

UNTIL PROVEN GUILTY	89638-9/$5.50 US/$7.50 CAN
INJUSTICE FOR ALL	89641-9/$5.50 US/$7.50 CAN
TRIAL BY FURY	75138-0/$4.99 US/$5.99 CAN
TAKING THE FIFTH	75139-9/$5.50 US/$7.50 CAN
IMPROBABLE CAUSE	75412-6/$4.99 US/$5.99 CAN
A MORE PERFECT UNION	75413-4/$4.99 US/$5.99 CAN
DISMISSED WITH PREJUDICE	
	75547-5/$4.99 US/$5.99 CAN
MINOR IN POSSESSION	75546-7/$5.50 US/$7.50 CAN
PAYMENT IN KIND	75836-9/$4.99 US/$5.99 CAN
WITHOUT DUE PROCESS	75837-7/$5.50 US/$7.50 CAN
FAILURE TO APPEAR	75839-3/$5.50 US/$6.50 CAN

Featuring Joanna Brady

DESERT HEAT	76545-4/$4.99 US/$5.99 CAN
TOMBSTONE COURAGE	76546-2/$5.99 US/$6.99 CAN